Baby, Take a Bow

Books by Jane Tesh

The Grace Street Mysteries
Stolen Hearts
Mixed Signals
Now You See It
Just You Wait
Baby, Take a Bow

The Madeline Maclin Mysteries
A Case of Imagination
A Hard Bargain
A Little Learning
A Bad Reputation
Evil Turns

Baby, Take a Bow

A Grace Street Mystery

Jane Tesh

Poisoned Pen Press

Poisoned Pen
PRESS

Copyright © 2017 by Jane Tesh

First Edition 2017

10 9 8 7 6 5 4 3 2 1

Library of Congress Catalog Card Number: 2016952670

ISBN: 9781464207969   Hardcover
       9781464207983   Trade Paperback

Poisoned Pen Press
6962 E. First Ave., Ste. 103
Scottsdale, AZ 85251
www.poisonedpenpress.com
info@poisonedpenpress.com

Printed in the United States of America

This one is for the newest baby in my family,
my great-niece, Elizabeth Ann Valent, born May 31, 2016,
and for her parents, Tiffany and Steve.

Acknowledgments

Thanks always to my family and friends and to all the great folks at Poisoned Pen Press.

Chapter One

"Oh My Babe Blues"

As much as I need the work, I don't take cases involving children. My first attempt at a family didn't end well, and although the emotional baggage is now down to an overnight bag, it's still hard to carry.

If the case involves a baby, forget it.

I live and work at my friend Camden's boardinghouse at 302 Grace Street here in Parkland, North Carolina, where I spend as much time as possible courting Kary Ingram. She hasn't said yes yet, but any time she gets a chance to help on a case, she jumps on it—sometimes too enthusiastically—which gives me hope for our future as a super crime-busting team.

After a long and stormy engagement, Camden and his girlfriend, Ellin, had gotten married, and despite Ellin's best efforts to dislodge Camden from his house, she has not succeeded. Ellin, who isn't the least bit psychic, produced shows for the dubious Psychic Service Network and was always after Camden to be on one of the programs and to find a better job. He was content to work at an upscale clothing store and take occasional carpentry work and jobs that didn't pay much. These jobs were calm and dull to offset his psychic visions, which were real and often intense.

To complicate matters, his friend, Rufus Jackson, and Rufus' wife, Angie, were house-hunting and planned to move out, and our oldest tenant, Fred, had passed away, so the boardinghouse was in need of new boarders. This was a problem that got me involved in what became a never-ending series of favors.

What could be so hard about that? You do a little something for someone, they do a little something for you. What's the problem?

Doing someone a favor?

It can be murder.

• ● ● ● •

This morning, I parked myself at my regular table near the front window of Perkie's Coffee Shop and sipped a large Perkie's Special. Things were hopping at Perkie's, a small shop in all shades of brown with small round tables, cane-back chairs, and an array of doughnuts, muffins, and pastries within easy reach. Young professionals dashed in for their morning lattes, and other folks settled in at tables with their books and laptops. Everyone had serious faces filled with purpose. Everyone was Getting Things Done, but, as usual, the Randall Detective Agency was spinning its wheels. There hadn't been a lot of work for me lately, except my least favorite chore, tracking down deadbeat dads.

The latest, a chinless wonder with an oddly shaped skull— sort of like those twelve-sided dice—was going to be a snap to find because he'd written his girlfriend's phone number on the back of the dollar he'd used for his generous tip to my cabdriver friend, Terrance "Toad" Hall. Then the poor sap called the taxi company looking for it.

Outside, Toad's taxicab, Old Betsy, pulled into a parking spot. Toad came in, greeted me, and sat down at the table. Despite the hotter-than-average June temperature, he looked cool and elegant, as always. Most taxi drivers in town favor jeans and t-shirts covered with beer slogans. Toad had on his usual dress shirt, narrow tie, and dark slacks. He handed me the dollar. "Here's another one for the stupid file."

"The stupid file is full."

He signaled to the waitress. "Anything new on the horizon?"

"Nope. Just sitting here, wincing."

Toad's niece, Evangeline, known as Vangie; her friend, Chloe; and another young woman had formed a band called Slotted Spoon. They worked their way up to four chords, and the owner of the coffee shop hired them. They shared a bill with Wonder Tree and Charred Scabs. The music was horrible, but then, my musical tastes stop 'round about the Forties. The members of Slotted Spoon were up on the tiny stage in the corner, mashing their four chords and wailing about the injustices of life. Seemed a bit early in the morning for angst, but maybe the owner wanted to go ahead and get it over with. All three girls had on black tattered clothes, black lipstick, black nail polish, and lots of black eye makeup. Vangie was singing lead, something about lots of pinchers in the circuit. That's what it sounded like. Pinchers in the circuit, oooh, baby.

The waitress brought Toad's order and sauntered back to the counter. He took out a package of slim cigars. "I'm surprised Vangie's not pregnant or in jail the way her mother lets her run around." He tapped a cigar from the pack. "When's Cam due back?"

"Sometime this afternoon." For their honeymoon, Camden and Ellin had gone to Ellin's family beach house at Atlantic Beach. Ellin no doubt spent a lot of time frisking in the waves and picking up every seashell she could find. With his aversion to large bodies of water, I was curious to find out if Camden even put a toe in the surf.

Toad offered me a cigar. "You're staying on at the house?"

I declined the cigar. "Yeah, even though Mrs. Camden would love to toss me out."

When I first moved into Camden's house and set up shop in the downstairs parlor, Ellin complained this would bring unsavory characters to the house, but the only characters so far had been Camden's friends, most of them on loan from *Ripley's Believe It Or Not*.

You couldn't smoke in Perkie's so Toad held the cigar for effect. "How's Kary? Still distracting?"

"I would call Kary Ingram the ultimate distraction."

Distracting, yes. Also beautiful, headstrong, and frustratingly resistant to all my offers of marriage. She was visiting friends in Virginia and would be home tomorrow. I couldn't believe how much I missed her. I hoped she missed me, too.

Thankfully, the girls finished their set. Toad and I applauded. Vangie grinned and came over. She tucked a long strand of her blue-black hair behind an ear festooned with silver hoops, revealing dark green eyes outlined in black.

"Morning, you two."

"Sounds lovely, dear," Toad said.

She kept grinning. "Oh, shut up. I know you hate it."

"Reminds me I need to get my brakes fixed."

"I'd be worried if you liked it, Uncle Toad, but David, here, he's a real fan."

I pulled out a chair. "Sit down and join us. Coffee?"

"No, thanks. We can have all we want. That's why we're so jazzed. And there's another reason we're excited." She leaned forward as if her news were top secret. "The Cave says we can play the next Rattle this weekend."

Toad gestured with his cigar. "The Cave? Where's that?"

"You know. It used to be the Bunker."

"Oh, yes, on Emerald."

I'd been to that dark little club. "Is that the latest Goth hangout?"

Vangie gave me a pitying look. "And here I thought you were so with it. Goth is passé. Everything is Shade now."

"At the next Cave Rattle. Gotcha."

"So, anyway, the girls and I are chuffed. If we make a sound at the Cave, we might get tagged to play Venue Two in Charlotte. It's a big step."

The other girls called to her. "Okay, gotta go. See you two later."

Toad watched her walk back to where her bandmates were tuning their instruments and adjusting the sound system. "They grow up so quickly."

"Want me to check out the Cave?"

"No, I know the place. It's safe enough. Part of the mayor's plan to clean up the city."

Richard Holt was running for re-election as mayor of Parkland. Even though the election was months away, he already had his slogan: "Children Deserve a Clean City." He'd even put up posters of himself and his very photogenic blond wife, Chelsea, posing with brooms as if sweeping up the streets. Model-thin and eerily remote, Chelsea Holt had made it clear in earlier interviews that she came from a wealthy family and never had to use any sort of household cleaning device, so the posters were a source of amusement for the *Parkland Herald* and local radio personalities. "Someone had to show Mrs. Mayor which end of the broom to hold," was one of the nicer remarks.

"Holt's done pretty good so far," I said. "Couple of extra parks, day care centers."

"I'm surprised his platform isn't 'Children Are Our Future.'"

"Wasn't that what he used last time?"

"It was 'Children Are Flowers in the Garden of Life.'"

I couldn't believe I'd forgotten something so cheesy. And I didn't want to keep on talking about children. I made sure I didn't leave the dollar bill with the phone number for a tip. "Guess I'll go pick up Dicehead."

"Does he have a real name?"

"His real name is Ferd Fuller."

Toad snickered. "Ferd."

"Short for Ferdinand. His wife knew he wasn't taking the family car, so my taxi sting paid off."

"Yeah, this guy was easy to spot."

"Wasn't it convenient of him to use your taxi company?"

"Sometimes these things work out. Did Mrs. Dicehead actually pay you to get him back?"

"Yes, she actually did." I'd had a problem lately with clients not paying their bills. "I was as surprised as you are."

"The girlfriend wants to cooperate?"

"She doesn't know that yet, but she will."

"Good luck."

I said good-bye to Toad, gave the Slotted Spoons a wave, and went out to my white sixty-seven Plymouth Fury. I started her up, but I didn't go anywhere right away. I sat for a while, feeling the ancient air-conditioner do its best to cool the interior, listening to the New Black Eagle Jazz Band play "Oh My Babe Blues," and thinking about what Toad had said. They grow up so quickly. I couldn't help but think of Lindsey. She'd been only eight years when the accident took her from me. I wondered what she would have been like as a teenager, as a young woman.

I put the Fury in gear. Keep busy. That was the key to surviving these bouts of self-pity, self-doubt, whatever the latest buzz word might be. Don't start imagining what might have been.

● ● ● ● ●

Dicehead's girlfriend lived in Bay Point, a small residential area near the airport. She was a slovenly young woman with bright blue fingernails, mouse-colored braids sticking out from under a blue toboggan—a toboggan hat, in June—and an unfortunate combination of green-and-white striped shirt, skull-patterned shorts, and scuffed black flip-flops. The shirt didn't quite meet the shorts, so I got a free view of fat, pale, round stomach. Most women complain about this unwanted pooch. This young woman didn't seem to mind giving hers a little fresh air. Headphones to an iPod were attached to her ears. During our conversation, she kept the headphones on. She spoke around a wad of gum.

"Saw him yesterday. That's all I can tell you."

"Do you think he'll be by today?"

"He needs to. I gotta talk to him about something. What's the deal? When you called, you said something about money."

Money, the magic word. "I owe him money, and I can't find him."

"You try his place? Forty-two sixty Pacer Avenue."

Too easy. "Thank you."

"He don't actually live there. It's where he likes to, you know, keep things private. You going that way, how about giving me a ride? There's a couple of things I wanna discuss with him."

"Sure. Hop in."

Back into the Fury for another blast of lukewarm air and hot jazz. All you have to do is say "money," and people will jump through hoops, or jump into my car. The young woman ignored my music, her own brand pounding through her ears. She popped her gum. "So what kinda deal you got with him?"

"The usual."

"Me, too. Actually, we got a couple of things going. You really got money for him? He better pay me outta that."

When we reached Pacer Avenue, she pointed out Dicehead's love nest.

"That's it."

Forty-two sixty Pacer Avenue was on the east side of Parkland, a short dark street with shuttered homes and droopy trees, exactly the neighborhood I'd choose for romantic rendezvous. Dicehead was home. He stared, slack-jawed, at the sight of his girlfriend.

"What are you doing here now?"

"Me and you's got to talk. What about that deal we made?"

"What deal?"

"The one you was gonna set up." At his blank look, she sighed, hands on hips. "You said this guy had a good thing going at the racetrack and was going to let you in."

He eyed me. "You bring along this guy to shake me down?"

"No," I said. "I'm here to return you to the loving arms of your family."

Dicehead eyed her and decided I was the lesser of his two problems. "I gotta go with this guy."

It's not often the deadbeat dads I corner leap gratefully into my car. Dicehead chose the backseat and cowered there as I drove his girlfriend home. She cussed him all the way. When she got out, she leaned in the window.

"If I don't hear from you tomorrow, I'm hiring this guy to take you apart, you hear me?"

"All right, all right."

She went into her house and slammed the door. Dicehead sighed with relief.

"Can't figure her out."

"Oh, I don't know. She seems pleasant enough."

He looked at me askance. Sarcasm is wasted on a deadbeat dad.

I drove him to another part of town where another woman stood with her hands on her hips. "In case you're wondering, you're going to get the same reaction from your wife."

"I know it." He looked around as if hoping to see an escape. "Damn."

"It's either her or the police."

"Just because I like to gamble a little now and then…"

As Dicehead got out, I offered him a piece of advice. "You could avoid a lot of grief if you'd pay your child support." As he dragged himself up the walk toward his wife, other words fought to leave my mouth, but I held back. *You ought to be grateful you've got children to support. You have children, you stupid bastard. I want to grab you by your skinny neck and shake you till your head rattles like a real handful of dice.*

I gripped the steering wheel until my hands ached. Damn.

Chapter Two

"Baby O' Mine"

A couple of deep breaths and I had myself back in control. No need to waste any more anger on something I couldn't change. What I needed was a break and conversation with normal people. Lunchtime or not, I was close enough to Janice's to stop in and have a hot dog. Janice Chan makes the best hot dogs I've ever tasted. The little brick building's nothing fancy, but it's always packed. Now that the weather was good, people sat outside at the picnic tables, or leaned against their cars, mouths full of hot dog, fries, and sodas.

I started in when a voice called, "Randall!" Rufus Jackson, three hundred pounds of Southern-fried Good Old Boy, waved from one of the picnic tables. With his scraggly red beard, long red braid, tattoos, and biker t-shirt, Rufus looked like someone you'd cross the street to avoid, but beneath all the hair there was a shrewd mind and a raunchy sense of humor. "I want to talk to you."

"Let me get my lunch."

I wedged my way into the crowd and up to the counter. All I had to do was catch Janice's eye. She'd bring me the usual, two hot dogs all the way, and a steaming pack of artery-clogging fries.

Steve, the glum man who did most of the cooking and cleaning, rarely spoke to me or to anyone, but he came over and said in a low voice, "Would you talk to Janice and tell her we're in America now and there's no such thing as fox fairies?"

I had no idea what he was talking about. "Okay."

"I mean, she's not the same around here. Something's really got her spooked. I told her it's maybe kids playing pranks, but she says it's fox fairies."

"And what would fox fairies be?"

"It's a Chinese thing. You know how she is."

I thought Janice was as American as the hot dogs she sold. "I'll see what I can do."

Steve went back to his cooking. In a few minutes, Janice brought me my hot dogs and fries in a red plastic basket and a Styrofoam cup full of Coke. "Here you go, Randall."

I handed her my money. I didn't know if she was plagued by fox fairies, but something was bothering her. "You okay today?"

She grimaced slightly and motioned down the counter. "Mother's here."

Janice's mother was perched on one of the stools, a small slight woman, her black hair cut short with a fringe of bangs. She wore a beige pants suit, a black blouse, and beige sandals. Her jade earrings matched the pin on the lapel of the suit.

"Don't let her appearance fool you," Janice said. "She's as Chinese as the Great Wall and twice as stony."

"What seems to be the problem?"

Janice straightened the napkin dispenser and ketchup bottle and tapped the little laminated menu back in place. "She thinks selling hot dogs is beneath me."

"Even though they're the best hot dogs in the world?"

"I'm a Rat child. I should be a lawyer."

"A Rat child? That sounds cool, if a bit shady."

"Chinese zodiac. I was born in the Year of the Rat."

"I hope that was a good year."

"Rats are charming, intelligent, and quick-witted."

"True, all true."

"Also calculating, selfish, and self-obsessed."

"There's always a dark side."

"Mozart was a Rat. So was Washington. Perhaps I should be running for president."

"So how do fox fairies fit into all this?"

She sighed and tucked a wayward strand of her fine black hair behind one ear. "Mother says the reason I'm having trouble is because I've offended the spirits."

"Ask Camden to look into this."

"Does he speak Chinese?"

"What's a little language barrier in the spirit world?"

"I hadn't thought of that." She gave me a thoughtful look. "When's your birthday?"

"August seventh, but I'm about five years older than you are."

Janice did a quick calculation. "A Dragon. I might have known."

"I take it that's a good thing."

"Only the most popular sign: lucky, dynamic, irresistible."

"What a remarkable coincidence. Now give me the flip side."

"Egocentric, arrogant, demanding, short-tempered."

I was impressed by how quickly she rattled off the details. "How do you know all this stuff?"

"Mother's an expert. I've heard it all my life. When she found out Steve was a Sheep, she almost disowned me. She says our business relationship could never work, because Rats consider Sheep lazy."

"But you two get along fine."

"Of course we do. This zodiac thing is all nonsense."

"Except for the part about the irresistible Dragon."

I was glad to make her smile again. "Maybe there is something to these signs, after all. Would you like to meet Mother?"

"It would be my pleasure."

Mei Chan was delighted to discover I was one of the fortunate Dragon people and chatted at length about the wonders of dragonhood. Turns out I'm a born leader with a will to win and succeed, an idealist, a perfectionist, dominant, powerful, strong, healthy, and generous. This was definitely the sign I'd have picked out for myself.

"It is so nice for Janice to have friends like you," she said. "Perhaps you can help me convince her to use her talents for something more than selling hot dogs. I don't think she should spend her life doing this."

I'd heard the same kind of complaint from Ellin's mother about Ellin's choice of career. Mrs. Belton believed that producer of a psychic network was beneath her daughter, never mind that Ellin had excellent administrative skills and loved telling people what to do. Maybe the two mothers ought to form a support group. "Not even if she's happy?"

"Ah, she says she's happy, but I'm her mother. I know her better than anyone. I know she has offended the spirits."

"Could you tell me more about fox fairies? Why would Chinese spirits travel all the way to America to pester a hot dog shop?"

She shrugged. "Who knows the way of spirits? But I feel there is something at work here, a strange sort of force. Perhaps it's a type of spirit native to this area. Do you know of anything like that?"

Ghosts find Camden irresistible, so I've dealt with weird things before. Why was this ghost here? The building had always been a restaurant, so it wouldn't be missing the old homeplace. Maybe he or she died in a cooking accident or choked on a chicken bone. During my past experiences, the Visitors From Beyond had a clear reason to return. This haunting didn't make sense. That made me uneasy.

Mei gathered her purse and scarf. "I'm so sorry to rush off, but I have an appointment. It was very nice to meet you, Mr. Randall. Janice, I will talk to you later this evening. You know this problem could be quickly resolved if you find another job."

Janice didn't roll her eyes, but her expression suggested she really wanted to. After Mrs. Chan had gone, she said, "You see how she is?"

"My mom's the same way. She wants the best for me."

"This is the best for me. I'm my own boss, I set my own hours, I make good money, and I like hot dogs."

"What would convince your mother?"

"Aside from a personal visit from the Jade Emperor? I don't know. She needs a sign."

"Maybe I can manufacture one."

She frowned. "What are you thinking of?"

"Your mother's into all this zodiac stuff. She'd believe a real psychic, wouldn't she?"

"I suppose."

"I happen to live with a real psychic. I think your fox fairies are toast."

Her expression brightened. "I'd appreciate that, Randall. I'd give you free hot dogs for life."

We shook hands. "Deal."

By the time I returned to the picnic tables, Rufus had finished his hot dogs. He slurped the last of a huge cola and motioned for me to sit down. "Got a job for you."

"I'll take it."

"You don't even know what it is yet."

"Doesn't matter. The Randall Detective Agency is at low tide."

Rufus gave a snort that jiggled the pieces of French fry caught in his beard. "Always low tide with you."

"So what's this job?"

He looked around, but nobody was within range. "Got a kid I want you to find."

Great. "What kind of kid?"

"Don't know." He rattled the ice in his cup. "See, this is coming between Angie and me. She knows I got a kid, and she wants to see it."

"You have a child by another woman?"

He took a big mouthful of ice and crunched it noisily. "Didn't I just say that?"

No, he didn't, but I should have been up on my Rufus-speak.

"My first wife, Bobbi, writes me about a week ago to tell me about this baby she had, only she don't send any details, just that it's mine."

"I didn't know you'd been married before."

"Yeah, it ain't something I'm proud of, but seeing as how you've managed to get yourself snagged twice, I thought you could handle this. Angie says I oughta do the right thing by Bobbi, whatever that is."

"Can Bobbi prove you're the father? Does she want you to pay child support?"

"Oh, I got no problem with the kid being mine. But I can't find Bobbi. I went to her place on Forest Cove Drive last Tuesday, and the place is locked up tight as a tick. Neighbors say they ain't seen her for a long time."

"You still have her letter?"

"Yeah, I got it someplace."

"I'll need to see it."

"Okay." He rested both huge forearms on the picnic table. "I don't want to start nothing with Bobbi, but I'm a bit concerned about her and the kid."

"Maybe she doesn't want you to know where she is. Maybe she's starting a new life."

"She started a new life the day I left. Don't go speculating on me, Randall. Take the job and find her. I won't get any peace from Angie till something's settled."

Angie, Rufus' wife, was as big as he was and just as stubborn. "Okay. Last seen at Forest Cove Drive."

"Second house on the right."

"Would she be going by Bobbi Jackson or another name?"

"Her maiden name's Hull. Bobbi Jo Hull. When I was married to her, she was about five-five, hundred and forty pounds, bleached blond hair, brown eyes. Got a birthmark shaped like Texas on her rear, but you ain't likely to see that."

"I hope not."

Rufus reached in the pocket of his jeans for his pack of chewing tobacco. He pulled out a wad of brown strings, stuffed them in his mouth, chewed a while, then transferred the wad to one cheek. "Gotta admit I'm damned curious about the kid."

"You and Angie planning to have children?"

"We're talking about it. I wouldn't mind a couple of little ankle-biters." He turned his head and sent a long stream of brown juice into the grass. "When's Cam and Ellin getting home?"

"This afternoon."

"Now that was a surprise to me, those two getting hitched. I didn't think she cared for him."

"She does, in her own twisted way."

Rufus gave another snort. "Think she's likely to keep you on?"

"Lately she's been too busy with her network to hassle me."

"Ever think of getting your own place?"

"Sometimes." I didn't set out to make 302 Grace Street my home, but damn it, I liked living there. If I moved, I'd have to give up sharing those little domestic moments with Kary that made my life so much brighter.

Rufus was well aware of my feelings toward Kary, but decided not to make a smart remark. "You do this little chore for me, Randall, and I'll make it worth your while."

"I'm sure you will."

"Yep. Ask me how sure."

A conversation with Rufus can't end without one of his peculiar Southern expressions. "As sure as what?"

"As sure as a thumbtack lands point side up."

• • ● • •

I didn't want to get involved with a missing child case, but Rufus had helped out on previous cases. I owed him a favor. I could at least stop by Forest Cove Drive and see if his ex-wife was at home and find out what she wanted. There might not even be a child. It could all be Bobbi Jo's ploy to get money from Rufus.

On my way, I stopped by the public library to see what Mandy, the reference librarian, knew about fox fairies. I could've looked them up online, but I enjoyed talking with Mandy, and like Kary, she got a thrill out of helping with my investigations. Mandy's a pretty little woman with a cloud of pale blond hair and a wistful expression. If she doesn't know the answer right away—and she usually does—she knows where to look. This question was a snap. Apparently, Mandy had memorized *The Giant Book of Multicultural Fairy Tales.*

"In Chinese folklore, foxes are considered the cleverest of animals and can change themselves into men and women whenever they like. Fox fairies will bring you good luck or bad, depending on how they're treated. Let me get you a book." She disappeared into the stacks and came back with a thick blue book. "*Tales of a Chinese Grandmother.* There's a wonderful story in here about a fox fairy who helps a young man win the woman he loves. You see, years ago, the young man's grandfather had been kind to the fox fairy, so this was her way of repaying the debt."

I flipped through the book. The flowing illustrations were in shades of red and gray. I went past "The Sisters in the Sun" and "The Daughter of the Dragon King" before I reached "The Grateful Fox Fairy."

"Have you ever wondered why in fairy tales there's always a price to pay?" I asked.

"I guess it's a way of keeping everything in balance. Back in fairy tale days, you might be a poor shepherd, but you did have your word, and that was something people took very seriously. If you went back on your word—"

"The fox fairies would get you."

"Or something like that."

I handed her the book and she scanned the barcode and my card. "How would I keep them away? Is there a particular spell? Fox fairy repellant?"

"In ancient China, there would've been a shrine or a temple especially for the fox fairies, and you'd light incense or leave small bowls of food."

"Do they eat hot dogs?"

"Probably not. I'd go with rice." She handed me the book. "That's due June twenty-fifth."

"Excellent advice, as always, thank you."

"Let me know how it comes out."

"Happily ever after, I hope."

Chapter Three

"Baby, Oh Where Can You Be?"

My investigations had taken me to every inch of Parkland, but I'd missed Forest Cove Drive. It was way over past the coliseum complex and new high school stadium, close to Interstate 40. Like every other neighborhood in the city, Forest Cove was misnamed. No forest. No cove. Only a typical street lined with parked cars and the occasional oak tree. All the houses were a faded pink brick with a garage on the right-hand side, but only one was surrounded by yellow police tape, two police cars, an ambulance, and a small crowd of curious neighbors.

The second house on the right.

When I parked the Fury and got out, my sinking feeling sank further. The EMTs carried out a covered body on a stretcher. A policeman the size and shape of a Humvee detached himself from the crowd and greeted me with a tight smile.

"Nice of you to show up, Randall. Saves me the trouble of hunting you down."

"Just out taking a drive."

Usually Jordan Finley runs me away from crime scenes because he knows I usually solve the crimes. He took out his small notebook. "For once in your life, you're going to be useful. The victim is one Bobbi Jo Hull Jackson. Now, there are probably a million Jacksons in this town, but you came along and made this a little easier. What's the connection to Rufus?"

"His ex-wife."

Jordan's dark eyebrows rose. "How many does he have?"

"Only this one, as far as I know. He wanted me to see if she was okay."

"She is not what I call okay. Someone shot her. When did you last see Rufus?"

"He couldn't have killed her. He was with me at Janice's not twenty minutes ago."

Jordan gave me the weary look of a man who has seen everything. "Oh, he had plenty of time. She's been dead about a week."

I had to swallow. A week! Hadn't Rufus told me he'd been by the house last Tuesday?

"Nobody noticed she was gone? Didn't she have any friends? Relatives?"

"She'd quit her job. Neighbors say she was often gone for weeks at a time. They thought nothing of it. Fella came round to cut her grass, got worried about her, managed to get in the house and found her on the floor."

What about the baby? "Anyone else in the house?"

"Should there have been?"

"Rufus got a letter from Bobbi about a week ago telling him she had his child."

Jordan stopped writing and gave me another look. This one was far from weary. "Does he still have this letter?"

I saw where this was headed. "You're not going to pin this on Rufus. He was happy about the baby. He wanted to do the right thing, only he couldn't find Bobbi."

"So he sends you. You walk in and you're found leaning over the body. Nice little set-up. Too bad the yard man got here first."

"Sounds like Bobbi was trying to set Rufus up. Maybe there wasn't a baby."

"Or maybe there was, and we haven't found its body yet."

"That's a whole lot worse than what I was thinking, Finley."

Jordan closed his notebook. "I'm paid to think the worst. That's my job. Where's Rufus now?"

"At home, I guess."

"I'll be by in a few minutes to have a little chat with him, and if he's not there, I'll know who warned him off—and speaking of warning off, you are officially out of here."

I took my time walking back to the Fury. The yard man's mower, weed trimmer, and all his equipment lay on the half-finished lawn. A blue-and-white tag on the mower said "Daily Rentals." Several faded newspapers, still in plastic wrappings, lay on the front stoop.

A large man with a too-tight t-shirt straining over a beer belly ambled over from the next house and stopped me. "That policeman tell you anything?"

"Looks like your neighbor was shot and killed," I said. "About a week ago."

The fact that Bobbi had been lying dead in the house that long didn't faze him. "Oh, yeah?"

I looked over my shoulder. Jordan was busy with the crime scene. I could probably get in a few more questions before he chased me away. "How well did you know Mrs. Hull and her family?"

"Wasn't nobody but her."

"She didn't have a baby?"

"Not that I know of."

The Amazing Mystery Baby was beginning to get on my nerves. "You notice any visitors last week, any different cars in the driveway? Maybe a Bigfoot truck?"

He shook his head. "I work most days. People could've come and gone all the time and I wouldn't know it."

"Did Mrs. Hull have any particular friends in the neighborhood?"

"Kept to herself. We all do around here. It's too dangerous these days. See what happened to her."

But if you'd been looking out for each other, maybe she wouldn't have gotten killed, I wanted to say, but I knew this was useless. Not every neighborhood was like Grace Street, where neighbors took in each other's mail, looked after pets, even had block parties.

At this point, I heard Jordan growl, "Randall."

"Thanks for your help," I told Beer Belly. "Be sure to lock your doors tonight. The killer's still on the loose."

I was glad to see that at least this made an impression on him.

• • ● • •

Daily Rentals was located in one of the small strip malls that decorate the outer loops of Parkland. Not only could you rent lawn mowers and weed trimmers, but backhoes, cranes, posthole diggers, and other construction accessories. I took off my jacket and tie and rolled up my shirtsleeves before I walked up to the counter. The manager was one of those bald guys who make up for it by having a long, full beard and flowing moustache. Maybe he was growing his own toupee.

He glanced up from a clipboard filled with orders. "Afternoon. What can I do for you?"

"Need a good lawn mower, a weed trimmer, and one of those edgers."

"Sure thing. How long for?"

"One day. What's that going to set me back?"

"'Bout fifty-five dollars, providing you bring it all in by six. After that, it's five dollars an hour."

I whistled. "A little more than I planned on. Let me take a trip by the ATM."

"No problem."

I looked around the store as if concerned he might not have what I needed. "You got plenty of those things on hand?"

"Oh, yeah, we get a lot of calls for lawn equipment, especially in the summer. We've been pretty busy, but we can set you up."

"Great, thanks. The grass is getting pretty high on Forest Cove Drive. I'll be back with the cash in a minute."

He fingered his long moustache. "Forest Cove? Just sent a fella out there."

"A Mrs. Bobbi Jo Hull asked me to cut her lawn."

He stopped fingering. "That's where Harwood was going."

"Harwood?"

"H.A. Harwood. He works for me. I hire him out to do jobs for people who can't operate the machines themselves, mostly widow ladies, old guys who shouldn't be mowing or shoveling snow. It's good advertisement, too."

"I guess Mrs. Hull forgot he was coming over. I'm her neighbor, and she asked me if I'd mow the lawn for her, but if Harwood's got it covered."

"Oh, yeah, he's a good man, good worker."

"Thanks," I said. "Sorry about the mix-up."

Like Bobbi's neighbor, nothing bothered this guy. "No problem."

I thought I'd better get to 302 Grace Street before Jordan arrived. I didn't see Rufus' Bigfoot truck in the drive, but Ellin's silver Lexus pulled in the driveway. The newlyweds were home. She and Camden got out. She had on a light blue blouse and matching shorts that showed off her great legs. She was a delicious shade of golden brown that made her gold curls shine. Cam had on his usual jeans and a blue shirt with the sleeves rolled up. He was his usual color: pale.

"Hey, where's your tan?" I said. "Were you a mushroom in another life?"

He inspected one arm. "What are you talking about? I'm three shades darker."

Ellin heaved two large plastic bags of shells from the trunk. "I actually got him to sit out in the sun."

I picked up the bags. "I was hoping you'd find some shells. We don't have enough."

She glared as I hauled the bags up to the porch. "Set them down anywhere, Randall. I've got to call the network."

She whipped out her cell phone and went into the house. Camden brought their suitcases up to the porch and sat down on the porch swing. He pushed his pale hair out of his eyes and gave me a grin.

"No need to ask how you spent your summer vacation," I said.

"I am pretty damn satisfied."

"Do a lot of swimming?" I knew he avoided anything larger than a birdbath.

He took off his sneakers. "There's no way you'll get me in the ocean. Ellie was out swimming in it every day while I kept a respectful distance." He gave me one of his deep blue gazes. "Are you looking for another baby?"

I've mentioned that Camden has considerable psychic ability. Add that to the fact we've been close friends for almost ten years, and it's impossible to keep anything from him. Nowadays, I don't even try.

He kept his gaze on high beam. "There's something else. Something about Rufus. Is he in trouble?"

"You could say that." I had started to explain when Ellin returned to the porch, no longer calm, relaxed, human Ellin, but supercharged Boss Lady Ellin.

"Reg has managed to ball up everything at the studio. I've got to go over there right away. Leave the shells out here, Cam. I'll take care of them later."

"Okay." He knew better than to say, "Honey, it's four-thirty, why don't you wait until tomorrow?" When she'd hurried out to the Lexus and zipped down the driveway, he said, "It's so much easier to agree with everything."

"My boy, you've learned the first lesson of a successful marriage."

"Coming from you, that has real merit. Now what's this about Rufus?"

I heard the roar of Rufus' truck down Grace Street. "You're about to find out."

Rufus and Jordan arrived within two minutes of each other, the bright blue truck with its oversized tires pulling in ahead of the patrol car. The two men got out and stood for a long while talking, Jordan large and square in his uniform, Rufus large and round in his overalls. They must have been sending strong signals, because Camden got up.

"Rufus."

Both men came up the porch steps. Rufus leaned back against the railing and crossed his arms, glowering. Jordan spoke first.

"Cam, Bobbi Jo Hull, Rufus' ex-wife, was found dead in her home today. She'd been shot. I don't have the coroner's report yet, but it looks as if the murder happened about a week ago. Rufus tells me she sent him a letter informing him of a child she claims is his. I need to see that letter."

Alarmed, Camden glanced at Rufus, who continued to frown. "A child?"

"That's all I wanted to know, and look where it got me," Rufus said with a growl.

"My God, Rufe, I know you didn't kill anybody."

"Tell that to Finley."

"Do you still have the letter?"

"It's in my room. I'll go get it, if it's so doggoned important."

"It is, if you want to prove you're innocent."

"Why would I kill her? I didn't want nothing from her. I wanted to see the kid, that's all."

He was still grumbling as he went into the house. Camden turned his anxious gaze to Jordan. "I know he didn't do it."

Jordan rubbed his face wearily. "That's fine, Cam, but you know how well psychic evidence holds up in court."

"You must have other suspects."

"None at the moment. Unfortunately for Rufus, history has shown us that it's nearly always the husband, wife, or ex-spouse. Plus Rufus doesn't have a very good alibi for last week."

"He was working, wasn't he? Can't his construction buddies vouch for him?"

"I checked with his boss. There were a couple of rainy days last week when nobody was working."

"What about the child?"

"We didn't find a child in the house."

I joined the conversation. "If there ever was one. Bobbi Jo could've been running a scam of her own. Maybe it backfired on her."

Camden sat down and put on his sneakers. "I want to go to the house."

Jordan usually doesn't mind. "Figured you might. You'll have to wait until the crime-scene team is finished."

Rufus returned and handed a piece of paper to Jordan, who read it.

"Mind if I have a look?" I asked.

He handed it to me. The letter was pretty straightforward.

> Rufus,
>
> I wanted you to know I've had a baby, and you're the father. Thought you might like to see it. I'm still on Forest Cove Street here in Parkland. Stop by sometime. I work at Oriental Imports, but I'm usually home nights. Trace says hello.
>
> Bobbi

Jordan made notes on his notepad. "Who's Trace?"

"Her cousin, Trace Burwell," Rufus said. "Now, you tell me if there's one thing in there that makes me a murderer."

"She gives you her address and when she'll be home. That could've been all the information you needed."

Rufus made a step toward Jordan, but Camden got between them. Both men backed away to avoid squishing him.

"Rufe, calm down. Jordan's only doing his job. I'll go to Bobbi's house and see what I can find out, and Randall will help me."

Rufus looked at me as if seeing me for the first time. "Randall—well, damn, what am I thinking? I hired him to find Bobbi and the kid. He can find her killer."

"Now, wait a minute—" Jordan began.

"What do you say, Randall? Will you take my case? I know you got the smarts to figure this out."

High praise, indeed. "My smarts are at your service."

"Stop right now, all three of you." Jordan folded the letter and put it in his pocket. "Rufus, you're coming to the station with me. I need to ask you more questions. Randall, you keep your nose out of this. Cam, I'll let you have a go at the house, but if you pick up on anything, you let me know exactly what you see or hear—otherwise, no deal. Got that?"

"Yes, of course."

"I'm serious. Someone shot and killed this woman and possibly her child, and if it wasn't Rufus, then we have a murderer out there somewhere."

Jordan and Rufus got into the patrol car and drove away. Camden watched until the car was out of sight.

"I know he didn't kill anyone," he said.

"It's okay. I'll find a way to prove it. Did you know he'd been married before?"

"Yes, but I never met Bobbi." He ran a hand through his hair. "I need to go to the house."

"You'll get your chance."

Neither of us felt like doing anything, so we waited on the porch until another policeman brought Rufus home. He hadn't been formally charged with the crime, but had been told to stay where Jordan could reach him at a moment's notice.

Rufus wedged himself into a rocking chair and held up a large tobacco-stained finger. "First order of business. I ain't guilty and never have been."

"Second order of business," I said. "Where were you nine months ago?"

He gave me a narrow-eyed stare. "The letter said she'd had a baby. Didn't say how old it was."

I had to agree he was right about that. "What can you tell me about Trace Burwell?"

Rufus reached for his chewing tobacco. "He's a cousin of Bobbi's. I met him a time or two."

"Is he in town?"

"Last I heard he was working at some bar."

"All right. You see if you can find him. Camden can check out the vibes at the house, and we'll stop by Oriental Imports. Maybe Bobbi made a co-worker mad enough to kill her."

"I don't see how. She was a real nice girl."

"Somebody didn't think so."

"Or somebody wanted the baby," Camden said, which was what I was afraid of. "Maybe another man thought he was the father."

Rufus chewed a while. "I lost contact with her after we split. Didn't seem much point in hanging on. We both knew it was over. But Trace might know." He scratched his beard. "Gotta think of what to tell Angie. She knows about the letter and that I was curious about the baby."

I hoped Angie wouldn't react badly to the news. I had a feeling I was going to have enough trouble keeping Rufus in line. "Tell her the truth. Tell her you've hired me, and I haven't found out anything yet."

"Yeah, that'll work." He snapped his fingers. "I know. I'll go pick her up at work and take her out to eat. I'll tell her then. She loves to eat out."

"And stay in Parkland."

Rufus frowned, bringing his low brow even lower. "Now, listen up. I hired you, but I'll play by the rules only so far. Maybe that marriage didn't work out, but I'm not gonna let some lousy murderer get away with killing Bobbi and taking her baby, and he's gonna be found if it hare-lips the nation. You've seen me mad. You ain't seen me real mad."

Camden started to say something, and Rufus held up a hand to stop him. "Cam, I'm tellin' it like it is. Randall's got a day or two to sort this out, and then I'm taking over, and if I find the killer, he'd better give his heart to Jesus, 'cause his ass is mine."

"Rufus, don't do anything stupid. Randall can solve this."

"He'd better."

"When Camden and I have a look in the house, one of us is bound to find a clue."

Rufus lumbered out to his truck and drove away. "He means it," Camden said.

"I'm still trying to figure out 'hare-lips the nation.'"

"It's a Southern way of saying damn the consequences."

"We can't have Rufus running around hare-lipping everyone. Besides Buddy, who are his other pals?"

"He's got quite a few friends at his construction job, and there are a bunch of guys at the Crow Bar he hangs out with."

"Maybe one of them knows something. I'd better have something for Kary to investigate." I'd learned the hard way that if I didn't, Kary would create her own investigation, usually involving a colorful disguise. "Is she going to be all right with a case involving a missing baby?"

"Yes. Are you?"

Leave it to Camden to zero in on my deepest emotional hang-up. Due to a teenage pregnancy that went very wrong, Kary was unable to have children, but she loved being around them and teaching them and was determined to adopt. Adoption was the last thing on my mind. But in this case, I had to make an exception.

"This is Rufus' baby we're talking about. I can handle it."

● ● ● ● ●

I looked up H.A. Harwood in the phone book and found his address on Delver Drive. The house was small and set back from the street in a tangle of grass and bushes in desperate need of a trim. I guess H.A. did so much mowing he let his own yard go native. The small front porch was lined with flowerpots full of scraggly pink and white petunias, old crates, cans of motor oil, rags, and pieces of old lawn mowers.

I'd knocked several times and was about to leave when a small, skinny black man came around the corner of the house, wiping his hands on a dirty rag. He had on faded jeans, a dirty white baseball cap, and a worn checkered shirt.

"Can I help you?"

"Mr. Harwood?"

"That's me. Who's asking?"

"My name is David Randall. I'm investigating the death of Mrs. Bobbi Jo Hull."

His small wrinkled face fell. "Oh, Lord. That poor woman. I hope I never see a sight like that again."

"Do you mind answering a few questions?"

He looked at his wristwatch. "I got to be at a job in twenty minutes."

"This'll take only ten."

"All right, then. Come on up on the porch."

I hadn't seen any chairs. Harwood turned over a crate and sat, so I did the same. I took out my small notebook and pen. "So you came to mow the lawn, as usual, right? What made you go inside the house?"

"Mrs. Hull, she always comes out and says hello. Always wanted to know how I was doing, how my family was. This time she didn't, and I thought maybe she was sick. I knocked on the door and called her name. You know how you feel sometimes that something's wrong? I knew she kept a key under a flowerpot for emergencies. Went on in. The smell hit me first. I know that smell, and you never forget it. Then I saw her on the floor." He took off his cap and rubbed his short graying hair. "A terrible sight."

"What did you do then?"

"I called 911, but I knew from looking she wasn't alive. Something about the way she was laying there."

"Had you known Mrs. Hull very long?"

"'Bout a year, I guess. I always mowed her lawn, and she always gave me a big old glass of tea. She was a real nice lady, and the baby was cute as a June bug. Had this little tuft of red hair."

Red hair. Just like Rufus. "But the baby wasn't at the house?"

He shook his head. "I dreaded going in its room. I was afraid I'd find the poor little thing dead, too, but it wasn't there. Police think the killer took it."

"Did you ever see anyone else at the house?"

"Police asked me the same question. All I could remember was one afternoon when I'd finished, I left the weed-whacker and had to come back to get it. There was one of them big trucks there. I remember because whoever it was parked his damn big truck on the lawn right after I got it looking perfect."

"When was this, do you remember?"

"A week ago, maybe."

"What kind of truck was it?"

"It was one of those giant things with big tires so they're riding way up high. Never saw the point of that."

Just like Rufus' truck. "Was it blue?"

"Yeah."

Damn. "Did you happen to see the driver?"

"No. You got an idea who it was?"

"I'm following a couple of leads." Rufus had said he knocked on the door and looked in the windows. Wouldn't Harwood have seen him? Not if Rufus was inside. "Was Mrs. Hull home at that time?"

"Yes, her car was there. One of them little Toyotas. Kind of a greenish color. I got what I came after and left. I'm paid to do the lawn, that's all." He got up. "And I'm being paid to do a lawn right now."

I stood and shook his hand. "Thank you very much for your time."

"You find the bastard that did that to her, and I'll put my weed-whacker to good use on him, you hear me?"

I was ready to take a weed-whacker to Rufus Jackson myself, and said so to Camden when I returned to 302 Grace.

"It can't be Rufus," he said. "There must be hundreds of big red-haired men who drive blue Bigfoot trucks."

"I'm interested in only one, and he'd better not be lying to me."

Jordan called Camden and told him he could look in the house tomorrow. Then Ellin called to say she'd be home late, so Camden and I had a pizza delivered and ate it on the porch. The smell attracted Cindy, our gray housecat, and her black-and-white kitten, Oreo, who wandered in from the front yard and up the porch steps. Oreo's attention was immediately taken by the bags of seashells. He poked his head in each sack, enjoying the fishy smells. Cindy, however, came up to me and rubbed against my leg. I've never really liked cats, but from the first day I moved in, Cindy and I have had a relationship I find oddly comforting. She never makes a pest of herself, but seems to know when I'd like company. I reached down and scratched behind her ears. I had a sudden vision of a ship full of ghostly sailors, doomed to sail the sky. *The Flying Dutchman*, that was it. My second wife, Anita, had been fond of that opera. I don't know why this occurred to me. Maybe it was the scent of the ocean wafting from the shells.

"That's me, Cindy, the Flying Dutchman, doomed to search for deadbeat dads and lost children. Is somebody trying to tell me something?"

As usual, Cindy's wide green gaze told me nothing.

Camden's wide blue gaze was troubled. "This baby. I can't focus in on it."

"You'll have better luck in the house."

He sighed. "It was real peaceful at the beach."

"Ellin brought back enough shells for you to start your own beach right here."

He gave Oreo a piece of pepperoni. "I see more than one lost child, Randall. It's a little disturbing."

"Do you see yourself flinging them about?" For a short while before the wedding, he'd been telekinetic. Dishes, magazines, and assorted objects, even kittens, had been levitating all over the place, but fortunately, everything settled down. We'd decided it had been a case of wedding jitters.

"That's over, thank God."

"Then relax. I'll be able to figure this one out."

Famous last words.

Chapter Four

"Come On In, Baby"

When Jordan stopped by the next morning to take Camden to Bobbi's house, I told him I was coming along, too. Naturally, Jordan protested, but Camden reminded him I was often needed as an interpreter.

"Sometimes, you know, the signals are confusing."

"That's a load of crap," Jordan said, but since he rarely refuses Camden anything, he grudgingly agreed.

Even in the bright morning light, the house looked dismal. I parked the Fury behind Jordan's car and we got out. Jordan pushed past the police tape and unlocked the door. We stepped in. The house had an unpleasantly stale smell. Camden moved slowly until he got to the center of the living room where he stopped and shuddered. At first, I thought it might be his reaction to the carpet, a hideous light pukey pink-and-brown combination.

"She died here."

Jordan paused. "That's where we found her."

"So long ago. Hard to see anything. Unexpected."

"Can you see the murderer?"

Camden's voice altered. He smiled. "Come in. I'm glad to see you."

Jordan started to say, "What's going on…?" but I motioned for quiet. I'd been through this before. "Who is it, Camden? Do you recognize the person?"

"Here it is." He gestured as if handing over something. Then he gasped. Jordan and I reached for him, but he didn't fall. He stood for a long moment and then said in his own voice, "Her words are still here. Her last words. The child's alive."

"That's one good thing, at least," Jordan said. "You okay?"

He looked dazed. "Her words are still here. I could see them right before me, like silver."

"Nice trick," I said. "You want to check the other rooms and see if any more words are hanging around?"

"I want to sit down."

I steered him to the nearest chair. "Let me know when you're ready."

Jordan let me have a brief look at the rest of the house. Bobbi Jo hadn't been much of a housekeeper. Piles of dirty laundry crowded the bedroom. The bed was unmade, the bureau drawers open to reveal wads of clothing that may or may not have been clean. Her jewelry box contained a scramble of bracelets and necklaces, but an expensive-looking watch lay beside it, as well as rings, credit cards, and a checkbook.

"Whoever took the baby didn't want anything else."

Jordan agreed. "From Cam's reaction, I'd say Bobbi handed the baby to someone she knew and trusted, and then that person shot her. She didn't have time to get away."

A stack of magazines threatened to tumble from an uneven pile by the dresser. All of them had to do with houses and home improvement: *American Homes, Home World, House and Garden*. Several books leaned against the pile, including *Home Improvements For Beginners*, and *Find Your Dream House*. Stuck in the edge of the mirror were a number of coupons and flyers mentioning open houses and realtors' specials. One flyer decorated in red, white, and blue proclaimed "The Sale of the Century at Superior Homes!"

"Doesn't look like Bobbi planned to stay in Forest Cove forever."

Jordan thumbed through *Home Improvement For Beginners*. "The wife's after me to redo the bathroom."

"Get Camden to do it."

"We just had it done. She fussed for days over what kind of tile to put down, and now she's not happy with it. What's all this over here?" A nest of crumpled and yellowing house plans cut from newspapers crowded a large basket. Most of the plans were for huge mansions with fancy porches, gazebos, pools, and other expensive features.

Jordan put the book back on the stack. "She was dreaming big."

A smaller room that must have been the nursery was completely bare. The same nauseating carpet covered the floor. The only clue it may have been a child's room was a faint design of Mother Goose characters on the curtains. Four dents in the carpet corresponded to what might have been the legs of a crib, and there were little white hooks on the wall, presumably for a child's coats and hats.

The kitchen was slightly cleaner. A jumble of dishes lay in the sink and dish drainer. The cabinets were full of cereal, junk food, and cans of soup. The refrigerator held milk, sodas, and a bunch of sad-looking carrots. There wasn't any baby food or anything that looked like formula.

Jordan took out a plastic bag full of little bottles, tubes, and containers. "What's this? Makeup?"

"Keeps it from melting in the heat."

"Oh, yeah, you'd know stuff like that."

"Didn't I just solve a big case for BeautiQueen?"

"Every now and then you luck up." He replaced the bag and shut the fridge. "Guess that's about it."

Bobbi Jo's one small television sat on a rolling cart beside the kitchen table. It was the kind with a built-in DVD player. The DVDs on the cart included standard women's favorites like *Steel Magnolias*, *Sleepless in Seattle*, *The Turning Point*, and several Shirley Temple movies.

Lindsey had loved Shirley Temple movies. Her favorite was one that may have been Shirley's first. In the film, tiny little

Shirley dances to an old jazz song called "Baby, Take a Bow." Every time Lindsey saw that part, she'd say, "Look how good she is. She can't be more than four years old. I'm going to be a dancer, too." Then she'd get up and copy Shirley's steps.

One of the joys of my life had been watching Lindsey dance. Every now and then I take the video of her dance recitals off my bookshelf and put it in the DVD player. Sometimes I even push "Play."

Jordan's voice startled me. "You coming? Where's Cam? Didn't we leave him in the living room?"

We found him sitting outside on the tiny front stoop. "I needed to get out of there."

"Any more flaming words from Beyond?"

"That was all."

Jordan gave us a long stare. "The two of you are going where now?"

"Over to Janice's," I said. "I promised I'd look into something for her."

Jordan looked like he didn't believe me. "All right. Thanks for your help, Cam. See you later."

He waited until we were in the Fury. As I drove away, his square shape filled the rearview mirror.

I needed clarification. "Are you sure that's what Bobbi said? 'Come in, I'm glad to see you. Here it is.'"

"She may have said more, but that's all I could see."

"That's odd. You'd think she'd say, 'Here's Mary Jo, my beautiful little girl,' or 'Here's Billy Jo, my precious little boy,' not 'Here it is' like it's a new TV. Are you going to call your children 'it'?"

"No."

"Was she holding the baby?"

"I couldn't tell, but she was happy to see whoever came in."

"A friend? A relative?"

"Something else. There was this huge sense of—of triumph. I can't figure it out. Maybe this person had come to help take care of the baby."

"He took care of the baby, all right, and Bobbi, too."

Camden finally had his color back, such as it is. "I could use a double shot of Coke."

"We'll be at Janice's in about five minutes."

Janice's shop wasn't open yet, but Janice and her mother were sitting at one of the picnic tables. It looked like they were at the end of a long and frustrating conversation, Janice with her arms folded and a defiant expression, Mei Chan with her hands on her hips and her eyebrows up.

"Remind you of anyone?" I said.

"Looks like the Asian version of Ellie and her mom."

"Exactly."

Janice came to meet us. "Thanks for coming, Cam. You don't mind if I introduce you as a fortune-teller, do you? That's actually a legitimate business in China."

"Not at all." We followed her back to the picnic table.

"Mother, you remember David Randall. This is his friend, Camden, a professional fortune-teller."

Mei Chan brightened. "When is your birthday, young man? I'm willing to bet you are a Snake."

If Camden was alarmed by this, he didn't show it. When he told her his birth date, she laughed.

"I knew it. There is something very alluring about Snake people. They are always charming and attractive, and they are clairvoyant. Did you know this?"

"I don't know anything about Chinese astrology," he said.

"Sit down by me. I'll tell you all about it."

She moved over a little, and he sat down. "I'm not sure how I could be a Snake. I'm afraid of them."

She patted his hand. "That's because of your Western upbringing. In my culture, snakes are just little dragons, wise and good-hearted. People born in the Year of the Snake are compassionate, determined, perceptive, and sensual. Of course, they can also be anxious, jealous, remote, and full of self-doubt, but it is a very good sign." She glanced at his wedding ring. "I see you're married. When is your wife's birthday?"

Year of the Shrew, I wanted to say.

Mei Chan was not happy to discover that Ellin was also a Snake. "Perhaps you should have consulted me before your wedding."

"We knew it was rocky going in," Camden said, "but since we can't live without each other, we decided it was worth the risk."

She put her hand to her heart. "Spoken like a true Snake."

"I'm here to see if I can help Janice with the fox fairies."

"Why don't you come inside and I'll show you what they've done."

While Camden and Mei Chan checked on the Chinese section of the Other World, Janice and I sat down at the picnic table. "You see how she is with this astrology business, Randall?"

"That's all right. Camden's working his snaky charm on her."

"I hope he wasn't insulted. I know he doesn't like snakes."

"When have you ever seen him insulted? Snakes are beyond that."

"Thanks for bringing him over."

"No problem."

Camden and Mei Chan returned. She was telling him a story about a Lady White Snake, but broke it off to address her daughter. "Janice, I think Cam may be able to help you. He knows where the spirits have their strongest powers. I'm going home to consult my books, and we'll meet here again tomorrow. In the meanwhile, you reconsider what I said. Cam, if you'll walk me to my car, I'll tell you the rest of the story."

"What does she want you to reconsider?" I asked Janice.

"She says she'll pay my way if I'll go back to school and study law. Otherwise, no inheritance for me."

"Can you get along without it?"

"I guess I'll have to. There's no way I'm going to law school, or any school, for that matter. There's only one other way to appease her."

"Get married and have a bunch of grandchildren."

"It would have to be someone special." She grinned. "Like a Dragon. The Dragon and the Rat are supposed to be the perfect match."

"Aren't there any other Dragons in your life?"

"No, and I'm very happy being a single Rat."

"Don't give up yet. Maybe Camden really can take care of this fox fairy infestation. I've seen him do some amazing things." Like pluck a dead woman's last words from thin air.

Camden came back to the picnic table. "Your mother is really serious about her astrology, Janice."

She made room for him to sit down. "You don't have to believe all that stuff about snakes."

"I usually think of myself as a small but friendly dog."

"That would work for you. Dog people are honest, faithful, and sincere. Did you speak with the fox fairies?"

"There's something around here, but it's not very clear yet. It doesn't seem harmful, though, just kind of sad."

I had a theory. "The ghosts of all those dead pigs."

Janice looked at me askance. "My hot dogs are all beef."

"Dead cows, then. Did you hear spectral mooing?"

"I'll figure it out," Camden said. "Whatever it is, it isn't serious."

A sound like a tired outboard motor announced Steve arriving on his green moped. Janice stood. "Almost time to open. You guys want lunch? I'll be back in a few minutes."

She greeted Steve and they went inside. I gave Camden a wary glance. "Before we go any further, we'd better ask Janice or her mother how well Dragons and Snakes get along."

"Didn't Mei say snakes were little dragons? What more do you want?"

"I'm going to need proof the stars are aligned before I let you back in the car."

Steve brought us two large Cokes. "The fries'll be ready in about five minutes. You find out anything, Cam?"

"Nothing yet, but I'll take care of it."

"Good. Can you get rid of the Dragon Lady, too?"

"She's just being a mom," I said.

"She's being a Horse."

This was a peculiar insult. Then I remembered the zodiac. "I thought she was a Dragon."

"Janice says her mom's sign is the Horse. She says Horses and Rats are complete opposites. All this astronomy is making me crazy, Cam. Fix it."

Steve made his glum way back to the fries. Camden took a drink. "I'm not sure I can fix the universe. What's next?"

"We'll complete our tour of the Orient with a stop by Oriental Imports."

Chapter Five

"Oh Baby! Don't Say No, Say Maybe"

Oriental Imports took up half a block downtown. Most of the building was used as a warehouse. The shop used two floors. Overpowering smells of incense, candles, and potpourri hit our noses. Inside, baskets of all kinds stacked to the ceiling. Brass candlesticks, candleholders, lamps, and dishes crowded the shelves, along with picture frames, wood carvings, onyx animals, feathers, ribbons, and beads. At the back of the store, rolled carpets leaned against the walls.

The salesgirl, an attractive teenager in a tie-dyed t-shirt and diamond-studded jeans, greeted us and asked if she could be of assistance. Her skin was a beautiful golden color, and her hair was a series of odd little sausage-shaped curls that bounced around her face.

"We're friends of Bobbi Jo Hull," I said. "Is she here today?"

The salesgirl must not have heard the news of Bobbi's death. "Oh, I'm sorry. She doesn't work here anymore."

"When did she quit?"

"She didn't quit. She was fired."

"Fired? I'll bet she was upset about that."

"Not really. She kept coming in late, and the boss got tired of it. Wasn't her fault. She couldn't get anybody to look after the baby."

Camden casually drifted off toward the back. I gave the salesgirl my best smile, pleased that my Dragon charm was still working. "That's too bad. So you got to see the baby?"

"Lots of times. She was a real cute little girl."

A little girl. Great. "I guess her family was excited about it."

"I don't know. She never said anything about a family. She had a husband but said they were divorced, said she'd written to tell him about the baby, so maybe he'd come by and at least see her. I don't know if he ever did."

"And nobody else cared? That's really sad."

Her nod set all the curls dancing. "Yeah, I thought so, too."

"Nobody ever stopped by to ask her about it? No baby shower?"

"Oh, all the girls here at the store went in together and got her a nice car seat."

"Sounds like you were the only friends she had in Parkland."

"Yeah, I guess so." She frowned in thought. "Although, there was this one guy. He came in right before closing, oh, about a week ago, I think."

"Was he a big guy? Red hair?"

"Yeah, actually he was."

Rufus, that better not have been you. "That must have been her cousin Trace. I know him from school. Excited about the baby, I'll bet."

"I don't know what they talked about. She didn't seem too pleased to see him." Now her gaze was suspicious. "What's with all the questions? Is Bobbi in trouble?"

"Oh, no. Sorry I missed her, that's all."

Camden returned, carrying a large red and gold pillow with gold tassels. "I'd like to buy this, please."

She was effectively distracted. "Yes, sir. Cash or charge?"

Camden looked at me. I reached for my wallet. "Cash."

The salesgirl rang it up. "Twenty-six eighty-two. Did you see the matching lampshade?"

"Just the pillow today, thanks. What a great store. Do you always have those ceiling fans?"

"Yes, sir. They're thirty-nine fifty, unless you want the brass ones. They're seventy-five fifty."

"I may come back and get one of those. Oh, I don't need a bag. I'll carry it."

She gave him the pillow and the receipt, smiled, and wished us both a good day.

Outside, Camden wedged the pillow into the backseat of the Fury and then got in the front passenger's side. I got in and cranked up the air. We compared notes.

"About a week ago, Bobbi had a visitor, a big red-haired man."

"That doesn't sound good."

"Any Rufus vibes in the store?"

He shook his head. "I've been to Africa."

"What?"

"The only vibes I picked up were African."

"Next time, stay away from the tribal masks. Is Rufus still working West Adams? Maybe someone there has time to talk to us."

Adams Boulevard had long been a source of contention in Parkland. It was really too narrow to be considered a boulevard, but it had a median filled with Bradford pear trees, trees that would have to go if the street were widened. Naturally, people protested, but other people argued that Adams was a serious bottleneck. A compromise had been reached when the company Rufus worked for agreed to widen the section of the street nearest town, leaving most of the trees. Still, there were a few protesters along the road who waved and shook their signs as we drove up to the construction site.

I parked the Fury next to a line of dump trucks. Rufus was standing with a dozen workers in hard hats and safety vests watching one worker dig a hole. He saw us and waved us over.

"Told the fellas you might want to talk to them."

"If they're not too busy."

Sarcasm wasted. "Nah. You can use the tent if you want."

The tent was a large piece of orange plastic stretched over a couple of poles and anchored to the back of someone's pickup. While I talked to the workers, Camden sat on the tailgate, observing closely and occasionally shaking hands with the men who knew him. We didn't discover anything new. The men confirmed that rain had stopped all construction work for two days last week. One of those days Bobbi had been murdered.

Rufus was the last one in the tent. I told him what we'd learned from the salesgirl at Oriental Imports, that Bobbi couldn't find anyone to look after the baby and had been fired for constantly coming in late.

"About a week ago, a large red-haired man came in to see her. I take it that wasn't you."

"No. Never went by Oriental Imports. Was there anything at her house?"

"Camden saw something."

Rufus looked down at the ground as Camden related Bobbi's last words.

"I'm so sorry, Rufe. If it's any consolation, the baby girl is alive, and we'll find her."

"Must've been somebody she knew. Bobbie was a real sweet gal. Wouldn't have hurt a soul." He raised his head. "Why didn't I go see her right then? The minute I got that letter, I should've gone right over."

I needed to get my facts straight. "Exactly when did you go?"

"Last Tuesday. I told you."

"You told me the place was all locked up. Did you look in the windows or the back door?"

"Yeah, I looked, but the drapes was closed, and I couldn't see nothing. I knocked and called her name. It was 'round about suppertime."

"But you didn't go in."

"Nah."

"Was her car in the driveway?"

Rufus thought a moment. "Yeah, that old beat-up Toyota."

"The rainy days you didn't work, where were you?"

"Took a drive over to see a buddy of mine in Rock Ledge."
Could this be the break we needed? "Can he vouch for you?"
"Nah, he wasn't home."
No break here. "So you were driving around. You've told the police this?"
"Uh, huh."
In their minds, Rufus drove to Bobbi Jo's and killed her. "You'd better be telling me everything."
"Got no reason to lie."
"Okay, Camden's got a rehearsal at three. I'm checking out the Crow Bar."
Rufus looked ready for battle. "After work, I'm going to look for Trace Burwell. I'm pretty sure I know where he is."
From the way Rufus ground one fist into his palm, I didn't envy Cousin Trace. "Just leave him in one piece."

• • ● • •

When we got back to our house, we recognized the white Cadillac in the drive.
"Jean's here," Camden said.
"As if we haven't had enough mothers today."
Before Camden and Ellin got married, Ellin and her mother had long discussions on the porch, most of them at full volume, about Camden's suitability as a husband. As far as Jean Belton was concerned, if he was husband material, then the building supplies must have come from the bargain department of the hardware store. His lack of education and ambition really stuck in her craw, or, as Rufus liked to describe it, put her tail in a crack. Of course, the more she disapproved, the more Ellin dug in.
Now that the deed was done, Jean stopped by infrequently, but pointedly, to see how the marriage was progressing. As far as I could tell, Camden and Ellin have the same relationship they had before they got married, only now they're living in the same house.
Camden took his new pillow from the backseat. We walked up the front steps and were on the porch in time to hear the

latest complaint. Today, Jean was unhappy with the living room. We call this area of the house the island, partly because it's in the middle of the room, and partly because the furniture looks as if it washed ashore from many foreign lands. The faded blue armchair is my usual seat. Camden likes the worn green corduroy sofa. Kary has a little brown wicker rocking chair with red velvet cushions. Another chair holds all the extra magazines, and there's an assortment of throw pillows, end tables, and books. Underneath is an old but fairly plush Oriental carpet. The fringe has been a cheap source of amusement for the cats.

Jean's voice was pitched to its usual whine. "I don't see how you can stand this clutter, Ellin. What if your business associates drop by? What if you want to bring an important client home for dinner?"

As if the Psychic Service attracted important clients. I could tell by Ellin's tone she was trying to remain calm. "We'd meet at a restaurant. It's easier."

"Camden did such a nice job redecorating your bedroom. Why can't he fix the rest of this house?"

"He works, too, Mother."

"As a part-time salesclerk. Honestly, Ellin."

"At least he's working. He's not lying around here all day, drinking beer and watching TV. That's Randall's job."

"Slander," Camden said to me. "You don't lie around *all* day."

Jean continued her complaints. "David is a gem compared to some of the people you've had in here. Who else is in the house now?"

"Harry Hermaphrodite and His Amazing Flea Circus," I said to Camden.

"Rufus and Angie won't be here forever. They're seriously house-hunting."

"Which is what you should be doing. I cannot believe you're still living in this house. No amount of redecorating can cover the fact that it is old and falling apart."

"She left out 'and on the wrong side of town.'" I said.

"Give her a minute."

"And it's in such an unfashionable neighborhood. I wish you'd consider the new Elysium Fields development over by the Catholic Church. It's perfect."

"Cam and I have discussed moving. That's not something we can agree on right now or afford." Ellin's tone was fraying. "He's been looking for another tenant."

"If he had a decent job, you wouldn't be struggling so for money."

"We're not struggling. The PSN is doing well."

"That's not what I heard. Your dinky little cable network is always on the brink of collapse. I just want the best for you, Ellin."

"Cam is the best for me. He always has been. And if he wants Randall around, then I guess Randall stays."

Now I'd have to forgive her for the beer and TV remark.

"Guess we'd better make our presence known." Camden pushed open the screen door. "Hi, Ellie, we're home. Hello, Jean."

Both women turned, a perfect example of Before and After. Jean's hair still has touches of gold and her figure's good, but she's much shorter than Ellin and more wrinkled. Her voice immediately changed to a warm and honeyed tone. "Cam, sweetheart, come give me a hug. What on earth do you have?"

"A new cushion for the island."

She eyed the gaudy pillow. "Hmm, it will fit in perfectly with the décor."

Camden tossed the pillow on the sofa, hugged his mother-in-law, and gave Ellin a kiss. "Where have you been?" she asked. "The Carlyle House has called twice."

"I'm due there at three."

"Don't you have your cell phone on? They wanted to make sure you and Kary bring the music with you."

"We will. Randall and I stopped by Janice's. There's a ghost she wanted me to talk to."

Jean ignored this. "Ellin, I really have to run. We'll continue our discussion later."

"No, we won't," she said, as her mother went out. She turned to Camden. "I wish you had come with me to the studio this morning. Do you know what that idiot Reg has done? He's hired the Archer Sisters! After I specifically told him they were too stupid to breathe."

Jean drove away, and we moved to the kitchen where Ellin stabbed the remains of a salad, still going on about the Archer Sisters, whom I gathered were a species of harpy, while Camden drank another Coke and nodded at appropriate intervals.

"If he thinks he's going to improve ratings by having those two, he must be more dense than I ever suspected. I told him to book Jessie Vardaman. Did he even contact him? No! Then Mother comes by and starts in on the house. Do you suppose you could rework the living room a little?"

"Honey, you know no matter what we do, it's not going to be enough."

"We could move."

If Ellin could sing this would be her favorite song.

"We could," Camden said, "but we're not."

"It wouldn't hurt to look around, see what's available. I brought home materials for us to look through."

"That's fine with me."

It's fine because he's never going to move, and Ellin knows it. She stopped the massacre of her lunch. "Did you really have to buy a huge red pillow?"

"It was part of our undercover sting this morning."

"I thought we agreed you weren't going to get involved in any more of Randall's cases."

"This is different. Rufus is in trouble."

Ellin surprised me with her concern. "What kind of trouble?"

"His ex-wife Bobbi's been killed, and her baby is missing."

She put down her fork. "Oh, my God. This is not a good idea. You know how you get. You were a complete wreck after your friend Jared's murder."

"I'll be okay."

"Why didn't I know about this?"

"I didn't get a chance to tell you last night. You got in late, and you were unhappy about everything that had happened while you were on vacation. It didn't seem like the best time. Then you were gone this morning before Randall and I went over to Bobbi's house."

"Where you saw all sorts of horrible visions, I'm sure." She gave me a glare. "We never had this kind of problem until you moved in."

"Yep, I'm the killer."

Camden set his Coke aside. "I need to help Rufus if I can, Ellie."

"Yes, of course, but I wish you'd leave all the gross stuff to the police. Why don't you come back to the studio with me? It wouldn't be traumatic to toss out the Archer Sisters and have you on the show instead." She smiled one of her knockout smiles that makes me understand why he married her—almost. "Although it would be traumatic for Reg."

Returning to the Psychic Service is the last thing Camden wants to do. "As much as I'd love to traumatize Reg, I have a paying job to practice for."

"Oo, a paying job." She kissed him. "You mean you're not out squandering your talent for somebody's birthday party?"

"The concert at the Carlyle House is a big, important event. It'll probably make the society page."

"I'll cut out the article for Mother's scrapbook."

They can still get into arguments as hot and wild as a California brush fire, but lately, the disagreements have been lighter, more teasing. I'm sure it's just a phase.

Camden put his arm around her. "You don't have to get back right away, do you?"

"No. Why?"

"I don't have to be at the Carlyle House until three."

"I can't imagine what you're thinking."

"I know what you're thinking."

She gave him another kiss. This one was longer and much more impressive. "What a surprise."

"Get a room," I said.

Camden picked her up. "Okay."

With the two of them occupied upstairs, I got ready for Kary's arrival. I knew she'd be home from her friend's house before one o'clock today because she had a student coming for a piano lesson. At twelve-thirty I heard Turbo, her neon green Festiva, chug up the drive and park. I met her on the porch, Diet Coke in hand. I got as far as "Welcome home," and the rest of my greeting got stuck in my throat, a usual reaction to Kary Ingram in all her summertime glory. She had on a short dress in a light green color that floated around her perfect figure. Her long cornsilk blond hair hung loose over her shoulders. She doesn't need jewelry or any sort of accessory. Everything about her is so effortless and so beautiful. She must have been born in the Year of the Angel.

Okay, enough. I even make myself sick with these flowery descriptions.

I set the cola on the porch rail and went out to the car. "Need any help?"

"Yes, thanks." She opened the trunk. "If you could get that suitcase, please."

I picked up the larger suitcase, and Kary took the smaller one. "How was your trip?"

"We had a lot of fun. How's everything here?"

"Come sit down and I'll tell you."

We put the suitcases on the porch, and Kary sat down in one of the rocking chairs. "Sat down" poorly describes how gracefully she moves. I handed her the cola, and she thanked me. "Where is everyone?"

"Camden and Ellin are upstairs. Rufus is at work." Looking for Trace Burwell, I hoped. Might as well get straight to the bad news. "I need to tell you something about Rufus. He's okay, but his ex-wife Bobbi was found dead in her home, and her baby's missing."

She sat up straight in her chair, eyes wide. "Oh, no! What happened?"

"It looks like she was murdered."

"What about the baby?"

"I'm going to find her."

Kary swallowed hard a few times, her eyes filled with tears. "I know you will, David."

Her faith in me made me swallow hard, myself. I put my hand on hers. "I'm sorry to have to tell you."

"No, I'm glad you did. I want to know. Are you sure Rufus is all right? Was it his baby?"

"He says it is. That doesn't matter. I still want to solve this."

"I'll help you. How's Cam handling all this?"

"Pretty well."

"Then the baby's still alive."

"That's what I was thinking, too."

"We'll find the baby, and we'll prove Rufus had nothing to do with this crime."

I used to think I needed to shelter Kary from the more sordid elements of my profession. Boy, was I wrong. She'd been amazingly resilient and helpful on past cases. Plus the excitement of working with her was addictive.

"What can I do to help?" she asked.

"There's not a lot to go on yet. I'll keep you posted."

"Thanks." She checked her watch. "Right now, I need to get ready for my student."

"I'll take your suitcases up to your room, and may I give you a ride to the Carlyle House this afternoon, ma'am?"

"That would be very nice."

Her student arrived as I was coming back from making my suitcase delivery. He was a stocky little boy whose expression and stance indicated what he thought of piano lessons. But he was as charmed as any male by Kary's smile and patient explanations of the complexities of "The Bull Frog Song."

I got a Coke and peanut butter crackers and went back to the porch. After the boy left, I heard the piano's graceful ripple of notes as Kary played through the tunes she and Camden had chosen from the stack of sheet music sent over by Patrick

Lauber, guardian of the Carlyle House. Delores Carlyle, wife of Amos Carlyle, a prominent artist, had been one of the grand dames of Parkland society up until her death in the late Fifties. The house, left to the city with strict instructions that it never be split up into apartments or offices, had been a showplace, the setting for many extravagant parties. It was now on the historic registry and open to the public on a limited basis.

The songs were pleasant standards of the Thirties and Forties, and there were a few older songs that must have been favorites of Delores Carlyle's mother including one called "Trust Me With Your Heart Again."

Trust me with your heart again. I'd asked Kary that question, maybe not in such flowery terms, but still, I wanted her to believe I was trustworthy. I liked to think she was seriously considering my offer, but I could never be sure.

Their next number was more upbeat, "Oh, Baby! Don't Say No, Say Maybe." I had it on a recording of Mike Daniels and His Delta Jazzmen. Yep, I'd even settle for maybe.

Ellin was all smiles as she went past my office door, but by the time she reached her car, her expression had changed to one of grim determination. I would not want to be Reg right now. He'd better duck and cover.

Chapter Six

"My Melancholy Baby"

Camden came down a short while later and rehearsed the songs with Kary. When they were ready, I took the two of them to the Carlyle House. The Carlyle House was one of those huge mansions with columns and all sorts of fancy windows. Parkland has dozens of them. Many have been made into apartment houses or suites of offices. Several have been neglected. Fortunately for the Carlyle, Patrick Lauber, a wealthy man who enjoyed remodeling old houses, took over, and now it looks as good as it did in nineteen fifteen.

Lauber met us at the front door. He was a large man in an expensive gray suit, complete with pearl buttons and cuff links. Another large pearl sat in the middle of his silk tie. With his white hair and moustache, he looked like a Southern colonel welcoming us to the plantation.

"Afternoon, folks. Welcome to the Carlyle House." He shook my hand. "I'm Patrick Lauber, caretaker of this wonderful home. You must be Camden. We've heard a lot about you."

"Then you must have skipped the description. I'm David Randall. This is Camden."

Camden stepped forward, smiling. "Mr. Lauber."

I'm comfortable in a suit and tie. I feel it lends an air of importance to my sleuthing. Camden, however, chooses to dress in faded jeans, sneakers, a blue shirt with the sleeves rolled up, and the occasional vest. That's exactly what he had on today. Apparently, someone who looks like a small sloppy street person wasn't what Lauber had in mind for his grand opening, but he recovered quickly. "I beg your pardon, Mr. Camden. Welcome."

Camden introduced Kary. "This is Kary Ingram. She'll be playing the piano."

Camden may not have made much of an impression, but Kary made up for it. Lauber kissed her hand. "Enchanted. Please come in."

The front doors opened onto a cream-colored foyer, complete with double staircase. A huge mirror in an ornate gold frame dominated the wall between the staircases. The mirror's surface was flecked with dim golden spots.

Lauber motioned to the mirror. "Mrs. Carlyle was very fond of this mirror. She brought it all the way from Italy. There's probably not another one like it."

As far as I could see, it was a big, old, cloudy mirror in need of a good silvering, but Camden paused and stared into its depths for an uncomfortably long time.

What was he seeing now? I was afraid to ask. "Don't tell me. There's a big floating head saying you're the fairest of them all."

"There's something, but I can't hear it."

Yet, we both added mentally.

If there was anything remotely supernatural in the house, it would eventually poke Camden in the eye, but Lauber was too busy describing the staircases and the wall-hangings to notice our latest close encounter. "I think they're ready for you in the parlor now."

The parlor had yellow velvet curtains, really uncomfortable-looking little chairs with yellow cushions, and a big chunky piano shaped like a rectangle with curved legs. The wallpaper was yellow with little red roses. Kary sat down at the piano and opened her music books.

"What do you want to start with, Cam?"

"Let's try 'Trust Me With Your Heart Again.'"

As she played and he sang, any reservations Lauber might have had disappeared. He and the docents gathered at the door to listen. I'm sure, in a perfect world, where the arts and detective-work pay the big bucks, Camden, Kary, and I would be huge stars. Kary's beautiful, competent playing and Camden's clear tenor voice filled the parlor. The docents sighed. One fanned herself. Another wiped tears from her eyes. Lauber's chest puffed out as he nodded to his staff, satisfied. When Kary and Camden finished the song, everyone applauded.

"That's absolutely perfect," Lauber said. "Exactly what I wanted. Please sing another."

They performed "It Had To Be You," and "How Deep is the Ocean." By the end of their little concert, there wasn't a dry eye in the parlor.

Lauber applauded again. "Splendid. Now, what were you planning to wear? Do you have anything that fits the period?"

"We can borrow clothes from the Little Theater," Camden said.

This suited Lauber. "If Miss Ingram could find something yellow, that would be ideal. Mrs. Carlyle's favorite color was yellow."

One of the docents raised her hand. "We'd love to hear another song."

Camden sang two more, and then we were treated to refreshments in the breakfast room. All of Lauber's attention was on Kary, so he didn't notice how often Camden's gaze turned back toward the foyer.

I strolled over, balancing my tea glass on my plate of cheese and crackers. "Someone calling your name?"

He shook his head. "It's probably leftover voices from past occupants. Old houses like this have a lot of echoes."

Still, on our way out, he paused and looked at the huge mirror for a long time.

• • ● • •

I dropped Kary and Camden at 302 Grace and drove to the Crow Bar. Late afternoon wasn't a busy time. The tables were empty.

A few people sat at the bar near the statue of a crow hoisting a mug. Delbert, the bartender, raised a hand in greeting.

"Is Buddy around?" I asked.

With his beaky nose and lank black hair, Delbert resembles a crow himself. A droopy crow. "He and that girl went to a fiddlers' convention up near Galax."

By "that girl," he meant Evelene, a punk teenager who loved bluegrass and played a mean hammered dulcimer to Buddy's banjo-picking. "Know when they'll be back?"

"Probably Sunday."

I wondered if Buddy knew his pal Rufus was a murder suspect. "Did you happen to see Rufus last week?"

"Yeah, a couple of times."

"What about Tuesday?" Maybe Rufus had stopped by the Crow Bar and forgot.

"No, can't say as I saw him Tuesday. Would've remembered. It was Chug Day."

Bad news. Chug Day was a special occasion for the Crow Bar, the one day a year that Delbert let everyone drink for free, and Rufus wouldn't have missed it. Only this time he did.

• • ● • •

I got home about the same time as Rufus, and Kary and Camden joined us on the porch. We took our usual seats, Kary and me in rocking chairs, Camden on the swing, and Rufus plopped down on the front step. "What's the word on Trace Burwell?" I asked.

Rufus looked disgusted. "Trace Burwell puts the 'dip' in dipstick. If life was a game of dominoes, he'd be the double blank."

"I take it he doesn't know anything."

"Didn't even know she was dead. Got all upset and blubbery. I asked him when he seen her last, and he said she came into the bar every now and then, but he couldn't remember the last time."

"Did he know anything about the baby?" I asked.

"Hell, no. He was useless."

"What bar is this?"

"Some place called the Cave, down on Emerald Street. Music's real crappy."

The Cave, Mecca for the Slotted Spoons. "I'll go down and have a talk with him."

"Hello!" Angie waved from the screen door. "Is this a private party?"

Rufus waved back. "Not if you bring us some beer."

"Be right there."

"Speaking of beer," I said, "Delbert said you missed Chug Day. I thought that was a sacred Redneck Holiday."

"Told you I drove to Rock Ledge."

"Yes, to see the friend who wasn't there. That didn't take all day, did it?"

He avoided my gaze. "I mighta taken a little detour."

To kill your ex-wife? I started to mention this when Camden stopped swinging and frowned at Rufus.

"You went up to Possum's Lair, didn't you?"

"Damn it, Cam."

"You know that's illegal, and if you get caught with that gang—"

"I am a grown-ass man, and I can do what I like!"

"Whoa, hold on," I said. "What are we talking about here?"

Rufus shifted position as if Camden's glare was hot enough to burn, which it was. "Aww, ain't nothin'. Some fellas I know got a still way up in the woods around Rock Ledge. I just stopped in for a visit." He turned to me. "And don't think you're going to find them, 'cause you won't."

"Not even if it'll prove you're innocent?"

"I am innocent, so it don't matter."

Angie gave the screen door a little kick and came out, her arms full of drink cans. She handed Rufus and me each a beer and gave Camden and Kary Cokes. Then she settled her large self on the front step beside Rufus, her huge dress billowing around the slopes of her body like a pink circus tent. Her close-cut brown hair lay in tiny curls from the heat. She raised her can of Mountain Dew in a salute.

"Gentlemen and Kary, I am now gainfully employed."

We set down our drinks to give her a round of applause.

"I am now head seamstress in the Alterations Department of the Key Center Belk. I start tomorrow. Full benefits."

Rufus took a big gulp of beer. "Nice going, sugarplum. Now we can start looking at double-wides."

"Oh, I don't think so. We're getting a real house. Now what are you going on about that don't matter? Is it about your ex-wife and her baby? What have you found out, Randall?"

"We know the baby is a girl," Kary said. "Camden says she's alive, so that's the good news."

"The police don't have any more clues?"

"Not right now."

"But Rufus is still their main suspect."

"Yes," I said, "and he's not making things easy. Hiding up in the hills drinking moonshine with his pals is not the best alibi I've ever heard."

She reached over and gave Rufus a slap on the arm. "You big dummy. Why'd you go over there?"

"Hadn't seen Possum and his boys in a while."

"No, I mean, why did you go over to Bobbi's house? You could've called her."

"She didn't give me her number. Besides, I wanted to see the kid."

"So, now what?"

"Randall told you. I've done hired him to solve the mystery. He's got two days before I start taking people apart."

Kary tried to calm the beast. "Rufus, that's not going to help your case."

Angie's little eyes were so narrow, I could barely see them. "This murderer likely to come after Rufus?"

As if anyone would try with Angie on guard. "I doubt it," I said. "I think someone was after the baby."

"You reckon it was a second husband, somebody who thought the kid was his?"

"That's as good a theory as any."

Angie took a swig of Mountain Dew. "Well, ain't that a kick in the head."

• ● ● ● •

To keep the peace, Rufus took Angie out to eat again. As soon as they were gone, Kary said, "All right, guys. What's in the mirror? I saw the way you looked at it, Cam."

"I'm not sure," Camden said.

"Is it Delores Carlyle, or someone who lived there before her?"

"I think it's just an echo. It wasn't very strong."

"If it comes out during our concert, I want to know." She set her Coke can down beside her chair. "Why don't I go back to Oriental Imports and ask if they're hiring? They might need a replacement for Bobbi."

"Good idea," I said. "Look for a salesgirl with little sausagy curls. She might talk to you."

"Anything else?"

"I didn't have much luck in Bobbi's neighborhood. Can you think of a reason you'd be knocking on doors?"

She thought for a moment. "How about food pantry donations? I have a lot of plastic bags left over from our school food drive."

"Perfect. You might even get a little extra food for the cause."

"I want to do everything I can to help Rufus. If anything's happened to his little girl—"

Camden put his hand on hers. "The baby's alive. I know it."

She attempted a smile. "If you know it, it must be true."

• ● ● ● •

It was Camden's turn to cook supper, so while he put together his special lasagna, I sat in my office and listened as Kary taught another little student the right way to finger a piano piece called "Twinkletoes," or "Fairy Bells," or something like that. After supper, a choir member stopped by to give Camden a ride to choir practice. Ellin called to say she'd be working late to undo more of Reg's handiwork. I'd hoped for a restful evening, but she came home around nine. By then, Kary had already gone upstairs to plan her undercover operations. Camden and I were grazing through the channels and eating pretzels and Cheetos. He looked over the back of the sofa as Ellin steamed by.

"Everything okay?"

"For now."

"There's lasagna in the oven."

"Thanks."

He went into the kitchen with her. I heard the rattle of dishes and silverware as she fixed her plate, microwaved it, and plunked it down on the dining room table. This took about three minutes, so it was time for another complaint.

"This crazy man kept calling the studio wanting us to have his child on the program. He says she can guess anyone's age or weight. I told him to take her to the circus."

"I thought you were planning a special on psychic kids."

"We wanted to, but we couldn't find any."

"Ours will be, you know that."

The silence that followed this statement stretched so long, I thought Ellin had fallen into her lasagna. By leaning back in the blue armchair, I could see into the dining area. Ellin sat at the end of the table, Camden on her left. She finally said something, something I knew he didn't want to hear.

"I really don't want to have any children, psychic or not."

"But, Ellie, you're going to have three."

"Are you sure about that?"

Of course he was sure. "Two girls and a boy."

She stabbed at her lasagna. "I don't want to."

"I know your career is important to you. I'll look after them."

"We can't afford three children. We can't afford one. We can hardly afford us."

"Maybe not now, but by the time they're here—"

Ellin put down her fork. "No. Cam, sweetheart. Listen to me. You'll always be happy doing odd jobs and singing for weddings and wandering around with Randall. It's up to me to bring in the big bucks, and I like that, but three children would be terribly expensive."

"I have a job."

"A part-time job. Have you worked at the store since we got home from the beach?"

"They're not very busy right now. I'll get another job."

"No, you won't."

"It's something else, isn't it?" He took her hand and winced. "Who told you it was horrible?"

She tried to pull away. "Don't. It's late, and I'm tired."

He held on. "I'm seeing all sorts of gross birth pictures. Where did all this come from?"

"It's war stories. Women like to talk about difficult childbirths. 'I was in labor for three days.' 'That's nothing. I was in labor for a month, and the baby came out sideways.' It's nothing. I'm not scared. I'm just not ready to walk around with fifty extra pounds hanging off my waist."

"We need to talk about this."

"Not now. I've had a long day, and I don't want to discuss anything. I'm going to take a long shower and go to bed." She scraped up the last of her meal, got up, put the dish in the sink, and walked around the island to the stairs. "Good night."

Camden washed the rest of the dishes. He sat down on the green sofa and leafed through the *TV Guide*. "What've we got?"

I could tell he didn't want to talk about children. I didn't, either. "Your sweetie didn't want a shower-buddy?"

"I don't need my brilliant psychic insight to tell she needs some alone time."

I'd already checked the cable program guide. "Here's a rundown of tonight's specials. *The Lost Continent* is on Channel six, *Space Travelers* on twenty-two, and *The Giant Gila Monster* on thirteen."

"Oh, no contest. *Giant Gila Monster*." He tossed the *TV Guide* on the coffee table.

"Are you sure? *Space Travelers* has Gene Hackman and Gregory Peck."

"But it takes forever. It's slower than—if Rufus were here, he'd know what it's slower than."

"We don't need Rufus. We can think up our own Southern slang. Slower than a full tick on a coon hound's back."

He gave me a mock glare. "Are you insulting my heritage?"

"Slower than moss growing on an abandoned still. Slower than a hair growing on a granny's chin."

He took the remote and turned the TV to Channel thirteen.

"Okay," I said. "Gila monsters!"

"*Giant* Gila monsters."

"And a wonderful theme song. I hope you're going to sing along."

But Camden had left the building. He was still sitting on the sofa, but his eyes were way off into space, and he wasn't seeing Gila monsters.

"Camden?" I reached over to shake him back to Earth when he blinked.

"I need to go back to the Carlyle House."

"What, now? Tonight?"

"Yes."

"It's that mirror, isn't it? Is it going to suck us into an alternate universe?"

"Can we go?"

I got up. "Since you won't let me watch *Space Travelers*, sure, why not?"

Chapter Seven

"I Really Miss You, Baby"

In the dim light of the streetlamps, the Carlyle House looked like a ghost house from the Civil War. It also looked impenetrable.

"Don't suppose the colonel gave you a key, did he?"

"I'm pretty sure I can get in a back window if you boost me up."

"What about the security system?"

"It's off."

I started to say, "How do you know?" which is a silly question to ask Camden. Then he explained.

"I heard one of the docents tell another to leave it off for the painters who are coming early in the morning to do some touch-up work."

"Where was I when you were planning your daring raid?"

"Eating cheese and crackers and eyeing the blond docent."

Trying not to look too obvious, we strolled around to the back of the house, keeping in the shadows. I boosted Camden up to a window. He climbed in. A few minutes later, he opened the back door, and we walked in semi-darkness to the foyer. On the surface of the mirror, clouds shifted. Camden put his hand on the mirror. Since his hand didn't sink in, and nothing with scaly claws reached out to grab him, I figured we were okay for the moment.

Then he stiffened. "There's someone here, someone who needs our help."

"The people from Reflecto-land?"

"Delores Carlyle."

"Uh-ho. She doesn't like the new wallpaper?"

He stood for a long time, listening. "No, that's okay. She's glad someone's looking after the house."

"Then what's the problem?"

"She wants out."

"Camden, this is so easy, I'm surprised you bothered me. All we have to do is break the mirror."

"I don't think so. She's not trapped in the mirror. She's trapped in the house."

"I'm not tearing down the house."

"I'm going to be a while."

While he communed with dead Delores, I found my way to the kitchen. It was equipped with all modern appliances, including a coffeemaker. I made coffee and thought about how casually I accepted all this. Well, I'd dealt with the spirit of a dead songwriter, fake superheroes, magicians, and a telekinetic sidekick. What was one old ghost?

I brought Camden a cup of heavily sweetened coffee. He sat cross-legged on the floor in front of the mirror like a kid watching TV. He nodded as if in reply to a question.

I handed him the cup. "Life story?" These ghosts can be pretty chatty.

"We're up to her college days."

"Tell her to skip to the haunting days. We're not supposed to be in here."

He drank and listened. I drank and wandered. There certainly wasn't anything to look at. Delores had dozens of paintings and prints on the walls, and every single one was butt-ugly. Brown landscapes, shriveled dried flowers, grim people staring out as if personally insulted, pathetic barns and churches—the only thing missing were bug-eyed children and clowns.

"Camden, ask her if she was a frustrated artist."

No answer. They were deep down, possibly discussing Mr. Carlyle.

I went into the library and gazed at the rows of old brown books. No rip-roaring adventure yarns here, not even a weird old horror book by somebody like Lovecraft—only books on agriculture, history, politics, and religion, all fat, frayed, and useless. I'd been away about fifteen minutes when I figured I'd better go pry Camden from the mirror's evil influence.

He met me at the library door. "All set."

"You're kidding. Solve the mystery all by yourself?"

"Delores says she has to get out of the house, so all we have to do is burn it down."

I patted my pockets. "I left my Junior Arson Kit at home."

"I told her that wasn't an option, and we'd think of something else."

"We?"

"I told her you were a detective. She's hired you."

David H. Randall, Detective to the Dead. "How's she going to pay my fee?"

"She's offering you thirty thousand dollars."

I blinked. "Are you kidding me? What's she going to do, tell you where the treasure's buried?"

"Something like that. There's valuable jewelry hidden in the house. It's yours if you take the case."

"Can't you tell where it is?"

"She's not letting me see it." He washed our coffee cups and handed them to me to dry.

I dried the cups and put them back in the cabinet. "So what does she want me to find?"

"She wants a family matter settled. Her daughter, Beverly, lives in town. Delores wanted her to have the house, but Beverly hated it. They quarreled. Delores told Beverly to get out and never come back, so Beverly never did. Delores regrets this. She believes if Beverly would come back into the house, she'll be free."

"Camden, you know how I love all this voodoo crap. Suppose Beverly steps inside and bursts into flame? We're going to take the word of an old dead lady in a mirror that this breaks the spell?"

"Yes," he said, "we are."

It was easier to play along, and I could certainly use the money. "Okay. For thirty thousand dollars, I can give it a try."

We let ourselves out and walked back around to my car. Now all I had to do was convince Beverly to a) believe all this nonsense; b) come to the Carlyle House; and c) say something nice about her mother.

• • ● • •

I didn't have any trouble finding Beverly. After dropping Camden off at Janice's the next morning to work his magic on the fox fairies, I stopped by the Carlyle House. Patrick Lauber had Beverly's address and phone number. What he didn't have were encouraging words.

"Is there a particular reason you wish to contact her? She was invited to the opening ceremonies, but she refused to come. In fact, she's refused all invitations to come oversee the reconstruction. I don't think she and Delores were on very good terms. It's my understanding they had a terrible argument and Beverly left the house for good. She won't come to the party, if that's what you're thinking. Why do you need to talk to her?"

I was going to have to let him in on the plan. "It's a little hard to explain. I don't know if you noticed yesterday, but Camden was drawn to the mirror in the foyer."

"Yes, I saw him admiring it."

"He's very receptive to certain vibrations that may be in the house."

"Ah, like feng shui?"

"No, more like ghosts."

Lauber didn't laugh or make a skeptical face. "We've actually had sightings. Strange occurrences. We're certain the house is haunted. Is it Delores?"

"That's what Camden says."

"Did he actually see Delores? Did he speak with her?"

"She spoke to him. It sounds like she'd really like to make amends with her daughter."

Lauber was pleased. "He actually made contact with the spirit world?"

"It's a little something he does every now and then."

"We should ask him to try again when he's here. I'd love to know what Delores thinks of the redecorating. But, then, if she's unhappy, she may not want this party. Did she seem very upset, Mr. Randall?"

"She'd like to see her daughter."

Now he looked skeptical. "Well, you can try."

• • ● • •

Delores' daughter lived in a modest brick house on Elderberry Lane—again, no elderberries, whatever they are, and not much of a lane. If someone shaved a beaver and put it in a dress, that beaver would be Beverly Carlyle Huntington. She had a short square body, a cap of brown hair on a round head, a long upper lip, and pronounced front teeth.

"Mrs. Huntington? My name is David Randall. I have what may be an unusual request."

She looked me up and down. Sometimes it pays to be attractive. "I'm sure whatever you request is going to be fine with me."

"Is your mother Delores Carlyle?"

"Yes, but she's dead. She's been dead for several years now."

"I understand she left you the family home?"

"I didn't want it. A white elephant if there ever was one. She left it to the city of Parkland."

"There's some unfinished business regarding the house that requires your attention. When were you planning another visit to the house?"

"Never."

"This would only take a few minutes."

She eyed me again, this time with suspicion. She'd met me at the door of her large brick home and hadn't invited me in.

As houses go, I'd much rather have the elegant Carlyle House than this featureless rectangle. "You're going to have to explain what this is all about."

I'd been hoping not to get into this so soon. "There've been disturbances in the house."

She rolled her eyes, a beaver discovering yet another hole in what should have been the perfect dam. "Oh, for heaven's sake. Is this about mother's ghost? Don't tell me you've been roped in, too."

"The caretaker seems to think—"

"The caretaker's a moron. Every six months or so, I get a call or a letter saying Delores is causing trouble. When is Lauber going to grow up? There's no such thing as a ghost. Besides, my mother, of all people, would never become one. She didn't believe in ghosts, and neither do I."

"What's the harm in stopping by? You could have a word with Mr. Lauber and settle this ghost business. Maybe there's a chair or a lamp you'd like to pick up."

"I don't want anything out of that house. If that's all you came to discuss, Mr. Randall, I'll say good-bye."

"I wish you'd reconsider. Isn't there anything I can say to convince you?"

We were interrupted by the roar of a motorcycle as it charged down the street and up into the driveway. A teenage boy and his passenger got off and removed their helmets. The boy was very thin, held together by black leather and silver chains. His pale face was topped with a patch of wiry black hair like a tuft of burnt grass. The girl was just as bony, her stomach hanging out between a torn green t-shirt and tight low-riding jeans, proof positive the bare midriff look is not for everyone. Her multicolored hair—and again I turn to Rufus for the descriptive phrase—looked like the cat had been sucking on it. They went by us without a glance, arguing.

"You're not coming with me, Frieda. I've told you a thousand times."

"As if I'd want to be in your scraggly old band. You suck."

"Go on, then, get lost."

"Get bent."

"Bite me."

They disappeared into the house. Beverly Huntington's expression changed, as if realizing a new and better way to build that pesky dam. "Mr. Randall, I believe there is something you can do for me."

I was afraid to ask.

"Those are my lovely children, Frieda and Kit. As you can imagine, they're driving me crazy. They're fine by themselves, but when they're together, they're always fighting. Now, I'm sure a man like you has plenty of resources. I don't suppose you know of a good, reasonable apartment that's available in town? I promised Kit as soon as he found one, he could move out, but he hasn't had any luck. He was going to stay with a couple of his band buddies, but that didn't work out."

"Does he have a job? Can he afford a place?"

"He works at Comic World. He could probably manage two hundred a month. I'd help him out if he got stuck. It would be worth it to have some peace in this house."

"Then you'd come to the Carlyle House?"

"Yes."

"It just so happens there's a vacancy in my building."

If she'd had a beaver tail, she would've slapped it on the water. "Wonderful! When can he move in?"

"Let me check with the landlord."

"Kit!" she called. "Christopher! Would you come here a minute, please?"

He slouched up, glowering. "What do you want?"

"This is Mr. Randall. He says there's a vacancy at his apartment house."

"Yeah? So?"

"So I thought you might like to check it out."

Kit eyed me. Apparently I wasn't wearing enough safety pins. "What's the deal?"

His act didn't impress me. I've been sneered at by the best. "Hey, if you're not interested, I don't care. Your mother thought you'd like to get out of the house."

"Yeah, well, she thought right. If I have to spend another day listening to Frieda whine about joining my band, I'll rip her head off."

Did I need to introduce this element into the house? We could use the money, and if Hot Shot here caused too much trouble, I'd kick him in his bony ass.

"It's 302 Grace Street. Stop by and have a look."

He shrugged and slouched away. Beverly didn't apologize for his rude behavior. "If he likes the place and decides to stay, then I'll come by the Carlyle House—once, that's all."

I hoped once would be enough for old dead Delores.

Chapter Eight

"If I Had My Way, Pretty Baby"

Kary met Camden and me at Janice's. We took our hot dogs and fries to one of the picnic tables, and she gave a report of her morning activities.

"Oriental Imports isn't hiring right now, but I did get a chance to talk with a few of the salespeople. I started by asking how they liked working there, and one of the girls was real chatty."

"The one with little sausage curls?"

"Yes. I asked if she knew where Bobbi Jo lived because I was a friend of hers and had a baby gift for her. She said, 'Haven't you heard? She was found dead in her house, and her baby's missing.' I acted shocked and asked her for more details. She said that was all she knew. The other salesgirls had read about it in the paper. Then she told me Bobbi got fired a couple of days ago because there was no one to look after the baby, and she couldn't afford daycare. I asked if the police had any suspects, and she said no, but that someone had been in the store asking about her. 'A relative?' I said, and she said, 'A big red-haired man.'"

"So she definitely said red-haired? Damn. That's what she told me, too."

"It wasn't Rufus," Camden said.

"Don't you think you may be a little too close to this situation to be accurate?"

"One other thing, guys." Kary's voice got our attention. She took a breath as if to steady it. "The salesgirl told me the baby's name. Mary Rose."

Mary Rose. Naming her made her seem even more real and made me even more determined to find her. We sat for a few minutes in silence until Janice brought our orders out to the picnic table.

"Mother's really pleased with what you've told her so far, Cam."

I reached for more fries. "What have you told Mother?"

Camden shook the ketchup bottle to encourage the last stubborn bit at the bottom. "That there is a spirit, a very sad spirit, but I'm going to be able to talk to it about moving along. It's not a fox, by the way."

"It's a cow, right?"

"No, it's a girl."

"Ate too many hot dogs."

Janice gave me a look. "This girl lived a long time before hot dogs. Mother has gone home to consult more of her books, which gives me breathing space."

Janice went back inside to wait on the growing crowd. Camden passed me the ketchup bottle and took a bite of hot dog. I finished my fries. "I've found another tenant for us, a moody, antisocial teenage boy, who looks like a reject Edward Scissorhands."

"Thanks so much."

"He's Beverly Huntington's son. It's part of a deal to get her to the house."

"We take in Mood Boy. She talks to the mirror."

"Nicely put."

Kary wiped mustard off her mouth. "So it is Delores in the mirror."

"Yes, and if we can get her daughter, Beverly, to come visit, the curse will be broken."

"If her son moves in with us."

I put more mustard on my hot dog. "He may or may not want to move in. He looked a bit angst-y."

Camden blew the paper off his straw. "I don't care what he looks like, as long as he doesn't do drugs or bother the girls."

"He won't bother me," Kary said. "I deal with moody children on a regular basis, and that's not counting you two."

Camden drank the rest of his Coke. He looked across the groups of people eating and laughing and beyond the little restaurant where the hot dog spirit girl was probably making faces at him. After a long while, his gaze returned to me, dark blue and serious. "Randall, Rufus didn't kill Bobbi."

"This time, I'm going to have to have a little more evidence. Look back about a week and tell me who did kill her."

I was being flippant, but he kept his serious look. "I've already tried that, but I couldn't see anything."

I took a drink of my soda, wishing I had something stronger. Not seeing anything meant one of two things. Either there was nothing to be seen, or, in some way, Camden was involved or would be involved in whatever happened next. "Let's hope that's because Rufus is a close friend."

Kary gathered up our trash and tossed a handful of crumbs to the sparrows that hopped hopefully around the table. "What are you going to do now?"

"We're on the trail of Bobbi's cousin, Trace Burwell, the double blank."

"Then I'll go to Bobbi's neighborhood and hunt for food and clues."

Camden finished his Coke. "Could we stop by the PSN for a few minutes? I promised Ellie I'd put in an appearance today."

A visit to the Psychic Service Network is always an experience. "Sure. I'd like to see what's left of Reg."

• ● ● ● •

Camden and Ellin have an ever-changing system that keeps both of them happy and the rest of us at peace. Ellin desperately wants him to return to the Psychic Service, specifically to star in one of her TV programs. Camden flat-out refuses this exciting offer, agreeing to stop by the studio a certain number of times each month as an observer, although she's roped him into being a guest on "Ready to Believe" and her latest idiotic program, "Past Forward," a show that gives reincarnation all the recognition it deserves.

Things were hopping at the network. The paid audience had filled all the seats. Bonnie Burton, an anxious-to-please fluffy-haired blonde, and Teresa Perello, a serious brunette, hosts of "Ready to Believe," were getting their microphones arranged on their flowing psychic dresses.

Ellin was at her best, ordering everybody around. "Five minutes! Mitch, fix that light over the table. Bonnie, straighten the flower arrangement, thank you. Reg, get in here now."

I looked at Camden and feigned surprise. "Reg is still with us? I thought he was psychic history."

"He must have done some serious groveling."

Reg Haverson came onto the set, adjusting his microphone to the collar of his immaculate gray suit. As usual, Reg looked like the perfect advertisement for an exclusive men's cologne. His hair was sculpted, his Ken-doll features covered with a layer of makeup. He managed to make his tone polite and testy at the same time. "I'm right here, Ellin."

"Three minutes."

"Thank you."

In exactly three minutes, the PSN was on the air. Reg beamed at the audience, his voice now Jolly Game Show Host.

"Good afternoon, and welcome to 'Ready to Believe'! Our special guest today is Pet Psychic to the Stars Jessie Vardaman!"

I turned to Camden. "What? No Archer Sisters?"

Reg worked the crowd into a psychic frenzy. "Yes, this is the program that dares to explore the unknown, reach into the corners of the supernatural, and grasp infinite dimensions! Are you 'Ready to Believe'?"

The audience called out "Yes!" and cheered and clapped like they're supposed to.

"Then, without further delay, let me introduce our charming and beautiful hosts, Bonnie and Teresa!"

More clapping and cheering. The camera zoomed in on the two women. Once they'd greeted the audience and the viewers at home, a dreamy-eyed woman dressed like a Gypsy, came out to read palms. Ellin came over to us and gave Camden a kiss.

"I see you've granted Reg a reprieve," he said.

"He's on probation. One more stunt, and he's out of here."

She knows that would kill Reg, because he has his eye on her job. I guess he sees it as a stepping stone to another network. Fashion World, maybe.

"Shoot," I said. "I wanted to see the Archer Sisters."

She ignored me and spoke to Camden. "How did things go at Janice's? Is there a spirit haunting the restaurant? Anything the PSN might be interested in?"

"I'm not sure yet."

She glanced back where the Gypsy woman was giving an audience member a special Tarot card reading. "We need more local paranormal happenings, breaking news kind of stuff."

"I don't think this is going to be a very big deal."

"Can you stay a while? Jessie's brought a huge lizard."

"Gee, I can't miss that."

Camden and I took seats in the audience and were properly awed by Jessie Vardaman's "reading" of Balthazar the Iguana. Seems Balthazar missed his favorite chew toy and would prefer a seventy-five rather than a hundred-watt light bulb in his cage. His owner was chastened and grateful by the news.

"I didn't know what was wrong with him," the man said. "He was so flushed and listless."

Yeah, I'd be flushed, too, lying under a hundred-watt light bulb without my rubber carrot. It was easy to see why Jessie Vardaman was in tune with the iguana. He looked like a lizard himself, thin and beady-eyed, with a long, pointed face.

"It's quite all right. Balthazar knows you mean well. He thinks a lot of you. He's very happy to be your iguana."

"That's such good news. He's such a wonderful pet."

During all this, Balthazar hadn't moved.

"And so expressive," I said to Camden, who grinned. I wondered if he had tuned into the lizard's thoughts. He says animals usually keep their thoughts to themselves, but I know for a fact he talks to Cindy when she lets him.

Balthazar's owner heaved the unresponsive lizard into his arms and carried him off. The next person was a young woman with a sad-looking parrot in a cage.

"Let me guess," I said. "The cage needs a southern exposure, and the crackers are stale."

Vardaman took care of this one pretty quickly. Susie Q the parrot was longing for the Amazon and wished her owner would leave the TV on the Discovery Channel more often.

"This is great stuff, Camden. I'm glad we stayed."

The third animal needing a psychic adjustment was a fox.

Camden and I both sat up a little straighter. A young man in a dark blue sweat suit held a little fox in his arms.

"A very unusual pet," Vardaman said. "Wild animals are best left in the wild, but occasionally, and for a brief time, a sick or wounded animal can be taken into a home. This lovely little creature is Mimi. She was hit by a car and broke her leg. Fortunately, Mr. Miller here saw the accident, stopped his car, and brought her to a vet. He's kept her for a couple of months now and wants to know how she's really feeling. Please sit down, Mr. Miller. Hello, Mimi."

"Wonder if Mimi likes hot dogs," I said.

Vardaman held out both hands as if feeling vibrations from the fox, closed his eyes for a few moments, and then opened them and addressed Mr. Miller. "Mimi would like you to know she's very grateful for all your help. She says she's feeling much better and would like to go back to the forest."

The fox turned her gaze from her owner and looked directly at Camden. For a moment, Vardaman was distracted. He started to say something and changed his mind. At this point, the little fox broke contact with Camden and snuggled into Miller's arms. Vardaman shook his head as if to clear it.

"Excuse me. I want to make sure I say this correctly. Mimi says if there's ever anything she can do for you, all you have to do is ask."

Mr. Miller rubbed Mimi's head. "I don't know what a fox can do for me, but I'll put her back in the forest soon enough."

"Mimi thanks you." Vardaman still looked a little rattled. "That's all we have time for today. Back to you, Bonnie and Teresa."

"And back to you," I said to Camden. "What did Mimi have to say?"

"She said, 'Hello, Cam. This guy's a goof, isn't he?' Then she said all that last part."

"No wonder he looked surprised."

"Ready to Believe" wound to an end. The audience filed out. Reg called for a drink. Jessie Vardaman came straight to Camden.

"You're Cam, right? Ellin's husband? I know you're psychic. Did you happen to hear anything during my segment?"

"A little bit."

"It was that fox, wasn't it? What did she mean by calling me a goof?"

"I think she was just joking. She is a fox. That's what they do."

Vardaman hadn't held Mimi, but he brushed his jacket as if removing all traces of fox. "I did not appreciate it. What was all that about if there's ever anything she can do, all Miller has to do is ask? Sounded like something out of a fairy tale. She can't do anything for him except maybe kill rats."

"Maybe she was trying to be nice. It sounded good."

"I'm not having any more foxes. I'm sticking to domesticated animals with normal dull problems." Still grumbling, he walked off.

"I don't think that little message was meant for Miller," I said. "Or Jessie Vardaman."

Camden shook his head. "I can't figure any of this out. Let's go talk to Trace Burwell. If he's like Rufus said, he won't be cryptic."

I knew what I wanted him to be. "He'd better be a big red-haired man with a Bigfoot truck."

Chapter Nine

"Baby, Won't You Please Come Home?"

The Cave Bar on Emerald was a small, dark establishment with black wrought-iron chairs and tables and a bar made of faux black marble. I asked for Burwell and was directed to the bar where a man was wiping the countertops. Trace Burwell was a short, dark-haired man with a sad excuse for a moustache. It hung over his top lip like a fake moustache glued on for a low-budget community theater production. He had dull little eyes and a weak chin. If this had been a TV movie titled *The Mystery of the Murdered Ex-Wife*, the part of the Loser would've been played by Trace Burwell.

"Mr. Burwell? We're friends of Bobbi Jo's. Could we ask you a few questions?"

He looked startled. "Friends?"

"Yes. I'm David Randall, and this is Camden."

He stared at us with frightened eyes, finding no comfort in my dashing air of authority or Camden's calm demeanor. "You know she's dead? She was murdered in her own home and her baby stolen," he said.

"Yes, we'd like to help." I sat down at the bar. Camden also took a seat. "When did you last see Bobbi?"

He clutched the towel to his thin chest. "Are you with the

police? They've already asked me questions. I don't know anything. Her ex-husband's been in here bothering me, too."

"I'm not going to bother you. I'm a private investigator. I want to find the killer and the baby."

He took a couple of deep breaths. "I've had enough hassle for one day."

"Just a few questions."

"But I don't know anything."

"How about a couple of beers, then?"

He thought it over. "I suppose." He put the towel down on the counter to pull two Budweisers. Camden moved the towel a little further, keeping his hand on it for a few minutes.

Burwell came back and set the beers in front of us. "Thanks," I said. "When did you last see Bobbi and the baby?"

"Last week. Monday, maybe."

"Did she seem happy? Worried? Excited?"

He picked up the towel and made a halfhearted attempt to wipe the counter. "She was okay."

I took a sip of beer. "The salesgirl at Oriental Imports said Bobbi was fired but didn't seem upset about it."

"Told me she never liked that job and had better plans."

"Do you know what those plans were?"

"She never told me no plans."

"Did she have any particular friends at Oriental Imports?"

"Not that I know of."

"Was there anyone else in her life? A boyfriend, maybe? Someone else who came to visit her?"

He put the towel aside and started fiddling with the napkin holder. "I didn't see her that often."

"Bobbi wrote a letter to Rufus to tell him about the baby. According to that letter, you asked her to write, 'Trace says hello.' So you were there when she wrote the letter?"

"I guess so, yeah."

"Did she have any enemies, anyone with a grudge against her?"

He made a feeble attempt to sound tough. "The way I see it, the only one who could be mad at her would be that Rufus

Jackson, if he didn't want to be the father. She never should've sent that letter."

I put money for the beer on the bar. I glanced at Camden, who nodded. While I kept Burwell talking to me, Camden had reached over and touched the towel again. "Thanks for your time, Mr. Burwell."

He was on a roll. "Yeah, I think both of you should leave now."

Out in the Fury, I said, "Get anything?"

"He's terrified."

"I managed to divine that myself."

"No, he's really scared. The vibes off that towel were pure fear."

"Does he think he's next?"

"Possibly."

"Rufus was right. The guy's a zero. We could've gotten more information out of Mimi the fox." I turned on the car and put it in gear. "Let's swing by Forest Cove and see how Kary's doing."

● ● ● ● ●

Forest Cove was as dismal as before. I pulled up beside Bobbi's ancient little Toyota. We got out. I looked in the car. No car seat.

"Whoever took the baby, took everything she would need. Seems to me someone had a plan."

Camden put his hands on the hood of the car. He shook his head. "Nothing here."

"I'd be seriously concerned if you could read the car."

"It's not locked."

I started to compliment him on his powers when he indicated the passenger door. The little button was up. I assumed the crime squad had been all over the car, because there wasn't a thing in it. Kary's Turbo was parked up the street. We walked toward her car and saw her talking with a woman on the woman's front porch. Kary handed her a plastic bag and we heard her say, "Thanks so much." She met us on the sidewalk.

"Not a lot to report, guys. Only a few people are home right now. The woman I was talking with said most of the people in the neighborhood were at work when Bobbi was killed, and only a few of them had ever spoken with her." She held up her few remaining plastic bags. "On the bright side, I've left bags on all the doors, which gives me an excuse to come back. Any luck with the cousin?"

"Trace says he saw Bobbi and the baby last week. He'd like to pin the crime on Rufus, but he's spooked by something."

Kary's gaze took in the sad little houses baking in the afternoon heat. "This is a depressing place, isn't it? No wonder everyone stays inside."

"Trace also said Bobbi told him she had plans for a better life. Sounds like she was trying to get out of here. Oh, and there's no car seat in her car, which makes me think whoever took the baby made plans of their own."

But what kind of plans? We took one last look at dismal Forest Cove Drive. Kary returned to Turbo and started up the little car. Camden's eyes were distant. He must have been hearing my thoughts. Bobbi Jo knew her killer. She'd been expecting him or her because she said, "Here it is." Or did she hand over the mysterious "it" to one person and was killed by another? A home invasion? Someone surprised to find a baby in the house, or someone desperate for a child? Someone hired to kill Bobbi and bring the baby back? Was there a black market baby ring in Parkland?

That was the first thing I was going to investigate when we got home.

● ● ● ● ●

I was in my office trolling the Internet when Kit Huntington drove up, the sound of his motorcycle shaking leaves from the trees. He was still in his black Angry Young Teen outfit. He knocked on the screen door, and I opened it. He hadn't lost any of his charm.

"So where's the room?"

"Upstairs."

I took him up to the second floor and showed him Fred's room. I didn't expect much of a reaction, but he stood for a while, his stance and expression reminding me oddly of Camden's.

"Did someone die, some old guy?"

"Yes, this used to be his room, but he didn't die in here, if that's what you're worried about."

"Nah, I'm not worried. He died in the park."

He must have read about Fred in the newspaper. He went to the window and looked out. "How much did you say?"

"Two hundred."

"Do I give you the money?"

"I'll get the landlord."

We stepped out into the hallway. Camden came down the stairs from his bedroom. He and Kit paused and regarded each other with a sudden stiffness. I'd seen the same reaction when Cindy met a strange cat in the yard. Neither offered to shake hands.

After a long moment, Kit said, "Christopher Huntington. I go by Kit."

"Camden."

"Randall says the rent's two hundred. Will you take one-fifty now and the rest at the end of the week?"

Camden nodded. Kit reached into a rip in his leather pants and brought out a scuffed wallet. He dug out three bills and handed them to Camden.

"I'll take care of my own meals. I don't do drugs, but I drink beer. I'll be sleeping most days and going to my gigs at night. And if a scrawny girl named Frieda comes over, don't let her in. She's my sister, and she's a jerk."

"All right."

"I'll go get my stuff."

Kit went down the stairs and out to his motorcycle. In a few moments, he roared down Grace Street and was gone.

I wasn't sure what had happened between them. "What was that strange spooky moment?"

Camden took so long to reply, I thought he hadn't heard me. "I was exactly like that."

"You were taller back then?"

"An angry, domineering smart-ass who thought he was going crazy."

"Wait a minute. You're telling me Kit is psychic?"

"And having a real hard time dealing with it."

"I'm more curious where a kid his age gets two hundred dollars. Was he being honest about no drugs? Tell me if you want him out."

"No, I think I might be able to help him—if he lets me."

"Good luck with that. He doesn't look like the kind who'll ask for help, and as for help, I'm calling Beverly Beaver. I kept my end of the bargain, so she's going to have to talk to Delores."

I went into my office and called Beverly Huntington. She agreed to meet me at the Carlyle House at four the next day. I called Jordan to see if he knew anything about illegal adoption agencies, but had to leave a message. I listened to one of my CDs, hoping for inspiration, but when the musicians came to "I Wonder Where My Baby Is Tonight?" I had to turn it off.

Kary stopped by my door. "You can keep that on."

"I'm not in the mood for a baby song."

She came in and sat down. "Speaking of babies, here's the latest on Baby Love."

I kept an interested expression but groaned inwardly. Kary had been determined to expose Baby Love as a fraudulent Internet adoption site. I thought I'd dodged that particular bullet when we posed as reporters from the *Herald* and infiltrated Baby Love's secret headquarters, which weren't so secret because the company was legit. "I thought we discovered they had nothing to hide."

"Ah, but there's a sister company called Rainbow Wishes. I'm going to ask them if they know anything about Mary Rose. What if whoever took Rufus' baby brought it there?"

"That's a possibility." Wasn't I just looking into that? "I can't see any reliable company taking in a baby without calling the police."

"I'm checking it out tomorrow. I have the perfect cover story. I live on Forest Cove Drive and saw the baby being taken out of Bobbi's house. I'll tell them I was curious about what happened."

"They don't have to tell you anything."

"It'll give me a chance to look around."

Since this wasn't any nuttier than her past schemes, I let it ride. "Okay, keep me posted. And if our new tenant even so much as looks at you the wrong way, you let me know."

"Thanks, but I think I can handle a grumpy teenager. What are you making for supper?"

"Chicken pie. You can help, if you like."

She put an apron on over her clothes and rolled the dough while I chopped chicken for the pie. During these small domestic moments, I could believe we're married. I could imagine having a family again, which scares me because part of me wants it so much. I don't know what I'm going to do with that part of me. I can't make it shut up. I needed a diversion.

"I forgot to tell you about the fox Camden and I saw at the PSN today."

"A real fox?"

"Yes. Its name is Mimi. Ellin had a pet psychic on the show, and Mimi told him off via Camden. You should've seen the guy's face."

"I want to hear more about the ghost of Delores Carlyle. Do you think she's dangerous?"

"Not really. Back when she was alive, Mrs. Carlyle kicked her daughter out of the house. Now she wants to see her and tell her she's sorry." I deposited the chicken into the pie pan and added a can of green peas. "Ready for the crust."

Kary draped the dough across the pan and cut off the edges. "Do you have a pan for these pieces?"

"Here you go."

She arranged the scraps of dough in a second pan, and I put both pans in the oven. She wiped her hands on the apron. "Anything else?" Her voice sounded odd, a little choked.

"I think there's some applesauce left." She was blinking as if holding back tears. "Are you okay? What's the matter?"

She sniffed. "I'm sorry. When you said Mrs. Carlyle wanted to see her daughter, that made me think of Bobbi's baby girl."

I handed her a tissue from the box on the counter. When Kary had gotten pregnant, her parents had broken all contact with her. Even the fact that she lost the baby and nearly died hadn't softened their hearts. I knew she wondered if her mother ever thought of her.

She sat down on one of the stools at the counter and blew her nose. "Sorry, David. Most of the time, I think I'm over it, and then I get all teary."

"Go ahead and cry if you want. It is sad. Mrs. Carlyle has to come back from beyond the grave to make up for years of neglect."

"Did you see her?"

"No, but she and Camden had a long conversation."

Kary wiped her eyes. "I guess people don't understand what they have until it's too late. You've heard Ellin and her mother quarrel."

"Oh, now those two are in a class by themselves."

"But they're still mother and daughter." She managed to smile. "And I love your mother, David."

Mom had spent the past Christmas with us at 302 Grace. "She's crazy about you." As a friend, though, not as a potential daughter-in-law. Mom thought I was an idiot for even considering Kary as Wife Number Three. "If you're going through withdrawal, why don't you call her?"

"That's a great idea."

"Do it now. Her number's in my phone."

Kary took off the apron and hung it on the back of a chair. She took my phone and went to the island. In a few minutes, I could hear her voice, already cheered by Mom's greeting.

I was surrounded. Ellin and her mother; Janice and her mother; Beverly and her mother. And let's not forget Vangie and her mother. All these independent daughters so desperate to be on their own, to show mom they can make it.

But there was one little daughter out there with no mother and nothing to prove. I had to find her.

Chapter Ten

"Buy Buy for Baby or Baby Will Bye Bye You"

Around eight o'clock Friday morning, I fixed myself a cup of coffee and carried it to the porch. Camden must have gotten a call to come into work, and Kary must have given him a ride because they were both gone. I'd settled in a rocking chair to ponder Rufus' case when Kit Huntington straggled up the front steps, looking as if he barely had the energy to carry his guitar. He slumped into one of the rocking chairs and gave me a bleary-eyed stare.

"Is there more of that coffee?"

"Hang on."

When I brought him a cup, he actually thanked me. "Man, we were kicking some major musical ass last night."

"Glad to hear it."

He gulped the coffee. "I gotta be at work at noon. That sucks."

"Everybody's got to work."

I guess this sounded too much like criticism. He scowled. "Yeah, but someday I'm going to get a major recording deal and make tons of money."

"You get a major recording deal, you'll be working harder than ever."

He considered this. "Maybe." He took another gulp. "Vangie says she knows you."

"I'm a big fan of the Slotted Spoons."

"For a girl group, they're not bad."

He'd reached the end of his conversation. He sat regarding the large oak trees and the quiet street, his expression glum. I'd had a few glum moments during my teenage years, but for the most part, I'd been riding around with my friends, talking too loud, and drinking too much. I hadn't gone in for moody introspection. There were too many girls to chase.

Kit turned his gaze to me and smirked. "Yeah, I kinda figured you for a hound."

This damned little pinhead was listening in!

His smirk faded, and he looked genuinely frightened. "Hey, man, I'm sorry."

"Oh, you heard that, too?"

"Yeah, look, I didn't—it slips out sometimes. Things kinda crowd in, you know, when I'm tired." He got up. "Don't go ballistic on me. I'm heading for bed."

"Wait a second," I said. "I'm used to this. You know Camden's psychic, too."

He didn't want to talk about it. "I'm not psychic." He picked up his guitar and hurried inside.

The hell you aren't.

Angie wandered out and took a seat on the top step. She had on a white blouse and white shorts. She looked like a giant meringue had landed on the porch. She had her coffee in a mug decorated with cows. Kary had gone overboard with cow kitchen décor. "The new boy's a bit squirrely, isn't he?"

"That's one way to put it."

She took a sip. "Rufus says he's so skinny he has to stand up twice to cast a shadow."

"How's the new job? I haven't seen you to ask you."

"It's going good. What have you found out about Rufus' ex?"

"Not much, so far. According to Cousin Trace, Bobbi wasn't too upset to be fired from Oriental Imports. Trace said she told him she had better plans."

"Did he know of a likely suspect?"

"No. How are you holding up?"

She shrugged and took another sip. "Okay, I guess. I know Rufus wouldn't hurt anybody."

"What about the idea of him having a baby? You two aren't planning on a family yet, are you?"

She shifted position. "Not sure how I feel about kids. I never was much of a maternal type. If Rufus is really the father and wants to keep the baby, we'll see. Tell you the truth, we can't afford a child right now. We're trying to find a house. Still, I don't like the idea of a little baby being lost out there somewhere."

Neither did I. "You're not going to start your own investigation, are you?" During my last case, Angie had gone undercover at a BeautiQueen makeup party to get information on the company.

"Not unless you give me an assignment. I got enough to do holding Rufus down."

"I'll let you know. Anything you can do to keep Rufus from killing anybody would be appreciated. He said he'd give me a couple of days before he went on the warpath."

"That was Tuesday, right? Been more than a couple of days."

"This is serious, Angie. If he takes the law into his own hands, I won't be able to help him."

"I hear you," she said. "I'll do my best."

● ● ● ● ●

I was pretty confident Angie could handle Rufus, and remembering her assistance on the BeautiQueen case reminded me of something I could check. The little plastic bag of makeup in Bobbi's refrigerator had been full of the distinctive peach color of BeautiQueen products. Since I'd saved the company's reputation, the owner, Folly Harper, was happy to answer my questions. I called and asked who the representative was for Bobbi Jo Hull. I was told that would be Tina Ramola, a travel agent for Dream Vacations in Friendly Center.

Dream Vacations was a tiny office wedged between a camera shop and a store that sold custom-made birdhouses. Tina Ramola was wedged between a little desk dominated by a huge computer monitor and a wall covered with travel posters. "See Exotic Thailand" and "Fish Scotland" vied for position with "Exciting Los Angeles" and "Take a Dive Into Bermuda." One of these days when I'm rich and famous, I want to travel to every single one of the countries and cities so flamboyantly displayed on the walls, but today, my travel was limited to people who might have known Bobbi Jo.

Tina Ramola looked like a kitten with a little pushed-in face, large eyes, and a wealth of curly black hair. Of course, like all true BeautiQueens, she wore a layer of the patented peach-colored makeup, lots of gray eye shadow, and magenta lipstick.

She looked up from her computer. "Hello. How may I help you?"

I took a seat in the one tiny chair in front of the desk. "My name's David Randall. We have a mutual friend, Folly Harper."

"Oh, she's a dear, isn't she? Don't tell me. Your wife needs something in the BeautiQueen line, and Folly's all out." She pulled out a desk drawer. "I keep extras of everything here. What can I get you?"

"Thanks, but I don't need any makeup. I'd like to know what you can tell me about one of your customers, Bobbi Jo Hull."

Tina Ramola pushed the drawer back in. "Bobbi Jo? But didn't I read about her having an accident? Didn't she get shot?"

"I'm investigating her murder."

Tina's peachy little kitten face paled. "I don't see how I could help."

"I'm hoping you can. Did she come here for her BeautiQueen supplies, or did you go to her house?"

"Sometimes she'd stop by, but I went to her house a few times to deliver things."

"Were you ever inside the house? Did you see her baby?"

"Yes, I went over not long after she had Mary Rose to bring her a little gift. She was a darling little girl with the prettiest red hair." Tina looked concerned. "I didn't stay very long. I asked if she needed anything, and she said no."

The bell rang as a customer entered the agency. Since there was barely room for two, I stepped outside while Tina conducted business. The air was hot and full of shopping center smells: cinnamon buns, exhaust fumes, perfume, and fries. I watched cars battling it out for parking spaces, and a couple of bored teenagers on skateboards almost ran over a soccer mom herding her team into a minivan. Words were exchanged. I looked across the vast area of cars and shops. Another baby song came to mind, "Baby, Oh Where Can You Be?" I wondered how I could possibly find one small red-haired baby.

Mary Rose. Lindsey was Lindsey Marie.

When Tina had finished and the customer had gone, I returned to the little chair. Tina folded a few papers into an envelope and slid the envelope into a standing tray.

"I've been trying to think," she said. "One time when I went by, I left her makeup in her mailbox. Another time, a man was there, her cousin, I believe."

"A nerdy little guy with a fake-looking moustache?"

"Exactly. When I went with the baby gift, a man was in the kitchen. She called to him to come out, but he didn't. He said he was busy. She said something to me about moving to another house, but if she did, she'd be sure and send me her new address. I don't think she was working anymore. I remember because she said she wouldn't be buying any makeup for a while, but she wanted to keep in touch."

I recalled the stacks of home improvement magazines in Bobbi's bedroom. I also remembered a flyer for a realtor stuck in the corner of her mirror. The Sale of the Century at Superior Homes.

Tina's little kitten face was worried. "Mr. Randall, do you suppose that man in the kitchen killed her?"

"That's what I'm trying to find out. Can you remember anything else about him?"

"I only caught a glimpse of him. He was a large man, I know that."

"Did you happen to see what he was driving? Was it a big blue truck with oversized wheels?"

"I didn't notice. As I said, I didn't stay but ten or fifteen minutes. I'm not much help, I'm afraid."

"You've been very helpful, and I've taken up enough of your time."

"If there's anything I can do, please let me know."

I gave her my phone number. "If you happen to remember anything else about your visit to Bobbi Jo's, you can call me."

I went back out into the heat. I'd seen a flyer like the one in Bobbi Jo's house somewhere else. Oh, yes, right on top of the stack of magazines on the coffee table in the island. Ellin must have left it as a pointed reminder to Camden about house-hunting.

My cell phone rang. It was Rufus.

"Done caught the killer yet?"

"No, and you'd better not be Vigilante Jackson this morning."

There was a pause as Rufus shifted his wad of chewing tobacco to the other cheek. "Chompin' at the bit, Randall. You'd better fish or cut bait."

"Lay off the Southernisms for a minute and listen to me. I may not be working as fast as you'd like, but if I do my job right, we'll have plenty of proof to put the murderer away. You don't want this guy to walk because of a rush job, do you?"

"I'd like to see him walk when I get through with 'im."

Was there any way to get through the Thick Skull of Vengeance? "You're going to have to give me more time."

There was silence on his end of the line. I wondered if he'd swallowed his tobacco. Then he said, "Finley wants to talk to me again."

"Okay, he's just doing his job. Try to be civil. Think of Angie. Don't let her spend the rest of her life visiting you in jail."

Another silence. "Yeah. All right. I know you're doin' all you can, Randall."

"I'll solve this."

"Yeah, even a blind hog finds an acorn now and then."

With that sterling endorsement, he signed off.

• ● ● ● ●

I stopped by Tamara's Boutique to get Camden up to speed. Tamara's was a trendy little dress shop containing a few expensive items of clothing, as well as overpriced shoes and designer bags. Camden worked here because the store was empty most of the time, and he liked the vibe-free atmosphere. He was up on a ladder in the window, replacing a light bulb in one of the artsy chandeliers.

"How many psychics does it take to replace a light bulb?" I asked.

"Only one, because he knows when it's going out."

"Latest news. Jordan wants to talk to Rufus again."

Camden gave the bulb a final turn. "That doesn't sound good."

"Rufus has grudgingly given me more time to find Bobbi's murderer. I had to remind him that the police don't take kindly to private citizens forming their own posses."

"'Don't take kindly.' You've been talking to Rufus, all right."

"I also went by Dream Vacations here in the shopping center and talked to Bobbi's BeautiQueen representative. Ms. Tina Ramola remembers seeing a large man at the house. She also saw Trace Burwell at the house one time she stopped by to deliver makeup."

"Flip that switch over there, will you?"

I did, and all the chandelier lights came on. Camden climbed down the ladder and folded it up. "Anything else about this large man?"

"Ms. Ramola didn't get a good look. She also said Bobbi told her she'd be moving soon."

He set the ladder aside. "What's next?"

"A visit to Superior Homes."

"I can't leave the store right now."

"No, problem. For this job, I need a different partner."

• ● ● ● ●

Superior Homes was located on Ashberry Street and looked exactly like one of the fancy mansions Bobbi Jo admired. The building was red brick with white trim. The doorknocker, door handle, and mailbox were polished brass. A gold sign on the door read "Welcome to Superior Homes. Brian Young, President."

I'd worked out a plan, and once I explained it to Kary, she was more than willing to go along. We walked down a short hallway decorated in beige with beige carpet and flower arrangements on all the tables. The receptionist smiled from her glass desk.

"Good afternoon and welcome to Superior Homes. How may I help you?"

"We'd like to see your top of the line listings, please," I said.

She brightened. "Yes, sir. If you'll have a seat, I'll get someone to assist you."

We sat down on one of the beige leather sofas. A stack of slick brochures and a large notebook lay on the table in front of us. I leafed through the shiny pages of color photographs.

Kary smoothed her hands on her skirt. She'd put her hair up and dressed in one of her Sunday best—a beautiful silky skirt and tailored short-sleeved jacket, all in shades of lightest pink. Her little shoes were light gray heels. Pearls shone in her ears and around her wrist. "Do I look like a wealthy client?"

"You look perfect. We've come to look at everything they've got, the more expensive, the better."

"I'm ready. I want to find this baby. Remind me to tell you about my visit to Rainbow Wishes this morning."

I didn't have time to express an opinion on this. Our appearance must have impressed the receptionist because she returned with a man she introduced as the president of Superior Homes himself, Brian Young.

Kary managed not to stare, and I hoped my features didn't give away my surprise. Brian Young was a large, red-haired man. I gave Kary a quick glance and then shook his hand. "Mr. Young, I'm John Fisher, and this is my wife, Julie. We're new to Parkland and looking for the right home in the right neighborhood."

He grinned a broad grin. "Then you've come to the right place. Please, step into my office."

Brian Young looked nothing like Rufus. His features were smaller, his face slick and shiny, his hands smooth and fleshy. His hair was cut short and combed back. But he was as tall as Rufus and as broad, although his stomach was partially camouflaged by the cut of his dark blue suit.

Young's office was spacious and decorated with framed photographs. Most of the pictures were of magnificent houses. A few were of sleek brown horses grazing in front of other mansions. He sat down behind a huge mahogany desk and tapped a few keys on his computer keyboard. Kary and I sat in the two chairs facing the desk. As I'd hoped, all of Young's attention was on Kary.

"We have many wonderful homes available, Mrs. Fisher. Anything in particular you're looking for?"

"We like Colonial style."

"Ah." He tapped a few more keys. "Let me show you this one."

He turned the monitor so we could see a huge brick and stone monstrosity that would have taken six years' pay to heat.

"It's in Deer Point Estates, an extremely good neighborhood. Do you have children?"

"No, but we're hoping."

"Deer Point Academy is a fine private school. Or there's this one."

A few more taps and we were looking at a castle-sized house in Braeside Acres.

"Only one owner. Been in the family for years, but the last relative died recently, and this came on the market."

"We'd heard of a neighborhood called Forest Cove," I said. "It sounds very pleasant. Are you familiar with it?"

His expression changed. I couldn't tell whether I'd hit a nerve, or he didn't care for that area of town. "It's a little seedy. I don't believe it would be right for you folks. Very average. Most of the homes were built in the Fifties. A working-class neighborhood."

"Ah, I see."

Young gave me a searching look. I smiled. He transferred his gaze to Kary, who had no trouble looking perfectly innocent.

"Now let me show you this wonderful Neo-Classical house with a splendid view of Lesser Lake."

I took out my cell phone. "Would you excuse me for a moment? I need to take this call."

"Certainly."

"Go ahead and look, dear. I'll be right back."

I knew Young wouldn't mind having Kary's complete attention. I walked back out through the reception area and I wandered around the building, pretending to talk on my phone. A black BMW was parked in the side lot of Superior Homes. The vanity tag said "SUPERIOR." There was a car seat in the back. Maybe this wasn't Young's car. Maybe Young had a child of his own. I'd check for a wedding ring, but nowadays, that could mean anything—or nothing.

I continued my stroll, circled the building, and came back in. The receptionist wasn't at her desk. I took a quick peek at her computer, but her screensaver of dancing kittens blocked my view of anything important.

"May I help you, sir?"

She'd come up behind me. "I was admiring your screensaver. My wife would love that."

"Dancing Kittens dot com," she said. "They have loads of patterns."

"My wife has a friend in town, Bobbi Jo Hull, who recommended Superior Homes to us. Do you remember Mrs. Hull?"

"Yes, I do. A very nice lady. I was very sorry to hear about her."

"Do you know what kind of house she was planning to buy? We might like the same."

She sat down at her desk and gave the keyboard a tap. The dancing kittens were replaced by a row of houses, each with a model number. "She was looking at number forty-six, the Classic Colonial."

The Classic Colonial was over four hundred thousand dollars. "That's beautiful." And completely out of Bobbi's range. "That would have been perfect for Bobbi and her baby."

"Oh, did she have a baby? Poor little thing."

"Yes, a little girl. You never saw her? I guess she left her with a babysitter when she came here."

"I guess so," the receptionist said. "I would've remembered."

"Is that Mr. Young's black BMW parked in the side lot?"

"Yes, sir."

"A wonderful car. I'm thinking of getting one." That's all I would be doing, thinking of getting one. "Thank you," I told the receptionist. "I'd better get back before my wife picks out something too elaborate."

The only ring Brian Young was wearing was a gold ring shaped like a horseshoe. The ring matched his cuff links. Business must be good at Superior Homes.

For the next hour, Kary and I looked at dozens of incredibly expensive houses until I was certain Young had bought our disguise.

"Well, honey, what do you think?"

Kary did an excellent job of looking confused. "They're all so beautiful, I can't decide."

Young was smitten by her shy smile. "Take your time, Mrs. Fisher. I certainly want you to be satisfied. We can arrange to see any one of these you choose."

I stood and offered Kary my arm. "Why don't we think it over, dear?"

Young picked up his phone. "Where can I reach you?"

"We're staying at the Hilton. But please don't trouble yourself. We're interested in that first house, the one at Terrace Lakes, and the castle."

Kary pointed to one of the photographs. "And this yellow one, the one with the indoor pool."

"A wonderful choice. Take all the time you need. Oh, here, let me give you one of these." He gave Kary a brochure. "In case you have any more questions, my number's on the back."

We shook hands all around. I escorted Kary back to the Fury, which I'd parked around the corner, not having a BMW for the full effect. I held the door for her.

"Now, what's this about the yellow one with the indoor pool?"

"That was my favorite. Can you imagine having enough money to own one of those houses?"

I got in and started the car. "Own one and keep it up. No, I can't."

"It would be nice, but I love our home."

Our home. I liked the sound of that. "Young has a car seat in his BMW. Maybe a coincidence. Maybe not."

"We have to find her, David."

"We will." I turned down the next street and stopped at the red light. "If Bobbi Jo was planning to buy a house from Superior Homes, then she must have had contact with Brian Young. Maybe not from the front, but going away and in the dark, Brian Young could easily be mistaken for Rufus."

"But what would a rich and successful businessman be doing at the downscale home of salesgirl and unwed mother Bobbi Jo? He wouldn't have gone there to talk business. They might have been having an affair."

"And if he'd been the large man Tina Ramola says she heard in the kitchen, wouldn't Tina have noticed a black BMW in the driveway? Where's that brochure he gave you? Is Young's picture on it somewhere?"

Kary took the brochure out of her pocketbook and turned it over. "Yes, on the back. You think someone might recognize him?"

I recalled how Young had flinched at the mention of Forest Cove. "I hope so."

She unpinned her hair and let the silky strands run through her fingers. I did my best to keep my eyes on the road. "Now, about my undercover mission this morning. I told the folks at Rainbow Wishes I was looking for work and had plenty of experience with computers, which I do. Get this. They actually need people to help with their website. This would be the perfect way to monitor what's really going on."

"Did they hire you?"

"I'm supposed to hear from them sometime today."

Could be worse. She could be trailing baby thieves through the back alleys of Parkland. "Sounds like a good job."

"It's a great job. I'll be in on everything that happens."

"Suppose nothing happens? What if you find out Rainbow Wishes is a legitimate company?" I didn't say, *Will you pick out a baby and buy it?* But I imagined Kary was thinking about that very thing.

Kary's expression was thoughtful. "We'll see."

Chapter Eleven

"Bashful Baby"

We swung by Janice's for lunch. Camden was sitting at a picnic table with Mei Chan and, of all people, Jessie Vardaman. The pet psychic was in deep conversation with Janice's mother, so deep they didn't even look up. Camden brought his lunch to another table, and Kary and I sat down across from him.

"What's Pet Man doing here?" I asked.

"Ellie told him he could probably find me here. He and Mei hit it off right away. They've been discussing animals and the zodiac ever since they met."

"That fox really rattled him, didn't she?"

"Mei's impressed that a fox spoke to him."

"Please tell me he was born in the Year of the Lizard."

"He's a Tiger and very happy about it."

Camden passed me his fries. I took a handful. I turned the brochure to the back and put it on the table. "Kary and I have been undercover at Superior Homes. Take a look at this guy. Brian Young, president."

Camden gave the photo his full attention. "Didn't I say there had to be another big red-haired man?"

"Point taken."

"Did he say he knew Bobbi?"

"I didn't mention her name, but there was a definite flinch of recognition when I brought up Forest Cove. Bobbi was seriously house-hunting. She had a flyer for Superior Homes in her bedroom and tons of home improvement magazines and house plans. The receptionist remembered her and showed me the house Bobbi wanted to buy. She must have had contact with Young."

He looked through the brochure. "From the looks of these homes, I think Superior was a little out of her league."

Janice came up with my usual order of two hot dogs, fries, and a large Coke. "I'm assuming you want lunch."

"You read my mind," I said.

"What can I get for you, Kary?"

"One all the way and a Coke, please."

"Refill for you, Cam?"

"Yes, thanks."

She took his cup. "Mother and Mr. Vardaman are still at it, I see. Things have been a little calmer lately. Have you spoken to the ghost?"

"She's very shy. I'll keep trying."

Janice thanked him and left. I ate a few more fries. "Since when are ghosts shy with you?"

"She says I'm too light."

"Light? You must weigh at least a hundred and thirty pounds."

"Light in aura."

"Oh. Excuse me."

"It's interesting because I always thought I had a dark aura."

"It may have been dark at one time."

I was being flippant, but Camden liked this response. "You may be right. My life's a lot better. I've learned to control certain aspects of this talent. Maybe I've lightened up."

"So you need to find someone with a dark aura to talk to this ghost. Try Vardaman. He looks pretty dark to me."

"He's already tried. He can't communicate with anything except animals."

Vardaman and Mei Chan were still deep into their conversation. "Are he and Janice's mother an item?' Kary asked.

"Looks like it. Janice should be very happy."

Janice returned with Kary's order and Camden's refill in time to hear this. "I am. As long as she's distracted, I can get on with my life."

Kary took her hot dog and drink and thanked her. "What's this ghost you have?"

"Cam says it's a young girl. I have no idea what she could want."

Camden slid the napkins over to Kary. "If I keep reassuring her, I think she'll talk to me."

"Think she'd talk to me?" I asked.

"No, your aura's way too dark. It's the black hole of auras."

Kary snickered. "The Black Hole of Auras. Sounds like a Creature Feature."

"I don't appreciate jokes at the expense of my aura. It's very delicate."

Janice returned to her other customers. I chewed on a hot dog for a while and then explained my plan of action. "I'm going to run Young's picture by the salesgirl at Oriental Imports and see if he's the same man who asked about Bobbi. I'm also going to show it to Tina Ramola. When she stopped by to see Mary Rose, she caught a glimpse of a large man. Maybe the picture will jog her memory."

I know Camden wanted to say something like, you can't find every lost child in the world, or you don't have to prove anything by this, but what he actually said was, "Sounds like a good lead."

I finished my lunch and took one last drink of cola. "Beverly Huntington's supposed to meet me at four to talk to dearly departed Mom. You probably ought to be there."

Mei Chan led Jessie Vardaman over to our table. "David, have you met Jessie? He can communicate with animals! So fascinating."

I shook hands with Vardaman. "David Randall. I caught your act at the PSN."

"Yes, I remember. You were with Cam. Are you psychic, too?"

"I don't think so. This is Kary Ingram."

He shook Kary's hand. "A pleasure to meet you. That business with the fox annoyed me enough to seek Camden out today, but my stars must have been properly aligned. If I hadn't come looking for him, I wouldn't have met Mei. It just shows you everything happens for a reason."

He and Mei smiled at each other in a way that made me wonder if there was a Mr. Chan in the picture who might not appreciate this. She put her hand on his arm. "I believe the fox brought us together. Didn't I tell you that was the way of fox fairies?"

Or sheer dumb luck, I wanted to say.

Vardaman patted her hand. "I'd never really explored the Chinese zodiac. Would you believe our signs are compatible?"

"Congratulations."

At this point, two of the stray cats that hang around the back of the restaurant raced around the corner and leaped up on the picnic table, knocking over Kary's cola, and screeching and growling. Hank was a lean gray cat with green eyes. Tilly was orange and white. Hank was missing an ear, and Tilly had bald patches. They don't usually pester the customers because Janice and Steve leave food out for them, so I wondered if they'd heard Vardaman was in the neighborhood and had come to have a chat.

Mei clapped her hands in excitement. "Jessie! Can you tell what these cats are saying?"

Vardaman immediately stepped forward, eager to impress Mei. He looked as if he were trying to hypnotize Hank, but couldn't out-stare that bright green gaze. "This one, ah, seems to be upset about something. He wants food, of course. He apologizes for upsetting your drink, Kary, and wants to know if he can have the rest of your French fries."

Hank turned away, contempt in every movement from his bored expression to the tip of his ragged tail, sat in front of Camden and continued to yowl.

I should have known who they really wanted to talk to.

Mei was anxious to know what Hank had just said, and Vardaman did his best.

"Quite an interesting character. He's has a hard life, as you can see, but he loves being wild and free. Is there a Year of the Cat, Mei?"

"Oh, no," she said. "The cat was cheated out of a place in the zodiac. Let me say good-bye to Janice and we can go. I will tell you the whole story."

Before he left, Vardaman spoke in an undertone to Camden. "What is going on with these cats?"

"They'd like for me to come to the back of the restaurant and check on something."

"Did you hear what that gray one called me?"

"He's a little cranky today."

Hank stared at him. Tilly turned upside down, purring like a little motorboat.

Camden wasn't fooled by the Adorable Kitten routine. "I love you, too," he told her, "but I know that trick, and I'm keeping all my fingers, thanks."

Tilly gave a disapproving sniff and rolled over. Both cats hopped off the table. Kary and I followed Camden and the cats around the restaurant past a neat row of garbage cans and stacks of empty cardboard boxes.

"What's going on?" Kary asked.

"Hank and Tilly don't like having Hot Dog Girl in their territory."

"Maybe she'll come out for me. Maybe my aura's what she's looking for."

He paused at the back door of the kitchen. Fragrant odors of hot dogs and fries filled the air. "Usually, she's right here."

"How do you call her?"

"She just appears."

"You might not be able to see her," I said when a slight chill breeze blew past my face and lifted a few strands of Kary's hair. "Then again."

The cats stiffened. Hank growled and Tilly gave a hiss.

"I'm sorry," Camden said, "but she's not going to leave until someone figures out why she's here. Won't she tell you?"

A pop sounded inside the restaurant, the back door slammed open, and the cats were pelted by a rain of raw hot dogs. Kary and I managed to duck the little missiles as they sailed by our heads, but plainly, Ghost Girl's targets were Hank and Tilley, who scampered off down the alley, not without each grabbing a hot dog to eat once they got out of range.

Camden tried to calm the ghost and got a hot dog right between the eyes. He rubbed juice off his forehead. "It's all right. They're gone. If you'd just tell me what you want, I can help you."

Right now, all she wanted was to fling wieners and make a mess. Maybe a little reverse psychology would work. "Forget it," I said. "She's never going to tell you. Just leave her alone. Let her haunt the restaurant as long as she likes. I don't care." For that, I got my ear soundly smacked by not one but two hot dogs. "Okay, bring back the cats."

Abruptly, all the hot dogs fell to the ground. I thought the threat of Hank and Tilly had done the trick, but Steve stood at the back door, dumfounded. "How'd these hot dogs get out here?"

"Your ghost threw a tantrum," I said, "and about a dozen wieners."

"Cam, can't you do something?"

"I don't know," he said. "For now, try to keep Hank and Tilly away."

With Steve grumbling about the waste of good food, we helped gather up the battered hot dogs and then drove back to Oriental Imports. It was the salesgirl's day off, and the other workers didn't recognize Young's picture.

"One down, one to go," I said.

Kary had followed us in Turbo, but couldn't continue the search. A piano student was coming to the house at three-thirty. She wished us luck with Young's picture and with Beverly

Huntington and drove off. When Camden and I stopped by Dream Vacations, Tina Ramola didn't recognize the picture, either.

She looked like a kitten that had lost its favorite cat toy. "I'm so sorry. I've never seen this fellow before."

I folded the brochure back into my pocket. "That's all right. We were hoping he might have been the man you saw in Bobbi's house that day."

"I didn't see him at all."

"Do you remember seeing a black BMW at the house at any time?"

"No, and I would've remembered that. Bobbi's neighborhood isn't the BMW type."

We thanked her and left. Next stop, the Carlyle House. The house smelled of fresh paint and flowers. In a small room opposite the parlor, Patrick Lauber supervised two red-faced men as they forced the elaborate wallpaper pattern to meet at the corners.

He turned to greet us. "Good afternoon. I have a message for you from Beverly Huntington. She's not coming. She called a few minutes ago and said to tell you she wouldn't be here."

What the hell? "What's going on with her?"

"You'll have to ask her yourself."

Camden drifted off to look in the mirror while I phoned Beverly. I repeated what I'd said to Lauber. "What's going on? We had a deal. Kit paid the rent, moved in, no problem."

"That's just it," she said. "It wasn't any problem. I think my coming back into that house is worth more than one favor."

How long was she planning to drag this out? "What do you want?"

"I need you to do something for Frieda. Ever since Kit left, she's been whining that it wasn't fair to leave her out."

"Didn't you say they couldn't live in the same house?"

"Oh, I don't mean for you to find her an apartment. She wants to be in a band, like Kit."

This was ridiculous, and I wasn't going to play anymore. "Would you hold on a moment, please?"

Camden stood in front of the mirror, his eyes reflecting the clouds shifting on its surface. "Camden, Beverly has a new demand. She says she won't come unless I get her daughter, Frieda, into a band. I'm ready to forget the whole thing. Tell Delores thirty thousand dollars isn't nearly enough."

The mirror darkened. At the same time, we heard a yelp and startled swearing from the room across from the parlor. I stepped in to see great hunks of wallpaper curling down. In about three minutes, the room was sheared. Patrick Lauber and the workmen stood knee-deep in wallpaper curls. They looked at me in astonishment.

Delores was having a major temper tantrum. Camden placed both hands on the mirror as if to calm her as vases trembled on the hall tables and pictures shivered on the walls. "Delores, take it easy. We'll find some way to get Beverly here." She must have given him a pithy reply because he turned to me in appeal. "Randall."

"Okay, okay, I'll see what I can do. Tell her I'll take care of it." As the house returned to normal, I spoke into my phone. "No more stalling," I told Beverly Huntington. "I'll get Frieda into a band, but that's the last thing I'm doing for you."

"Excellent. When can I expect results?"

"I'll call you."

We left Lauber and the bewildered workmen still wading through wallpaper. Camden leaned back against the Fury, hands in his pockets. "She was ready to bring the place down."

"I say let her do it. Beverly feels she's making a huge sacrifice, so I have to make it worth her while. I have a feeling it's not going to stop with Frieda."

"She may not ever come, no matter what you do for her."

"That's why I think I should stop right now."

He looked at the house. "You have to try."

"I don't owe Beverly Huntington anything. I don't owe Delores Carlyle anything. You say getting mother and daughter together's going to fix things. Fix what? Delores will still be a cranky old mirror and Beverly a cranky old beaver. I'm wasting my time with these two. I should be out looking for a real baby instead of ghosts."

Camden didn't say anything. I thought of my own little daughter. In my dreams, she's always eight years old, dressed in her best white lace dress, white ribbons in her long curly brown hair. She's always smiling. I glared at Camden. If he was sending me this picture, he was way out of line.

No, he wasn't. I couldn't help thinking of Lindsey, of wanting to see her. Damn it. I knew exactly how Delores Carlyle felt.

"Get in," I said. "We're going to Perkie's."

• • ● • •

"Frieda Huntington?" Vangie wrinkled her nose in disgust. "No way."

Her bandmate, Chloe, made a face. "Uh-huh. She's wretched."

We'd caught the girls in rehearsal—if twanging the same four chords can be called rehearsing—and suggested a new bandmate. They were less than enthusiastic.

"You've got to be kidding," Vangie said. "Can she sing? No. Can she play an instrument? I don't think so. Can she bitch? Oh, my, yes, she can. Tell her to start her own band."

"Couldn't she whack on a tambourine or something? It's only for a couple of days until her mom fulfills her part of the bargain."

Vangie tucked her hair behind her ear and gave me a dark green stare. "Okay, let me get this straight, David. You've got this client who won't do something unless you get her skanky daughter in a band. We take skank in, mom does her thing, we toss skank out?"

"I couldn't have said it better."

Chloe was still shaking her head. Dressed all in black, her black hair pulled back, she looked like a mini-mourner. "It's not worth it. Frieda Huntington is a pit-girl and drags major baggage. She'd poison our musical concept."

"Two days tops, I promise."

"Two days is way too long to deal with Frieda." Vangie exchanged a meaningful look with the other girls. "Could I have a word with you ladies, please?"

They moved to a corner of the bandstand. I sat down at the table with Camden.

He pushed a large coffee cup my way. "I didn't want to bring this up, but even if Vangie agrees, Frieda might not want to be a Slotted Spoon."

I took a long drink of coffee, wishing the cup were big enough to drown in. "I'm so glad I brought you along."

Vangie returned to our table and sat down. "Okay, here's our deal."

"Oh, great, Camden. They have a deal."

"You get us a gig at the Cave, and we'll take Frieda in for two days."

"I thought you already had a gig at the Cave."

"Fell through."

"How am I supposed to get it back?"

"You're the big smart detective. You'll think of something. Deal?"

I sighed. "Camden, do you see a pattern here?"

"I guess our next stop is the Cave."

Grimly, I turned to Vangie, who beamed at me. I held up two fingers, resisting the urge to lower one. "Two days."

Chapter Twelve

"I'm Nobody's Baby"

When we entered the dim confines of the Cave for the second time that week, I thought Trace Burwell was going to sink into the floor. He held onto his towel like a shield.

"I already told you guys everything I know, so don't think you'll push me around."

"Relax," I said. "Who's in charge of entertainment?"

His face went blank. "Entertainment?"

"Music, bands, groups, stand-up comedians. Who books the acts?"

"We don't have stand-up."

"Do you have a manager?"

I finally got through. "Oh. That'd be Dillon Pennix."

"Is he here? Can I speak to him?"

"He's in his office, in the back."

We wound through the tables and chairs to the back of the club. "I wonder what Pennix will want in return for this favor. Maybe he'd like a great big mirror to hang on the wall."

I knocked on the black door, and a voice said, "Come in." The door opened into a cramped office about the size of a supply closet. Dillon Pennix was digging through a black file cabinet. In his khaki slacks and striped shirt, he looked surprisingly preppy to be manager of a dark little bar. With his careful hairstyle and smooth face, he could've been Reg Haverson's wayward cousin.

He found a manila folder and lifted it from the cabinet. He turned to us. "Yeah, what now? I told you guys I've met all the new requirements, so back off."

"Mr. Pennix, my name's John Fisher, and I represent a very fine young band that would like to play at your establishment."

"So you're not from the health department?"

"No, as I said, I represent a new band on the Parkland music scene."

He sat behind his desk and began to go through the folder. "Yeah? Who's that?"

"They call themselves the Destitute Dolls. You may have heard of them. They were on the bill for the Dungeon Rattle in Charlotte a couple of weeks ago."

"Can't say that I've heard of them. What's their line?"

Line? "Old-style Goth mixed with electronic Shade."

It sounded good to me and apparently sounded good to Dillon Pennix. He glanced up from his work. "This an all-girl band? I mean, I've heard some real clunkers lately. These teenage girls think if they learn a few chords and scream real loud, it passes for music. Do the Dolls have a distinctive sound?"

"I'd say so. Would you be willing to give them a tryout?"

He looked at his desk calendar. "Looks like I've got a spot next week."

"Anything sooner? They're getting a lot of calls, and I'd hate for you to miss out."

He shook his head. "Next Wednesday's the best I can do."

"What if they came over tomorrow night and played for free?"

"What if they suck? I can't afford to lose customers. It's not exactly booming out there." He gave me a hard look. "You're pushing here, bud. What is it? One of the Dolls your special playmate?"

I held up both hands. "Okay, you got me. I wish it was something nice like a playmate, but the truth is my ex-wife's daughter is the leader of this little group. If I don't get the band a gig by tomorrow night, she's calling in the big dogs. It'd really help me out if you let the girls play a couple of songs."

"Fifteen hundred dollars will buy them a couple of songs."

"Ex-wife's got all my money." That part was true.

Pennix shifted his hard gaze to Camden and then back to me. "How old is your friend there?"

What did that have to do with anything? "Thirty-one."

Pennix looked surprised. "No kidding?"

Was he hitting on Camden? "He keeps a picture in the attic."

Pennix missed the reference. "There may be something you can do for me."

Camden took a step back. "I don't think so."

"Nothing like that, pal, settle down. There's a new club open down near Royalle's Jewelry. I want to scope out the competition, but there's a couple of problems. One, the people who run the place know me and we kinda don't get along, and, two, it's a club for kids. Even if they'd let me in, I'd stick out."

"What exactly are we talking about?" I asked.

"We're talking about a deal, big guy. Your friend here does a little reconnoitering for me, I let your Dolls sing here tomorrow night."

I looked at Camden. "Over to you."

He was puzzled. "A club for kids?"

"Yeah, teenagers," Pennix said. "You could pass easily."

"Why are you interested in a teenage club?"

"Business here isn't so hot. I could use some fresh ideas."

"Then watch MTV. I'm not going."

"See what kind of music they have, what sort of drinks and food they're serving. Nothing to it."

"Let me confer with Mr. Fisher." He pulled me out of the little office. "Okay, I just have this to say: No."

"If you say no, then this whole scheme implodes. The Spoons don't play, Frieda's singing career stalls, Beverly stays home, and Delores brings the house down."

"Randall, no. It's crazy. There's no way I could pass for a teenager."

"Have you looked in a mirror lately? Oh, that's right, you have. A great big mirror full of sad old Delores. Can you abandon her now when we're so close?"

"Close? You thought you were done when Kit moved in. When is this ever going to end?"

"This has to be the last deal."

"It better be."

We went back into the office. "Okay," I said to Pennix. "He'll do it. When can the Dolls go on?"

"Ten o'clock tomorrow night. They can play one set."

• ● ● ● •

Except for a well-deserved go-to-hell look, Camden didn't say much to me on the drive back to Perkie's.

"It can't be that bad," I said. "Ellin's always at the studio on Saturday nights taping 'Bilk the Suckers' or something like that. You check out this club, maybe dance with pretty girls, probably get decent club chow, and you're home before you turn back into a pumpkin."

No answer.

"This is a great way to help Delores without getting your head messed up with a psychic load. You won't get possessed or see ghastly crimes, unless the kids are into Satanism."

Since I don't smoke, I keep my spare change in the Fury's ashtray. One by one, the coins came up out of the tray and began to spin in a tight circle. My sunglasses leaped from the visor to join the circle, as did the road atlas from the backseat. The glove compartment popped open, spilling inspection papers, registration cards, and a screwdriver. All these objects joined the dance. I pulled over to the curb and stopped the car. I knew Camden was angry, but not this angry.

"Whoa, I thought we were done with this."

Whatever had set him off faded. The objects dropped and bounced all over the floor, except for a few pennies that hovered in front of him as if awaiting orders. He took a deep breath. "Me, too."

"So maybe there's something you're not telling me?"

I didn't get any response until I pulled up in Perkie's parking lot. By then, the pennies had landed. Then he said, "Don't tell Vangie about me going to the club. She'll laugh herself sick."

"I wasn't going to." But I didn't think that was the cause of the little poltergeist action in the car.

The Slotted Spoons were taking a coffee break at the counter. They tried very hard to act cool, but their eagerness shone through.

Vangie bounced on her toes. "Well? Did we get it?"

"You go on at ten tomorrow night."

They screamed so loudly, the other customers jumped and clutched their coffee cups.

I unplugged my ears. "Hold on. I could arrange only one set, but if he likes what you do, he might let you play another."

"That's great, David, thanks."

"Oh, one other thing. You have to call yourselves the Destitute Dolls. I thought if he heard Slotted Spoon, he'd turn me down flat."

Vangie tried it out. "Destitute Dolls. That's not bad. Did you come up with that yourself?"

"Totally original. You can use it."

"Hey, for one night we can be destitute."

"Call Frieda right now."

She made a face. "Does she have to play tomorrow night? She'll ruin our big break."

"No, but she's got to be a Spoon by this weekend."

Vangie shook my hand. "Deal. Thanks again. Okay, Dolls, we'd better practice."

I left them hammering out their four chords and wailing something that sounded like, "Crab apples my heart till I touch my wringer." I liked it better than "Pinchers in the circuit."

Camden had waited in the car. He still wasn't over his sulk, but nothing was in orbit around him.

I got behind the wheel and started the car. "The girls are happy."

"I heard them."

"What's it going to take to de-funk you?"

We were one street over from Grace Street when he decided to reply. "I don't look like a teenager."

"Yes, you do. Get over it."

"I'm thirty-one years old. I'm a married man."

"Most people would kill to look younger."

"Most women, maybe."

"You've always looked like this."

"Don't you find that a little strange?"

"Maybe they experimented on you at the Home."

Whoo, boy, was *that* the wrong thing to say.

He stiffened, eyes wide. "I never thought of that. Do you suppose—?"

"No, and neither should you."

"But there were hundreds of us there."

"Yes, I know. All named John."

Another mistake. Now Camden's eyes threatened to take over his whole face.

"Oh, my God. What if we're clones?"

"Then the world would be full of short blond idiots. I was joking, Camden."

"Still, it might explain things." He was silent until we got home. I parked the Fury and turned it off. He sat for while and then said, "I need to go back."

"To Perkie's? You've had your quota of caffeine for today."

"To Green Valley."

"I thought you never wanted to see that place again."

"When could we go?"

"I don't know if you've noticed, but I'm in the middle of a case right now. Two cases, if you count Delores."

Every now and then Camden will get a steely expression that means 'there's no way you're talking me out of this.' "I need to go back."

"Okay, fine. Ellin can take you. Or hop a bus."

We got out of the car. Halfway up the walk, Camden caught at his leg and began to limp. "Ow. Something's wrong with my leg." He gave me a look of pure innocence. "I hope it's okay by tomorrow night."

"Are you blackmailing me?"

"I sure as hell am."

"Why not? Everyone else is."

Camden didn't know enough about his past to make informed decisions. Maybe there was an explanation for his youthful appearance. Maybe the orphanage cafeteria had served magic beans. Then he brought up a little something else.

"Thirty thousand dollars, Randall."

Speaking of magic, hadn't I said money was the magic word? "All right."

Camden ran up the porch steps, stopped and turned to me. Now his eyes were wide with feigned amazement. "It's a miracle!"

Chapter Thirteen

"You Must Have Been a Beautiful Baby"

Kary had her famous tuna casserole ready for our supper. I say famous. Perhaps a better word would be "notorious." But Camden and I would rather choke on it and die than hurt her feelings. Fortunately, there were plenty of Ellin's delicious biscuits left over from a previous meal. The biscuits made an excellent stomach lining.

We sat down at the dining room table and I reached for the biscuits. "Okay, Kary, you're going to enjoy this. Beverly didn't show, and Delores expressed her displeasure by removing the wallpaper. Beverly now says I have to do something for Kit's sister, Frieda, and the something is to get her into a band. I asked Vangie if the Slotted Spoons would take her in, and she said yes, if I got the Spoons a gig at the Cave. Dillon Pennix, owner of the Cave, will let them play tomorrow night if—and here's the best part—if Camden will sneak into a rival club that caters to teens and take notes."

Camden took up the story. "And I agreed to pass as a teenager if Randall takes me to Green Valley to see if I can find out why I look like a teenager."

He didn't mention his little episode in the car.

Kary laughed. "This would make a great fairy tale. In order to bring the queen to the castle to release her mother from the enchanted mirror, you must first find the prince a home, and then grant the princess her dream of singing with the fairies. But you must also find out if the spell of Eternal Youth is a gift or a curse."

"Exactly. Only we don't know when this tale ends, or if it ends happily." I'd had more than enough fairy tales. "There better not be another knot in this string."

Kary dug out another scoop of casserole for each of us and plopped it on our plates. "Cam, I didn't think you wanted to go back to Green Valley."

"I'm hoping someone there can answer my questions."

"Couldn't you call them?"

"No, I want to go there."

I passed him the biscuits. "If I come back with more than one of him, head for the hills."

"I'm not sure I want to know what that means," Kary said. "What about Young's picture? Did Bobbi's BeautiQueen saleswoman recognize him?"

"No, but it's still the best lead we've got. The only lead we've got, I should say."

"We're going back to Superior Homes, aren't we? We still might find a clue." She pushed back her chair. "I think there are more of those little oranges in the fridge. Want one?"

"Yes, thanks." I waited until she was out of earshot before adding, "Anything to cut the taste."

Camden looked at the pile of casserole on his plate. "You know, times like these, a dog would really come in handy."

I passed him the biscuits. "Man up and chow down."

He toyed with a clump of casserole. "Somebody should tell her how awful this is."

"What's wrong with you telling her?"

"She's always so pleased with these things."

"Does she ever taste them?"

Kary returned with the oranges and passed them around. I asked her if she'd heard from Rainbow Wishes.

"Not yet."

"Think they're on to you?"

"I don't see how." She sat down and began to peel her orange. "Maybe I didn't get the job."

I didn't tell her I thought that was a good thing.

She glanced at Camden's plate. "You're not very hungry tonight."

Camden's glance to me plainly said, "*You* tell her."

How to phrase this? "Kary, about your tuna casserole…"

"Oh," she said. "Didn't this one turn out okay?"

"Actually—and I say this with love—none of them do."

She looked surprised. "None of them?"

Camden tried to soften the blow. "Maybe you could try cooking something else?"

I braced myself for her reply. Her mouth quirked in a smile. "Are you two saying that all this time you've been worrying them down to spare my feelings?"

"Only to prove the depth of my affection," I said.

She laughed. "There are other ways to prove that." She reached over for Camden's plate. "Cam, I can't believe you didn't say something sooner. You guys are ridiculous."

"And hungry," he said. "Would you bring the peanut butter, please?"

• • ● • •

Later that evening, Camden and I were watching *The Lost World* when Rufus and Angie came home. We could hear them arguing out in yard, up onto the porch, and into the foyer.

Angie was exasperated. "Don't you understand you have to cooperate with the police?"

"Not when they've already got me found guilty! You try holdin' your temper."

"No, that's what you've got to do. Jordan wanted to know where you'd been that day, that's all."

"And I told him! I told him five hundred times! Oh, hi, fellas."

The argument had reached the island. I took the remote and muted the TV. "I take it Jordan doesn't have any other suspects."

Rufus gave a snort. "Finley couldn't find his rear with his hands in his back pockets. Hope you've had better luck today."

"As a matter of fact, I have a promising lead."

Rufus plopped down on the other end of the green corduroy sofa. "Let's hear it."

"The owner of Superior Homes is a big red-haired man."

"Superior Homes?"

"The realtor Bobbi was dealing with."

"Oh, ho. Have you called Finley?"

"I don't have any proof the man did anything wrong."

"But you got a plan, right?"

"Yes, do me a favor and stay away until I spring the trap."

Rufus considered this. "All right." He spoke over his shoulder to Angie who was standing behind him, resting her large forearms on the back of the sofa. "See? I'm cooperating."

"'Bout time," she said.

She went upstairs to go to bed, but Rufus stayed awhile and watched about fifteen minutes of the movie. During a commercial, he reached for the remote and muted the sound again. "You think this realtor fella done it?"

"Like I said, no proof yet."

"How'd Bobbi plan to afford a Superior Home? They're top of the line."

"I don't know."

"Can't you look up her bank records or something?"

"That's not always possible."

"What about her cell phone? Maybe there's something on that."

"The police have her cell phone."

"Ain't Finley lettin' you in on this case?"

"He's being as agreeable as he can."

Rufus snorted again. "Well, that ain't much, is it?" He punched up the sound. On the TV, jerky stop-motion dinosaurs roared and trampled fake palm trees. I was pretty sure Rufus felt like doing the same.

"I ain't gonna wait forever, Randall. I gotta do something. You know how you'd feel if something happened to Kary and the police thought you did it. Same for you, Cam, if it was Ellin. You'd be spontaneously combustin', or throwin' things around without touchin' 'em, like you did last month."

"You're not going to combust, but I know you're going to do something," Camden told Rufus, "and it's not going to help."

"Think you've got me all figured out, do you?"

"Yep. I don't have to hold your hand to know you want to go over to Superior Homes, break in, and shake a confession out of Brian Young. That's not going to happen."

"Not now, not after you done took all the fun out of it."

What was it going to take to quell the Mighty Mammoth? "If you set one foot into Superior Homes, I promise I'll call Jordan to come take you away," I said. "Adams Boulevard, the Crow Bar, and 302 Grace. Those are the only places you need to be."

Rufus rubbed his face, further ruffling his scraggly beard. He was searching for the right phrase, and sure enough, he found one. "Y'all two are meaner than a pair of striped snakes."

"Make that a striped snake and a striped dragon, and you've got that right."

• • ● • •

Saturday morning, I took Camden to Bell City, Virginia, site of the Green Valley Home for Boys. I'd been by Camden's orphanage before. The Green Valley Home wasn't a grim gray institution surrounded by a stone wall topped with razor wire. It was a pleasant-looking red brick and wood structure that looked like an old-fashioned hotel. A group of boys played soccer on the lawn. Another group rode by on bikes. The morning sun shone between large maple trees.

I parked the car and we got out. Camden stood for a long time, gazing at the front door. He never said much about his childhood. He'd been brought to the Home when he was three days old and placed with a family who returned him a year later, worried about the baby's "seizures." For the next few years, he was adopted and returned like an overdue library book until an older couple, Rosalie and Herbert Camden, took him in and kept him. Rosalie had been a kind if somewhat stern and humorless foster mother. Herbert had been afraid of the "abnormal" boy. At age sixteen, not long after Rosalie's death, Camden dropped out of school and began wandering across the country.

"Want to go in?" I asked.

"Now that I'm here, I'm not sure."

"Come on."

The foyer was wide and clean. It smelled of old wood and lemons.

"The smell," he said. "It's like being flung back in time. And the wallpaper's the same."

A design of faded ducks and teddy bears danced around the room. In the center of the room was a desk and floor lamp. An elderly man sat behind the desk, working at a computer. Camden approached him cautiously.

"Mr. Reynolds?"

The man looked up, peering through little round glasses. "Yes. What can I do for you?"

"You probably don't remember me. I lived here for a few years until the Camdens took me in."

Mr. Reynolds frowned in thought. "When was this?"

Camden told him his birthday.

"Let me look it up. Your name, son?"

"John Camden."

Mr. Reynolds hesitated a moment. I wondered if the Name All the Boys John had been his bright idea. Then his fingers slowly tapped the keys. "A wonderful thing, this computer. We used to have mounds of paper to sort through. Ah, here we are."

He turned the screen so we could see. The information was listed in three short lines. Mother requested anonymity. Father unknown. Camden had weighed all of six pounds. All the papers signing him over to Green Valley were in order.

Camden knew his birthmother's name because I'd found her. At first, she didn't want to see him, but later relented and even came to his wedding.

"Any pictures?" I asked.

Mr. Reynolds swung the screen back around. "According to this, there's one in our picture file. One moment."

He went to a row of file boxes at the back of the room.

Camden frowned at me. "Pictures?"

"To prove you're not one of Boys from Brazil."

"I can't believe Mr. Reynolds is still here. He was ancient years ago."

"Maybe the lemon smell acts as a preservative."

Mr. Reynolds returned and handed Camden a photograph. Three-year-old Camden gazed out of the picture with large innocent eyes, untidy pale hair, and a slight smile, as if caught daydreaming.

"Okay, I give up," I said. "You look the same."

Camden stared at his younger self. It was a beautiful child's face, the kind that would've been on magazine covers or even in commercials and movies. He was quiet for so long, I knew what he was thinking: If I looked like this, why didn't anyone want me?

"Can we take this with us?" I asked Mr. Reynolds.

"Yes, of course. Nice to see you again, John."

I steered Camden out. "Ellin will like it."

We got back into the car. I decided we needed to save a trip and deal with everything. "Okay, while we're tripping down memory lane, let's stop by your old homeplace."

"It was falling down when I lived there. It must be a complete dump by now."

"I want to see it."

Camden directed me to the neighborhood, which wasn't all that bad: middle class, lots of vans, basketball goals, plastic wading pools, yard art like big chickens and froggies on love seats.

He pointed up the street. "It's right up there. 3808. Hold on. I think that's it." He sat back. "Wow."

The old house had obviously been remodeled, painted, and the yard landscaped. It was clean and white with green shutters, a front door with a fancy glass panel in the center, flowers boxes filled with red and pink geraniums, and white wicker porch furniture with green cushions.

Relief was evident in Camden's voice. "It looks good."

"Kind of remade itself, wouldn't you say?"

He nodded.

"Sort of the way you did."

Another nod.

"You can't help the way you look, any more than I can. But despite a rocky beginning, you managed to become a decent human being with a great house, lots of friends, and a beautiful wife who loves you. I had an ideal childhood, and look where I am, all alone with only a disturbed psychic for a pal."

This made him grin. "You're pretty decent."

"Thanks."

He looked back at the house. "If this had been the dump I remembered, your speech wouldn't have worked."

"I would've found another analogy."

"'Analogy.' That's good."

"An ideal childhood and an impressive vocabulary."

He pointed to the top floor. "That was my room up there."

"Oh, they kept you locked in the attic. That explains everything."

"I liked having the upstairs to myself. It was a lot easier than having the thoughts of hundreds of kids bombarding me all day. And the porch. I always liked sitting out on the porch." He sat for a while in the stillness that meant he was back in his memories. "My foster mother didn't understand how disconnecting my visions could be. She thought I was hard of hearing, so she'd be back in the kitchen and holler for me to come eat. The whole neighborhood could hear her."

At that moment, a woman stepped out the front door and shouted, "Robert!" Camden and I both jumped.

"Come in right now, young man!" the woman called. She gave the Fury a curious look. I'm sure the sight of a giant white car with two strange men inside laughing was enough to phone the cops.

It was time to move on. "Seen enough?"

"Yes, thanks. Let's go home."

• • ● • •

The delicious smell of fried bread and cheese greeted us as we entered 302 Grace. We found Kary in the kitchen cooking sandwiches. She slid one out of the frying pan onto a plate, which she handed to me.

"So, guys, how was the mission to Green Valley?"

Camden took the picture out of his pocket and showed it to her. "That's me at three."

Kary's face brightened. "Oh, look at you! I love it. I definitely want a copy." She admired the photo from all angles. "I think it's beautiful." She handed him the picture and then put a comforting hand on his arm. "Are you okay? I know you didn't really want to go back there."

"I'm glad I did. We went by my old house, too. It used to be so shabby and rundown, I didn't want to see it, but somebody had bought it and fixed it up. It looks brand new."

"I'm glad you decided to go by."

"It was Randall's idea."

The expression Kary turned my way was so full of admiration and gratitude I almost choked on my sandwich. "Nice going, David."

I managed to swallow. "I needed closure."

She handed me the potato chips. "When are Mr. and Mrs. Fisher going back to Superior Homes?"

"I'll call Brian Young and see if he can show us a couple of houses this afternoon."

We heard the roar of Rufus' truck, and in a few minutes, he came in the back kitchen door, sniffing the cheese-filled air. "Got an extra sandwich?"

Kary flipped another sandwich in the pan. "We've got plenty."

Rufus washed his hands at the sink and joined us. "I recalled Bobbi had another cousin living in South Carolina, so I phoned her to tell her the bad news. She'd already heard through another relative. Said she hadn't spoken to Bobbi in months, but the last time she did, Bobbi was excited about a house she was going to buy. Like me, the cousin said she didn't see how Bobbi could afford a house."

"Did this cousin know about the baby?" I asked.

"Didn't say nothing about it."

"I'd like to talk to her."

"I'll write down the number for you. You got anything else?"

"If Brian Young's in today, Kary and I will go back to Superior Homes."

Rufus took a handful of chips from the bag. "I appreciate the help, Kary."

"When we find your baby, you do plan to keep her, right?" Kary's question sounded casual, but I could hear the undertones of concern.

Rufus took a big bite of sandwich, chewed, swallowed, and wiped his mouth with the back of his hand. "Angie and I are still discussin' it."

"I don't see what there is to discuss."

"Lots of things."

"Rufus, she's your daughter."

"Now, don't get yourself in a swivet. It'll all work out."

"You know I'll help you look after her."

"One thing at a time. Let's find her first."

Kary let the subject drop, but I knew she didn't want to. "Cam, Patrick Lauber sent over another song they want you to sing. You want to try it after lunch?"

"Sure."

I finished my sandwich and got up to get more Coke. I got another can for Camden. "Kary? Rufus?"

"No, thank you."

"Got any Mountain Dew in there?"

I found a can of Mountain Dew for him. "Angie enjoying her new job?"

"Yeah, she says it's pretty good. What's this here?" He'd found Camden's baby picture on the counter.

"That's Cam," Kary said. "He and David went on a pilgrimage to Green Valley this morning."

"Well, ain't you cuter than a bug's ear?"

"I imagine anything would be cuter than a bug's ear," Camden said.

"Ain't changed much, have you? A little taller, maybe."

"Just what I needed to hear, Rufe."

"Ought to see my baby pictures. I was so ugly, my mama took me everywhere so she wouldn't have to kiss me good-bye."

After lunch, while Kary and Camden rehearsed the new song, I called Brian Young, even though I didn't think he'd be working on the weekend. As I'd figured, he wasn't in. I'd started into the island to tell Kary the news when we heard a crash overhead. We ran up the stairs. Kit Huntington thrashed around in his room like a rock star trashing a hotel. I heard wood splinter and glass shatter.

I banged on Kit's door. "Hey! What are you doing in there?" The noise stopped. I cautiously opened the door. Kit sat on the edge of the bed, holding his head and moaning. A chair had been thrown into the mirror over the bureau. Drawers had been yanked out, their contents spilling on the floor. There were dents in the wall and shreds of paper torn from books. "What the hell do you think you're doing?"

I wanted to grab him and throw him out, but Camden stopped me. "Wait a minute. I know what's going on."

"Is he having a psychic fit?"

Kit rocked back and forth. Camden put his hands on the boy's shoulders. "Kit, listen to me. You've got too many signals coming in at once. You can shut them off."

Kit's voice was hoarse and strained. "Signals? What are you talking about?"

"Thoughts from other people."

Kit shook him off. "Man, that's crazy! I'm crazy! All these voices, coming from everywhere. You don't know what it's like."

"Yes, I do. It happens to me all the time. You know I'm telling the truth."

Kit shuddered and nodded. "I don't know how, but I know."

"You can control it."

"There's no way."

"Yes, there is. Find the door."

"The door?"

"There's a door. Look for it."

Kit scrunched up his eyes. "There's too much stuff in the way!"

"Push it aside. Come on, you're always bragging about how tough you are."

He opened his eyes long enough to give Camden a glare, then closed them again. After a few minutes of concentration, he said, "I see something, but I don't know if it's a door."

"See if you can shut it. Do whatever it takes."

Kit was shaking, sweat running down his face. "It won't move."

"Try bringing it up like a drawbridge."

"Or like the doors on *Star Trek*?"

"Whatever works for you."

He gritted his teeth. "Shut, damn you, shut!" Suddenly, he opened his eyes wide. "Oh, my God, it worked! Everything stopped!"

"Don't lose concentration yet," Camden said. "It'll try to open."

"No, it won't." His thin face was filled with fierce triumph. "I won't let it." He stared at Camden. "You knew that first day, didn't you, when we met?"

"I can control most of the visions, and you can, too."

"Hell, yeah, now that I've got this handy door trick."

"That'll help, but you've got to shut the door dozens of times a day. After a while, it becomes automatic, but some visions are going to be stronger. Those are the ones you pay attention to."

Kit paused as if listening. "Yeah, I can feel them pushing at the door." He took a deep breath. "Man, it's a whole lot quieter now." He rubbed his eyes. "The only way I could get any peace was to sleep or play my music as loud as I could to drown 'em out. But I couldn't keep that up all the time. I was going insane. Who taught you this trick?"

"I figured it out, but it took a long time."

Kit became aware of Kary's anxious gaze and the remains of the room. "Oh, man, look at this. I'm sorry. I'll clean it up."

"That's okay," Camden said. "I'm not going to tell you how many rooms I trashed."

A suggestion of a grin crossed Kit's pale face. Then even this faded. "I guess you want me out, huh?"

"No. You've got it under control now."

The boy gave me a guilty look. "I'm not so sure Randall wants me hanging around here anymore."

"Two psychics in the house? Gee, I don't know. Could get rough."

This time, he grinned a real grin. "Better get used to it."

"Come get something to eat," Camden said. "We'll clean this up later."

He sat down at the counter while Kary fixed more grilled cheese sandwiches. The boy was like another person. Occasionally, I'd see his brow furrow and his eyes shut as he worked on his door-closing technique. Otherwise, he shoved in the food like a typical teenager. After his third sandwich, he paused and offered me his hand.

"Sorry about—you know, Randall."

I shook his hand. "No problem. I've been through this before."

"You, too, Kary. I apologize."

She favored him with one of her dazzling smiles. "That's all right. I'm glad you're okay."

Kit turned to Camden. "Were you going to mow the lawn today? You oughta check the mower before you start. One of the blades is loose."

"Thanks. I'll take care of that right now."

Camden took his toolbox, and he and Kit went out to the backyard.

I helped Kary put the sandwich stuff away. "This could very useful. Since Camden can't see his own future, maybe Kit can keep him out of trouble."

She gathered up the napkins we hadn't used. "What really

made Cam decide to go back to Green Valley? It must have been something serious."

"It's like he said. He's hung up on looking young for his age."

"He should be happy about that."

I put the bread back in the bread box. "You never know what's going to set him off."

"He probably has a young-looking father."

"That's next on my list."

She handed me the cheese to put back in the fridge. "Are you sure that's what Cam wants?"

"If his father can be found. But I want to find Bobbi Jo's killer and her baby first." I almost asked Kary if she had any baby pictures. Her parents had probably made a bonfire of her things.

"If Rufus and Angie don't want her, I'll take her."

No pressure here. Just provide the woman you love with the one thing she desires most in the world. "Where is Rufus, by the way?"

"I thought he was upstairs."

"He would've heard all Kit's racket, wouldn't he?"

"Yes, and come to help out."

"Uh, oh." I looked out the side window. Rufus' truck was gone. I was ready to charge out, but Kary stopped me.

"Hold on. I'll call him. Angie's working today. He might have decided to take her to lunch."

"Call Angie, too."

A few brief phone calls later, Kary had discovered Rufus was not answering his phone, he was not with Angie, and Angie was looking for him.

I started to the back door to get Camden when he ran in.

"Rufus is on the loose," I said.

"Just got that newsflash."

"Any idea where he might be? Turkey Leg Mountain? Chewing Tobacco Ridge?"

"He's headed toward Superior Homes."

"Damn it."

The three of us hopped into the Fury, and I drove as fast as I could toward Ashberry Street. Kary continued her unsuccessful attempt to reach Rufus.

"Forget that," I said. "Call Angie and tell her he's gone to Superior Homes to do God knows what."

"Get himself arrested."

Or worse. "Not if we get there first."

"We don't know how long he's been gone, though."

I ran into traffic on Marion Drive and had to take one of the side streets, but it was a good thing I did. As I turned onto Ashberry from my detour, I saw a bulldozer chugging down the street.

"There he is," Kary said.

"You have got to be kidding."

Sure enough, the driver was Rufus, his face as dark as a thundercloud. Was the big idiot planning to uproot Superior Homes and shake Young out like the last peanut in the jar? Or flatten the building and everyone in it?

Fortunately, there wasn't much traffic on Ashberry, and the bulldozer couldn't go as fast as the Fury. I honked the horn, pulled alongside, and the three of us made all kinds of signals for Rufus to stop. He ignored us and continued on his pathway to destruction. Superior Homes was coming up on the left. Did I want to sacrifice the Fury and possibly all of us, and pull in front of the bulldozer?

"Slow down and let me out," Camden said. "I might be able to stop him."

Kary caught his arm. "Cam, no."

The bulldozer bumped over the curb, narrowly missing a telephone pole, the treads leaving deep furrows in the grassy lot next to Superior Homes. I jerked the Fury to a halt, and Camden jumped out. Kary and I got out, too, but I held her back. I'd seen him stop a car before, but I wasn't sure his re-emerging telekinetic power could hold a bulldozer, not with the driver hell-bent on crushing something.

As it turned out, he didn't have to. Standing at the door to Superior Homes was Angie, arms folded, expression wrathful. With a puff of black smoke and a shudder, the bulldozer sputtered to a stop. I was surprised the earth didn't quake as Angie stomped up and stood in front of the bulldozer like some ancient stone monument come to life.

"Rufus Lee Jackson, what the hell do you think you're doing?" He stood up in his seat. "Get outta the way, woman."

"Oh, I'll get out of the way," she said. "I'll get all the way out of your way. If you move that bulldozer so much as an inch further, this is the last you'll see of me."

I don't think anything else could've gotten through. Rufus blinked in surprise.

"You don't mean that."

"I certainly do. I told the people inside Superior Homes that a construction company was doing a little work in this lot here and apologized for the noise. Do you know what that means? That means you can leave and nobody'll know the driver of this bulldozer was a big stupid boneheaded man with some cockeyed notion of revenge. I have saved your worthless hide. If you don't take advantage of that, then you are dumber than a stump, and I don't want to have anything else to do with you."

Rufus blew his breath out in an angry puff and sat down. "All right."

"All right, what?"

"All right, I'm leaving."

"Great," she said. "See you tonight—and let Randall handle this."

The bulldozer roared back to life and slowly moved toward the street.

"Thanks, Angie," I said. "You're the only one who could've gotten through to him."

"Honestly! That dolt done give me a panic attack and a twitch."

Just then, the bulldozer grazed a fire hydrant which immediately popped open and spewed a geyser of water up into the air. We cringed, but Angie shook her head.

"Don't that beat all."

Rufus didn't look back, but waved good-bye, unconcerned.

Angie stood in her attack position until the bulldozer was completely out of sight and then gave a nod as if to say, 'that's that.' She gave us a cheerful smile. "Call me if you need me."

Chapter Fourteen

"Sing Me a Baby Song"

Once all the drama was over, Camden mowed the lawn, and Kary
went up to her room, no doubt to plan how to talk Rufus and
Angie into letting her keep Mary Rose. I called Bobbi's cousin,
and after learning all I could from her, which was practically
nothing, she told me of another cousin, so I spent the rest of
the afternoon talking with various distant relatives and learning
even less than nothing.

Thankfully, Ellin was involved in taping a Very Special Episode of "Ready to Believe," that evening, so she wasn't around
while Camden prepared for his wild night of clubbing. I went
up to his room to see how he was progressing. He had on his
jeans and his Carolina Panthers t-shirt.

"Planning to wear shoes?"

He sighed as he reached for his sneakers

"Your baseball cap worn backward would be a nice touch."

"Too bad I don't have a giant gold chain."

He put on his shoes, stood up, and ran his hand through his
hair, which immediately fell into its usual disarray. "I guess this
is as good as it's going to get."

He looked all of sixteen. "Bet you get carded."

"Ha, ha."

I drove Camden to the address Pennix had given us.

"Camden, this is perfect for you, look."

Silvery lights spelled out the club's name: The Other Side.

"Been there," he said

The Other Side looked like every other night spot, a dark little place with music pulsing out and lights making jittery patterns on the street. Camden joined the line of teens waiting to get in. Nobody said anything to him, but a couple of the scantily attired girls gave him their complete attention. By the time he went inside, he had three girls chatting with him and three more giving him the eye.

● ● ● ● ●

I arrived at the Cave ten minutes before the Dolls were scheduled to appear. The tables were crowded, and all the stools at the bar were occupied. The patrons were mostly college age, boisterous, but not too drunk. Any sort of music would probably sound good to them.

I got a beer from Trace Burwell, who shot me a frightened look, and waded through the crowd. Pennix saw me and raised his beer glass in greeting. "Your friend get into The Other Side all right?"

"Yep. He's had a lot of practice. Are the Dolls here?"

"They're warming up in the back. They looked kinda familiar to me, but I see so many bands, I guess they all look alike after a while."

"I'd like to check with them."

"Take the door on the left."

"In the back" was a medium-sized room backstage with a low counter under a row of mirrors and a few folding chairs. The door was open, but I knocked and was greeted by the band formerly known as Slotted Spoon. Vangie and the other girls had on their usual black clothes, but had added fishnet hose, charm bracelets, and big floppy black bows in their hair.

Vangie finished tying her bow. "Do we look more like Destitute Dolls?"

They looked like Fun Time in Mom's Closet, but I didn't mention that. "You look very destitute. What did Frieda say?"

Vangie was reluctant to answer. "She said she'd never be a part of our band, even if we gave her a million dollars."

"Oh, great. Now she's decided to be picky."

"I hope that doesn't cancel our deal, David."

Chloe tugged at her black fishnet hose. "We asked her real nicely. I even offered to show her how to play guitar."

The girls looked at me with anxious eyes.

"No, you go ahead and have your big night. You did what you could."

Vangie readjusted her bow. "She was quite rude. She said, 'I can find my own band. I don't need your talentless crew.' Then she made other disparaging remarks about my character. Because my mother lets me do whatever I want doesn't make me a tramp."

"I'm sorry I set you up for that. I've met Frieda only once, but I should've known how she'd react."

The other member of the band leaned toward the mirror to check on her spiky eyelashes. "It doesn't make sense. When Vangie asked me to be in her band, I was thrilled."

Vangie gave me a worried glance. "What will you do now?"

"Right now, I'm going to go out front, get another beer, and enjoy the Destitute Dolls in concert."

I went out front, got another beer, and enjoyed—no, endured—the Destitute Dolls in concert. Fortunately, nobody threw anything at the stage. The crowd liked the discordant crashes and mumbled lyrics, even singing along. The Dolls played a mind-numbing hour and bowed to semi-enthusiastic applause.

Dillon Pennix strolled up to my table. "Not bad."

"Would you have them back again?"

"We might work something out. You and your friend come by the house tomorrow morning so he can tell me about the club." He saw someone across the room. "Excuse me. Gotta catch this fella."

I went back to give the Dolls the good news. They screamed and jumped up and down.

"Nothing's definite yet," I said, "but you made a good impression."

Vangie kissed my cheek. "Thanks, David. I wish we could've done what you asked."

"Don't worry about it." I was more concerned about what Camden and his new teenage friends were up to.

•   •   ●   ●   •

He was standing outside the club with a group of young ladies when I drove up. As he got in the car, they all said, "Good-bye, Johnny! See you!" and other sweet things.

"I can see you had a good time," I said. "Did you smoke some illegal substances?"

"Nope."

"Get down, get funky? Bust a move?"

"All night long."

"Meet cute chicks?"

"One cute chick in particular. The salesgirl from Oriental Imports was there. The one with all the little curls? Her name's Tashara, by the way."

"Uh, oh. Did she blow your cover?"

He made a wry face. "No, she thought I was eighteen like everyone else."

I stopped for a red light. "Learn anything useful?"

"Seems Tashara and Bobbi Jo had a lot of conversations about babies before Mary Rose was born. Tashara's anxious to have a baby of her own, and Bobbi told her it wasn't all that exciting. Tashara said she didn't like to hear Bobbi talk like that, and Bobbi told her she had other plans."

"Other plans for the baby? Such as?"

"Tashara didn't know. But she did say she'd heard several of her friends talking about a way you could make money by selling your baby instead of giving it up for adoption. She was afraid Bobbi was going to do that."

The light changed, and I drove on. "Who were these girls selling their babies to?"

"I don't know. It was very hard to pick up anything in that hormonal stew."

"I get the feeling this was a deal that went horribly wrong. Did Bobbi want a house that badly? Did she hand over her child, thinking she'd get a down payment on the mansion of her dreams, and then got killed instead?"

"I didn't get the feeling in the house that Bobbi wanted to sell her baby."

All this reminded me that Jordan hadn't returned my call about a possible black market in babies. "I can't imagine how anyone would do that."

"How did the Dolls do?"

"They made a good impression."

"So this intricate plan is working."

"But Frieda refused their offer."

Camden had the same reaction I did. "What? You've still got to find a band to stick her in?"

"I can think of several places I'd like to stick her."

We didn't say much the rest of the way home. The house was dark, and Ellin's car was in the driveway.

"Oh, Lord," Camden said.

"It's okay. We can sneak in. I've done it hundreds of times."

"I don't want to explain all this."

"You won't have to. Come on."

Camden tiptoed on up the stairs to their bedroom, and I tiptoed into mine. I didn't hear any outrage from Ellin, so I figured he was safe. I took a quick shower and got into bed. Before I went to sleep, I took a few minutes to think about what I could do with thirty thousand dollars. I'd always wanted to see more of the country. Travel out west, take in a few national parks, maybe see the Grand Canyon. Visit Alaska and see the Northern Lights. No, take a trip to New Orleans and spend a couple of weeks soaking, in the real traditional jazz played by the masters. Yeah, that was it. Kary could come, too. Oh, no, wait. I should buy something incredibly showy and expensive for Kary. Maybe a new car? So far, Turbo had been reliable, but it was almost as old as the Fury. I could use a new car, myself. I wouldn't have to ditch the Fury. I could keep her nice and clean and take her out on special occasions.

Or maybe I could put a substantial down payment on a house just for the two of us. Nothing as grand as a Superior Home, but we could make it work. There were a few houses for sale on Grace Street, not as big as 302, of course, but if we wanted to stay in the neighborhood—

Be reasonable, my reasonable side broke in. Here's what Kary would say. "If we're going to live on Grace Street, we might as well stay here." Have you forgotten Kary's a very independent woman, who likes doing things her way? What makes you think a grand gesture like a new car or a house is going to be what she wants, anyway? Do you even know what she wants, aside from a child?

Thirty thousand dollars would go a long way toward adopting and supporting a child.

No, I should put every cent in the bank. That would be amazingly sensible and amazingly dull. The way my career was going, I needed backup.

Thinking of my career brought my thoughts around to the case. So what was my next move? Strangle Frieda was at the top of the list.

Chapter Fifteen

"I Know That My Baby's Cheatin' On Me"

"Did you get up last night?"

This question was leveled at Camden by Ellin as I came into the kitchen on Sunday morning. He was sitting at the counter, Pop-Tart in hand. He was still in his pajamas. Ellin had poured a cup of coffee from the coffeemaker. She was dressed in one of her dark blue power suits. Little gold stars dangled from her ears.

"Up?" he said.

"I thought maybe you had a nightmare."

He was incapable of more than one word at a time. "No."

"I could've sworn you were up and dressed. Were you channeling someone?" She turned to me. "It isn't this case of yours, is it, Randall? I promise you, if you drag him into something that's going to screw with his personality—"

I got my coffee cup from the cabinet. "No more than usual."

"And is that the mirror that was in Fred's room out in the trash? What happened? Did that devil boy break it?"

"An accident," Camden said. "He's going to pay for it."

She leveled one of her laser stares his way. "You'd better fill me in on what's been going on around here."

I poured my coffee and sat down at the counter, curious to see how Camden explained it all.

He stalled by getting a large plastic cup and filling it with his morning cola. "Randall's had to make several deals in order to get Beverly Huntington to come to the Carlyle House and calm her mother's ghost. This hasn't kept Delores from throwing major temper tantrums, including the latest when all the wallpaper fell off. Randall had to find a band that would take Beverly's daughter, Frieda, which involved making another deal with Vangie and the Slotted Spoons. It turns out Kit is psychic and can't control his visions, so that's why he broke the mirror. The ghost girl at Janice's attacked us with flying hot dogs, and Rufus tried to knock over Superior Homes with a stolen bulldozer."

I noticed he left out the part about going to the rival club in disguise and levitating pennies.

Ellin took a moment. "Sorry I asked. Are any of these deals helping you find out who killed Rufus' ex-wife?"

He couldn't say much more without revealing his trip to The Other Side. "We hope so."

Time for a diversion. "Camden, have you shown Ellin your baby picture?"

He knew a life preserver when he saw one. "No, I haven't."

She had started to take a drink of coffee and put her cup down. "What baby picture? I thought there weren't any."

He retrieved the picture from the top of the piano. "We went by Green Valley the other day, and they had this."

Ellin's reaction was perfect. "Oh, Cam! Look at you! You were darling! How could anyone have given up such a precious child?"

I saw Camden's throat work as he swallowed what must have been a large chunk of emotion. "I guess I'll never know."

Ellin kissed him. "It doesn't matter. I have you now, and I'll never give you up."

Damn. Every now and then, she gets it right. Of course, it didn't last long.

"Can you come by the studio today?"

"After church, Kary and I have our concert at the Carlyle House."

For once, she didn't complain. "All right, stop by if you get a chance. Did you look at those brochures I brought home?"

"Not yet."

"Don't worry about Superior Homes. We could never afford one of those, and besides, I hear the company's not doing too well."

This caught my attention. "Really? Know any details?"

"The market's not good right now, especially for luxury homes. One of the cameramen at the station has a brother who works for State Realty, and he said State was thinking of buying out Superior."

"That's actually a useful bit of news, Ellin, thanks."

She looked bemused, as if helping me was the last thing she'd planned. She checked her watch. "I've got to go. See you." She gave Camden another kiss and hurried out.

"You should've gotten a baby picture a long time ago," I said.

He watched her go. "She's still taking her birth control pills."

I poured a cup of coffee for myself. "Sorry to hear that."

He sighed and pushed his hair out of eyes. "It's not fair of me to insist on children. She has to decide."

"But you see three in your future."

"And we know my future is always in question."

I sat down at the counter. "Maybe Kit can see it for you."

"That's a very good idea."

"Lord knows what we'll have to give him in return."

Camden sat back at his place and picked up his Pop-Tart. "You've read *The Moon is a Harsh Mistress*, right? Robert Heinlein says there's no such thing as a free lunch."

"Too bad Bobbi Jo paid the ultimate price."

He kept glancing at his baby picture. "If she didn't plan to sell Mary Rose, how was she going to have enough money to buy a Superior Home?"

"Maybe she had another scheme going." When he didn't answer right away, I said, "Camden?"

He brought his gaze up from the picture and smiled. "Our first daughter is going to look just like me."

"Oh, yeah? Going to be psychic, too?"

"All three are. At least, that's what I see right now."

"Ellin will be so pleased."

Kary came in, carrying *Tales of a Chinese Grandmother*. "David, I borrowed your book. I didn't know you were interested in Chinese fairy tales."

"I thought it might give me a clue about Janice's hot dog ghost."

She sat down at the counter and opened the book to the middle. "These are great stories. Very different."

"I still bet everybody has to pay."

"That is a recurring theme. In 'The Wonderful Pear Tree,' the selfish peddler who won't share his pears loses all of them, and in this one, 'The Spinning Maid and the Cowherd,' the maid leaves her loom to be with her lover, so there'll be no more silky clothes for the gods."

"Oh, that will not do."

"Yep. The Empress of Heaven got annoyed and drew a line across the sky which became the River of Stars, otherwise known as the Silver River, or the Milky Way. It separates the lovers forever. But before you get too sad, they get to meet every seventh day of the seventh moon. The birds make a bridge for the maid. A fancy story to explain the position of the stars."

"Did Janice ever tell you what sign you are in the Chinese zodiac?"

"I'm a Rat, like her. I know you're a Dragon and Cam's a Snake. Rufus is an Ox, and Angie's a Pig. Don't say anything! That's just how it turned out."

"No smart remarks, I promise. Janice told me Rats and Dragons get along very well." The perfect match, she'd said.

"Cam, you'll be glad to know Rats and Snakes are better friends than lovers."

"That's convenient," Camden said.

"Fortunately, all of the animals can live together here in our lovely barn." She took a napkin from the napkin holder and put it in the book to mark her place. "How did things go at the club?"

"I had a real swingin' time. The salesgirl from Oriental Imports recognized me."

"Whoops. Did she blow your cover?"

"What cover?" I said, which earned me a dark look. "He did find out that Bobbi may have considered selling her child."

Kary shuddered. "Good Lord."

"I don't think she would've gone through with it," Camden said, "but she may have gotten mixed up with some really bad customers."

"So what's next?"

"Camden and I are going to let Dillon Pennix know how things are in the rival club, and I have to find another band that would be stupid enough to take Frieda."

Kary held up both hands. "Wait, wait. I thought she was joining Vangie's group."

"Turned them down."

"As if she can afford to be choosy! You didn't call off the deal with Slotted Spoon, though, did you?"

"Of course not. But if one more person wants to make any sort of deal with me, I'm going to go all Dragon on them."

• ● ● ● •

After church and before the concert, I drove Camden over to give Pennix his report on The Other Side. The Pennix house was a swanky ranch house that I imagined, with my newfound knowledge of real estate, would cost somewhere in the five hundred thousand-dollar range. But what was even more interesting was the blue Bigfoot truck parked in the driveway.

"Well, what do you know."

Camden rang the bell. "Didn't I say there had to be more than one blue Bigfoot truck in town?"

Pennix let us in. "Come on in. I'll be right back. Important call. Make yourselves at home."

We stepped into the foyer. Somebody in the family liked horses, because there was a definite equine theme. A lamp with a horse for a base stood on a table shaped like a wagon. Horses galloped around the border of the wallpaper. The hall mirror had a frame made from a horse collar.

Camden stopped to inspect an umbrella stand shaped like a horse's head. "This is very strange."

"Yeah, I didn't figure Pennix for a cowboy." Stepping into the living room was like stepping into the stables. "I don't know, Camden, the Country and Western décor isn't working for me."

Above the fireplace was a photo of a dark brown horse standing in a pasture in front of a huge house. I took a closer look. "There's a picture exactly like this in Brian Young's office."

Pennix returned. "Oh, I see you're admiring Fortune Favors the Brave."

"Is that your horse?"

"I'm part owner. About a year ago a friend and I decided to try our luck at the track, so we bought shares in a racehorse. Went pretty well the first couple of years, but lately Fortune hasn't been living up to his name."

"Not having a good season?"

"I told my partner we needed to sell our shares, but he keeps saying our luck will change. He's more of a gambler than I am. Sit down, sit down. How's The Other Side, Cam?"

Camden resisted several smart-ass replies. "It's about the size of the Cave, same kind of furniture, same kind of bar. Lots of neon and laser lights."

"What about the food?"

"Typical bar snacks, peanuts, pretzels. There wasn't anything very special about it."

"The music?"

"What the kids are listening to these days."

"Hmm." Pennix shrugged. "I don't guess I have anything to worry about, then. Thanks for your help."

"Thanks for letting the Dolls play," I said.

"Oh, they weren't bad, at all. In fact, they can come back next Saturday."

At least one thing was going right. "They'll be delighted."

"Who knows? Another club might open and I'll need a spy."

To head off any protest Camden might have, I asked another more important question. "Let me ask you about that truck in your driveway. Is it yours?"

"Yeah, sometimes I need to haul stuff to and from the club."

"I've been thinking of getting one." To park beside my phantom BMW. "Kinda hard to load, isn't it, sitting way up high?"

"It's not too bad. I like it because people notice it. I'm thinking of painting the club's name on the sides. It'll be good advertisement." His phone rang again and he checked the caller ID. "I'd better take this. These damn restrictions are driving me crazy."

"We'll see ourselves out."

When we got in the Fury, Camden said, "Are you sure about that picture?"

"Yes, and if the horse isn't doing well, and Superior Homes is in financial trouble, Young may be the partner who likes to gamble. He may have heavy debts. If he's friends with Pennix, he may have borrowed the truck."

"But why go to Bobbi's house? You'd think they'd do all the house dealing in his office."

"Unless they were doing something else."

We stopped off at a convenience store and bought Cokes and peanut butter crackers. Rufus calls these kinds of packaged crackers "Nabs" for some unknown reason. Maybe it's short for "Nabisco." Maybe he runs out and "nabs" a few packs whenever he needs a snack. I parked in the shade and unwrapped my crackers.

"It's great having Kary for a wife, even a pretend wife. I feel guilty for getting her involved where there's a baby concerned, though. How come I get the woman who wants children, and you get the woman who'd be happy without?"

Camden's blue gaze was steady. "You can handle having a child."

"I don't think so. All I want to do is find one little red-haired child."

"Then what?"

"Hand her over to Rufus. He's the father." An unsettling thought occurred. "Does he want her?"

"I get the impression the answer's no."

"This is very sticky territory, but would he let Kary keep her?"

"Things are too unsettled for me to see."

"Too unsettled to see" was code for "You don't want to know." I didn't want to talk about this anymore. "Let's go tell Vangie and the Dolls the good news."

I started the Fury and turned the music up, hoping to drown out my bad mood, but the first song was "I Know That My Baby's Cheatin' On Me." Is that what was going on? If so, who was cheating on whom? Damn it, I kept putting these families together, and they kept falling apart. Of course, I hadn't been able to keep my own family together, so I guess I could be considered an expert at failed relationships.

I punched the CD player until it settled on "There'll Come a Day." There'll come a day, all right.

Rufus Jackson had damn well better want this baby.

● ● ● ● ●

Perkie's was much livelier than the Cave. Nearly all the tables were occupied. The rich smell of coffee and muffins flowed through the little shop along with the chatter of shoppers and neighbors out for walks. Vangie brought Camden and me coffee and bagels and sat down at our table.

I thanked her, and she waved my thanks away. "No, thank you, David. You could've pulled the plug on our deal, but you didn't."

"I'm not that heartless. And guess what? You were a hit with the manager, so you're on next Saturday, too."

I braced for the happy scream. Then Vangie squeezed my arm. "I knew we were good, I knew it! Our big break at last! Thanks, David."

"Remember me when you go platinum."

"I'll settle for a small, devoted fan base."

"Okay, so maybe you can help me find a group to suit Frieda. Are there any other skanky girls wandering around who need a leader?"

"Who knows what she wants, least of all her?" Vangie sat back in her chair and sighed. "She could've ridden with us to glory, a free ride, and she turns up her pointed little nose."

"What did she say, exactly?"

Vangie affected Frieda's bored, whiny tone. "'I wouldn't be seen dead with you trashy losers. I'm going to have my own band, and it's going to be way better than yours.' Just like the spoiled bratlet she is." She sat forward and leaned her arms on the small table. "Why, exactly, are you expected to grant her wishes?"

"Her dead grandmother's making a scene at the Carlyle House. Camden seems to think Frieda's mom is the cure, but Frieda's mom won't help unless Frieda is happy."

"Don't hold your breath. I don't think anything could make Frieda happy. Oh, would you like to know something else about our favorite teen?"

"Sure."

"She's pregnant."

I exchanged a glance with Camden. "No wonder she's cranky."

"She had the nerve to ask me if I knew anyone who could do something about it."

"Did you mention the handy clinics and counseling offices that can be found all over Parkland?"

"Yes. Of course, her mother doesn't know, but Kit does, and Frieda's afraid he'll tell. Too bad for her. If she bad-mouths me again, I'll tell her mother."

Frieda struck me as a gal who'd make tracks for the nearest abortion clinic. "Any idea what she plans to do?"

"Oh, she's going to have it, but she doesn't want to keep it. She actually asked me what people would pay for a baby. Can you believe that? She's thinking of selling it. That's cold. I mean, I know women have babies for other people, and those people pay the medical expenses, but to sell it like a puppy—that's Frieda for you."

Was that Bobbi's plan? This fit with the information Camden had learned at The Other Side and my own suspicions about an illegal marketplace somewhere in town. "Any idea who Frieda's selling the baby to?"

"No, sorry."

I drank my coffee and pushed the bagel toward Vangie. "That's okay. I'll figure it out."

"A dead grandmother, huh?"

"Stuck in a big mirror."

"That's the worst kind." She gave my arm another squeeze and got up. "I'll go tell the Dolls the good news. We owe you one, David. Bye, Cam."

She'd already helped me out a lot more than she knew.

Chapter Sixteen

"Bye Bye Pretty Baby"

I wasn't ready to go another round with Beverly, but I figured if anybody knew where Frieda was, it would be her psychic brother, Kit. It was almost time for him to be staggering home. Sure enough, we hadn't been home ten minutes when his motorcycle chugged into the drive. This time, Kit didn't drag himself up the steps. He bounded.

"Yo, Cam, Randall, what's new?"

"You, for one thing." He was still weirdly dressed Stick Boy, but the dark circles under his eyes were gone, as well as the sneer.

"Yeah, things are a lot calmer now that Cam showed me how to control all the signals." He gave Camden a thumbs-up. "It's still working, bro. My music's a lot better, too. I'd been wondering what was wrong." He shot me a curious look. "So it was real fortunate there was a place here. Did you have any idea? Are you psychic, too?"

"Nope, I'm damn lucky. Now there's something you can do for me."

"Yeah, sure, man, name it."

"I need to talk to your sister. Know where she is?"

"Yeah. She's hanging around the mall with one of her friends. Probably her only friend. She'll be there all day."

"Who's the father of her baby?"

He didn't even blink. "D.J. Goins. Went to school with us."

"One of Frieda's acquaintances seems to think Frieda wants to sell her baby."

"That'd be just like her. She's daft." He yawned a huge yawn. "I gotta crash. Anything else you need to know?"

"That's all for now, thanks."

Kary and Camden practiced a few songs to warm up for their concert. I sat on the porch and listened as they sang "My Baby Just Cares For Me." I thought about how many baby songs there were. "Baby Face," "Pretty Baby," "Everybody Loves My Baby," "When My Baby Smiles at Me." I knew most of them from my jazz recordings, including not-so-traditional ones like "Because My Baby Don't Mean 'Maybe' Now," and one I'd recently heard called "What a Blue-Eyed Baby You Are." Of course, usually the baby referred to in the song was the singer's girlfriend or love interest, but all I could think of was little Mary Rose. It seemed far-fetched that Frieda would have information that could lead me to the missing baby, or that she'd share this information, but at this point, I was willing to try anything.

• • ● • •

Kit said Frieda would be at the mall all day, so I planned to track her down after the concert. I guess Delores liked the music because the wallpaper stayed in place during the rehearsal. Lauber approved Kary's yellow nineteen-forties-style dress, two-toned pumps with little bows, and Camden's black suit, white shirt, and yellow tie he'd borrowed from the Little Theater. As Camden sang and Kary played, Lauber sat in one of the uncomfortable little chairs. He motioned to another chair, so I came in and sat down. Camden and Kary swung into another number called "Trusting." On this one, Kary's light soprano joined with Camden's voice for the chorus.

Lauber leaned over and whispered, "This is exactly what I wanted."

"Good. Any more problems with Delores?"

"Not a peep."

I didn't know if this was a good thing. Delores might be saving up for the concert. When Camden and Kary finished their song, Lauber thanked them. "That's excellent. Exactly an hour. Then we'll have refreshments and tour the house."

While Lauber conferred with Kary about the order of the songs, I asked Camden if he'd heard anything from Delores.

"Not yet."

He crossed back to the foyer and stood in front of the mirror, arms folded.

"Anything?" I asked.

"No."

"Maybe the music soothed her savage breast."

"Lauber said everything's been quiet." Camden stepped forward to touch the mirror. Then he stepped back and shook his head. "I don't know what's going on. Do you suppose she knows about her first great-grandchild?" He watched the mirror to see if this news had any effect. Nothing.

"If Frieda keeps it. It could be going to the highest bidder."

"Maybe that's why we haven't heard anything from Delores."

"I don't really care about some phantom grandma in a snit. I'm thinking if Frieda's in the market, she could lead me to Babies R Us."

● ● ● ● ●

Proceeds from the concert went to the Historical Preservation Society, so the event was attended by serious-looking women in suits and fancy scarves; a few younger women in more Bohemian outfits, long patterned skirts, and lots of beads; and a few men who looked like history professors wearing bow ties and jackets with elbow patches. The audience chatted amiably among themselves as I kept an eye toward the foyer, hoping Delores hadn't planned to really bring the house down this afternoon.

Camden also gave the foyer an anxious glance. Could he tell what she was thinking?

"What's the latest?" I asked.

"Still calm."

"Can you hold her off if she tries anything?"

"Guess we'll find out."

Lauber welcomed everyone and introduced Camden and Kary. "We will now hear a selection of Delores Carlyle's favorite songs, followed by light refreshments in the dining room and a tour of the house for anyone who has not seen this beautiful building. Our sincere thanks to the Historical Preservation Society and all they have done to keep the Carlyle House in such wonderful condition. We could not do this without you. Thank you and enjoy the concert."

I stood at the back of the parlor with Lauber and the docents, so I had a good view of the room. The audience members sat on rows of padded folding chairs facing the piano. The parlor sofa and uncomfortable chairs had been moved to a corner. Several small tables sat around the room, each one topped with a vase, lamp, or collection of small breakable knickknacks. The walls were decorated with large dull landscapes and dreary still-life paintings of sad-looking flowers and unappetizing-looking fruit.

Something I hadn't noticed before was the ornate chandelier hanging right over the audience.

Camden was singing "Always" when the chandelier began to sway ever so slightly. So Delores had decided to go all *Phantom of the Opera*, had she? I pointed to the chandelier, and he nodded. In a few minutes, it stopped swinging.

Next, the china figurines on the table began to shake. I caught them before they fell and set them out of the way on the carpet. No one seemed to notice, and if they did, probably thought I'd bumped the table

Home team, 2. Delores, 0.

Throughout the concert, Delores played her little tricks. A picture slid out of place. Camden put it back. An empty folding chair fell over. I moved it to the back of the room. Kary's music slipped off the piano. Camden continued to sing as she leaned over gracefully and replaced it on the stand. The music must have had some effect because Delores never let loose with a full-blown display of temper. The audience was so caught up in the performance they were not aware that ghostly things were going on around them and applauded each number with real appreciation.

Afterwards, while Camden and Kary accepted the crowd's thanks and praise, Lauber leaned over to me. "All that was Delores, wasn't it? Thank God she didn't go crazy."

It was easier to say that yes, all that was Delores. "She wanted to make sure we didn't forget her."

"As if we could. I hope you can find a solution to this problem, Mr. Randall."

He hurried off to tend to his guests. Camden and Kary finished talking with their new fans. Camden went right to the mirror. Kary and I followed.

"Was Delores trying to tell us something?" Kary asked.

Camden touched the mirror and withdrew his hand as if the surface was hot. "It was a warning. She's getting impatient, Randall."

"So am I. Nobody wants this case solved more than I do. But I need time. She's got to understand that."

Kary added her own plea. "We're doing everything we can, Delores. We really want to help you."

Camden put his hand on the mirror again. He listened for a few moments and smiled. "Thanks, Delores."

I didn't believe she'd agreed to stop. "So she's going to behave?"

"For now."

• ● ● ● •

Kary said she was going to change clothes and head back to Forest Cove Drive to retrieve the food bags. Camden and I went to the mall.

Parkland has four shopping malls, but when people say "The Mall," they mean the first and biggest, Olympia Mall. As usual, the parking lot was jammed, so we had to park five miles away and hike in. Olympia Mall has an ice rink in the middle and a small carousel. Surrounding this area are twenty or thirty fast food restaurants. Most teenagers like to hang around the rink and food court, but Frieda wasn't among them. We took the escalator to the second level and cruised all the jewelry shops where young women were getting their ears pierced and stapled. After about fifty of those, I wondered if Kit's signals were still scrambled.

"Think she's shopping for diapers?"

"Nails," Camden said.

"She's making a stroller?"

"No, fingernails." He pointed to a small salon. Frieda sat across from a slim Asian woman who leaned forward, doing something delicate to Frieda's outstretched hand.

"Well, of course," I said. "What every unwed mother needs, new fingernails."

The little shop smelled unpleasantly of chemicals. Frieda glanced up and sighed dramatically.

"What do you want?"

The woman was painting Frieda's fingernails a dark green shade. I couldn't see the name on the bottle, but I imagined it was something like Slimy Moss or Dead Snot. The woman gave me one look and went back to smoothing the polish.

"Vangie tells me you refused their generous offer to be a Spoon."

She wrinkled her nose. Vangie was right. It was little and pointed. "Their music sucks. I want to be in a real band."

"And your definition of real band is?"

"One that doesn't suck."

"So what do you play? Guitar? Harmonica? Trombone?"

I know if she hadn't been up to her cuticles in Slime Rot, she would've spit in my eye and left the shop. "What the hell do you want?"

The woman paused for a moment as if offended by this show of bad manners. Frieda glared at her. "Aren't you through yet? What do you want, Randall?"

"I want to help you, and I think you can help me."

"Why would I want to help you?"

"For one thing, I found Kit a place to stay, so he's out of your hair."

"Big deal."

"And I won't tell your mom you're pregnant."

This time, the woman stopped completely.

"I apologize," I told her. "Frieda, I'll wait for you outside."

Camden sat on a bench outside the nail salon eating an ice cream cone. I joined him. In about fifteen minutes, Frieda came out, green nails glinting. It would've ruined the paint job to bury them in my heart, but from her expression, I could tell that's what she wanted to do.

Her voice was low and furious. "Don't you dare tell my mother anything. How did you know, anyway? Kit told you, didn't he? That bastard. I don't know how he does it."

I'd thought her unattractive pooch of stomach was baby fat. Now I could see it was all baby. "Settle down. Your mother has agreed to do something for me if I get you into a band. Now, I don't know if you plan to bring the kid along, but it could make a difference."

She was silent. I could see her weighing her options. "You can get me in a band?"

"I'll do my best."

"What do you want for not telling about the baby?"

"I want to know what you're going to do with it."

Another long silence. "Why?"

"I have my reasons. Maybe if you stop being so defensive, I'll tell you."

"It's none of your business."

"You're right."

"You're right" was apparently not something Frieda heard very often. She gave me another measuring stare. "You get me in a band, I'll tell you my plans."

"Deal." I offered my hand, and after a minute's hesitation, she shook it. "Great-looking nails. Did you see them, Camden?"

"Do you mind if I have a look?" She shrugged and extended her hand. Camden touched it lightly as he admired her fingers. "Very nice."

She pulled her hand back. "Okay, so when am I going to know something?"

"How about if I call you tonight?" I said.

"Okay."

Another bony teenage girl came up lugging two shopping bags. "Hey, Frieda, who are your friends?"

She turned up her pointy little nose. "They aren't my friends. Come on, let's go."

The friend said, "The blond one's cute," as Frieda dragged her away.

"See?" I said to Camden. "You could have any adolescent you want."

He watched them go. "It's a good thing she doesn't want to keep the baby. She'd be a horrible mother."

"You get anything else?"

"That's about as mindless a young lady as I've ever read."

"Now all I have to do is find a band that'll take her." People crowded the mall, going in and out of shops, but none of them could help me, and there wasn't a store where I could buy a group that would jump at the chance to have Miss Disdainful as their lead singer. "Got any ideas?"

"I was thinking the Archer Sisters may be your best bet."

"What? The reviled and despised Archer Sisters? How do you figure that?"

"One reason Ellie doesn't like them is because they sing."

"That's their psychic act?"

"They sing to get in tune with the spirits."

"You've got to be kidding."

"Actually, it's more of a yodel."

Could this get any nuttier? "Does it work?"

"I don't see how. They're way off-key. Maybe they could use another tone-deaf member."

"Now I'm so damn curious to see them."

"Then let's go to the Holiday Lounge."

Chapter Seventeen

"I Wonder Where My Baby is Tonight"

I was surprised to find that the Holiday Lounge was one place in Parkland that lived up to its name. It was a lounge, and it had a holiday theme. Streamers and confetti were in evidence, as well as Christmas trees, American flags, and turkeys dressed like Pilgrims. Valentines and shamrocks hung from the ceiling. Easter baskets and jack-o-lanterns shared space on the tables. A small stage gleamed with pink and gold lights.

"This is very festive," I said.

A pert young hostess dressed like a witch greeted us. "Good afternoon, gentlemen. You're just in time for our happy holiday two-for-one special. Would you like to sit at the bar or a table?"

"A table would be fine," Camden said, "and could you please tell Ruby and Pearl that Cam is here to see them?"

"It would be my pleasure, sir. This way." She led us to a table up front near the stage. "Enjoy."

An equally attractive young woman dressed like Betsy Ross materialized from a corner. "Drinks, gentlemen?"

She rattled off the entire list. I chose a likely-sounding beer, and Camden ordered a Coke. When she left, I said, "Ruby and Pearl? Sounds exotic."

At that moment, two tall, identical dark-haired women wearing short white silky robes came from backstage. "Cam!"

they squealed. He'd barely gotten out of his seat before he was engulfed. They hugged him and patted him and ruffled his hair.

When they finally let go, he looked more rumpled than ever.

"Ladies, this is my friend David Randall. Randall, may I present Ruby and Pearl, the Archer Sisters."

Ruby and Pearl shook my hand and beamed twin smiles. They weren't knockdown gorgeous like Kary, but they had a definite Look At Me attractiveness. Their shoulder-length hair flipped up in the style made popular by Mary Tyler Moore. Their dark eyes were surrounded by lots of mascara. Red polish gleamed on their fingernails, and red lipstick defined their wide mouths. I couldn't tell them apart.

One of them said, "We have a few minutes."

The other sister finished the sentence. "Before the show."

Camden and I held their chairs, and they sat down.

One patted Camden's hand. "Did you come especially to see our act? That's so sweet! You know, we were scheduled to appear on Ellin's TV program, but there was a last minute snafu."

I could easily see why Reg wanted them on the PSN. I could also see why Ellin disapproved. Ruby and Pearl couldn't keep their hands off Camden.

"Yes, we came to see your act, but I also have a favor to ask."

I tried to signal to Camden to forget it. Frieda Huntington would never be as classy and polished as the Archer Sisters, not if she worked at it her whole life. No need to burden them with a hostile waif.

"We'd do anything for you," one sister said.

"We know a young woman who wants to join a band, but we don't know of any groups needing a new member. We thought you could help."

"What kind of band? Bob Kalinski and His Polka Ramblers are short an accordion player, aren't they, Ruby?"

Now I knew Ruby was the one on the left. She thought a moment. "Yes, and I believe Scruff Havers and the Polliwogs were looking for someone to play the xylophone. Or was it the triangle?"

"She wants something a little more modern," Camden said. "Something teenagers are into."

Both women paused. "Oh. Electric."

"Can we get back to you?" Pearl asked. "We're on in about five minutes. Come on, Ruby."

During our conversation with the Archer Sisters, the lounge had filled. Were two yodeling psychics that much of a draw? "Camden, I don't think they'll be able to help us find a band that will suit Frieda."

"They might."

"Do I sense a little history here?"

He doesn't talk about it, but the way his female acquaintances carry on when they see him leads me to believe there may have been a fair amount of upstairs activity before Ellin decided to marry him.

"Ellie doesn't like them because they remind her of her sisters."

"Oh, that's why they look familiar." Ellin's two older sisters are tall, dark, and super confident. Basically, they treat Ellin like a pretty little doll and aren't impressed by her accomplishments. "So you and Ruby and Pearl never—?"

"No."

"If you say so."

I'm sure he would've said something else, but the lights dimmed, and the Archer Sisters burst on stage in a blaze of short red-and-gold spangled dresses. "Good afternoon, everyone, and welcome to the Holiday Lounge!" they chorused. "We're the Archer Sisters, and we're here to tell your future!"

Then, to my amazement, they began to sing. Camden was right. It was more of a yodel, a strangled sound like birds gargling. Ruby—or maybe it was Pearl—warbled a scale, something in her throat wobbling up and down. Then they both let loose with a vibrato so wide you could've driven a truck through it. I turned to give Camden a disbelieving look, but he avoided my gaze. He had his hand over his mouth and was trying not to laugh.

After about ten painful minutes of oscillating sound, the Archer Sisters and the audience relaxed. Pearl—or perhaps Ruby—smiled a broad smile. "We were able to get in touch with many many spirits today. Is there someone here named Vernon?"

This being Parkland, of course there was someone here named Vernon. A large man two tables back raised his hand. The sisters proceeded to give a cold reading that pleased him, something about his grandmother and her cat. Halfway through, they had to stop and yodel a bit to clarify. By this time, Camden was practically under the table, and I had to bite my lip. Mercifully, the act didn't last long. We were able to get control and have another drink. Ruby and Pearl greeted their fans and circled around to our table. Camden told them how much we enjoyed the performance.

"We'll get right to work on your problem," one sister said. "Do you suppose this young lady would like a job here? It's a very safe working environment and we don't have any of the problems other clubs have."

The other leaned in. "There've been quite a few places fined lately for not being up to code. The Holiday Lounge is not one of them and not ever likely to be. The owners follow all the rules and regulations."

This reminded me of Pennix's complaints. "Have you ladies heard of any trouble at the Cave on Emerald?"

"We know the health department has really been calling out owners who aren't doing what they're supposed to. There are very strict rules involved, and a few places have been shut down for good. Now, getting back to your problem, we always need waitresses, and this young lady of yours could dress up in different costumes. It's fun."

My mind backed up at the thought of Frieda as Betsy Ross. "We'll ask her."

The sisters insisted on paying for our drinks. Camden endured another round of hugs. I got a couple, myself, and we left.

I unlocked the Fury and we got in. "Interesting little info about the clubs and the health department. That's what Pennix has been griping about. If he's had to pay stiff fines, he might be looking for other ways to supplement his income."

"But how does he fit in with Bobbi's death?"

"I wish I knew. On to Comic World. I want to talk to Kit about Frieda."

"He won't do anything to help his sister."

I agreed. "However, he might like to sic her on a rival band."

• ● ● ● •

Kit wasn't at Comic World, so we went home to see if he was there. He wasn't, but Buddy was back from the fiddlers' convention. Buddy's as big as Rufus and just as scraggly. He had on his usual bib overalls and a baseball cap that read: "My Give A Damn's Busted."

He heaved himself out of a rocking chair. "What's all this about Rufus murderin' somebody?"

"We're going on the assumption he didn't," I said. "Do you know where he was last Tuesday?"

Buddy wrinkled up his small features to think. "Tuesday, Tuesday. Nope, can't say as I recall. What's the deal?"

"His ex-wife, Bobbi, was found dead in her home, and her baby's missing. Rufus is the father."

"For real? He never said nothin' about no baby."

"That's because he didn't know about the baby until last week. Is he here? Have you talked to him?"

"Stopped by to do that very thing, only he ain't here."

Camden took out his phone. After a few moments, he said, "No answer."

"Damn it, we're going to have to put a GPS on him. Any ideas, Buddy? We need to know where he is."

"It's Sunday. Sometimes he and Angie go up on the Parkway."

The Blue Ridge Parkway is about an hour from Parkland. As much as I wanted to believe that Rufus and Angie were sitting at a scenic overlook having a picnic and enjoying a cool mountain breeze, I could tell by the expression on Camden's face this was not the case.

"He's up to something, isn't he?"

"Let me try Angie."

A phone call to Angie revealed she was at her mother's, and Rufus had told her he was going fishing with Buddy.

"First I heard of that," Buddy said.

"He's fishing, all right," I said, "only he's the one who's going to get caught."

Superior Homes was closed, but Rufus might try something stupid at Brian Young's home. I got the brochure from the island, which fortunately included Young's address and phone number. I gave him a call, but there was no answer.

I put my phone away. "This could mean several things. Either Young's not home, or Rufus has already killed him. We'd better go see."

"Well, doggone it," Buddy said, "I would've liked to have gone fishing."

Camden and I left him still grumbling about this missed opportunity and drove to Brian Young's massive cathedral of a house in Putnam Grove. The first thing we saw was the not very subtle sight of a blue Bigfoot truck parked down the street.

Rufus wasn't in his truck.

"Is he hiding in the bushes? Please don't tell me he's broken into the house. All these mansions have major alarm systems."

Camden scanned the neighborhood, trying to hone in on Rufus' signal. "He's behind the house."

"Taking a dip in the pool? Young will appreciate that."

I parked in front of Young's house. I opened my trunk and took out the dog leash I carry when I'm snooping in upscale neighborhoods. "Here. Carry this. If anyone asks, we're looking for your lost dog."

"Rufe's a mighty big dog."

"One that needs to be on a leash."

We circled the house and came upon a lavish backyard, complete with pool, patio, guest house, and a mini-vineyard. I'd been making a joke about Rufus hiding in the bushes, but that's where we found him, hunkered down behind a collection of carefully trimmed boxwoods. At least he'd left the bulldozer at home.

I tapped his shoulder. "Tag, you're it."

He jumped as if I'd poked him with a taser. "Damn it all! What're you two doing here?"

"Trying to keep you out of jail, you moron. What are you planning to do?"

Rufus brushed twigs and leaves off his overalls. "Thought I'd surprise Young when he came home, maybe get a confession out of 'im."

"Let's see, trespassing, assault, slander—"

"Well, you ain't doing squat."

"Didn't you promise Angie you wouldn't do anything else? You want to jeopardize your relationship?"

"Just payin' a friendly call."

"Rufus, please," Camden said. "I'm sure the minute somebody saw your truck, they called the cops. We need to get out of here."

Rufus crossed his arms over his chest and glared down at him. "Can't make me."

Camden took a moment. "Okay. Get back in the bushes and make room for me."

Rufus stared in surprise. "What?"

"If you're going to jail, I'll go, too."

"Aw, Cam, don't be stupid."

"I'm serious. If you won't leave, then I'll stay. Randall will, too."

"Sure, why not?" I said. "Let's all go to jail. Then Young can run free and commit all the crimes he likes."

Rufus looked at me and then at Camden. "Neither one of y'all's got the sense God gave an animal cracker." He shook his head. "Damnation. You're not gonna tell Angie about this, are you?"

"We won't if you stop trying to be Crouching Tiger Hidden Redneck."

He gave me a glare. "Let's go."

We'd reached the sidewalk when a woman came to meet us. She had on a tennis outfit and a chilly expression.

"Can I help you gentlemen?"

"You're on," I said under my breath to Camden.

He held up the leash. "Yes, ma'am, I'm looking for my dog. He got away from me right outside your neighborhood, and I thought I saw him up this way."

As I've said many times, few women can resist those big blue eyes. I signaled Rufus to get to his truck and go while Camden had her attention.

"What kind of dog?" she asked.

We hadn't discussed this, but on occasion, Camden can improvise. "A yellow lab. His name's Buster."

"Does he have a collar and identification?"

"Oh, yes."

Her tone was polite but firm. "If anyone in the neighborhood happens to see him, we'll be sure to call animal rescue, and they can contact you." *So you can leave now* was implied.

"Thank you very much."

Still giving us suspicious glares, the woman walked off. Rufus had already made his getaway, and now we made ours.

Camden tossed the leash into the backseat. "I can't believe Rufus did that."

"I can. Anyone who'd try to bulldoze a building is capable of lurking in the shrubbery." At the entrance to Putnam Grove, I turned the car. "I'm going to circle around and make sure he doesn't try to sneak back to Young's house."

We checked all the streets. There was no sign of the Bigfoot truck. Camden called Rufus, who must have told him to put the call on speaker.

"I want Randall to hear this. Yo, Randall! I'm going by the Quik-Fry for a snack, and then I'm going home."

"You'd better," I said.

"That dog leash thing's a slick trick. Might try it myself some time."

"Good-bye, Rufus."

"Cam, you know you wouldn't last a day in jail. You're too purty."

"Shut up," Camden told him and hit "end call."

"Well, you are," I said.

• • ● • •

Camden decided this didn't merit an answer, so we drove past the Quik-Fry to make certain Rufus' truck was there, and then we went home.

Kary met us at the door. "Wait till you see what I found in one of the food bags."

"Some really old spaghetti?"

"I went through the bags to make sure none of the cans were out of date. I found this."

"This" was a note written on a page torn from a spiral note-book. Camden took his seat on the porch swing, and I sat down in a rocking chair to read the note. "'To the blond lady who came by asking about Bobbi. Call this number.'"

Kary sat in another rocker. "I thought I'd wait until you came home to call. Have you been at the mall all this time?"

"No, we stopped by the Holiday Lounge to see if the Archer Sisters knew of a band for Frieda, and then we had to retrieve Rufus from Brian Young's house before Young came home."

She stopped rocking. "Rufus went to Young's house? He could've ruined our entire plan."

"Not to mention getting himself arrested for trespassing and possible assault."

"Sometimes he's so dumb."

I couldn't resist. "How dumb?"

"As dumb as a bag of hammers."

"Or a box of rocks," Camden said.

"I lost count of the Southernisms he laid on us," I said. "He wasn't happy."

Kary took out her phone and punched in the number. "Let's see what happens." She waited a moment and then said, "Hello? This is the woman who asked about Bobbi Jo Hull." She listened for while. "No, that wasn't me. Yes, I'm the one who brought the food bags. Thank you for your donation." She listened for another few moments. "I'm sure the police are doing all they can. Okay, thanks." She closed her phone. "Guys, we might have a clue. The woman asked if I had been to see Bobbi before, because she definitely remembered seeing a blond woman at the house several times."

"Great. Now the killer's a blond woman."

"She said when she saw us in the neighborhood the day I left the bags, she first thought we were the people she'd seen at the house, but she knew she hadn't seen anyone matching Cam's description, and you were not as big as the man she saw."

"So a big man, like Rufus, and a blond woman."

"It couldn't have been Rufus with another woman. He's faithful to Angie. What do we do now? It's baffling."

"One thing that's not baffling is Frieda's behavior," I said. "Three guesses why she's so cranky."

"Aside from being a teenage girl?"

"A pregnant teenage girl."

Again Kary stopped rocking. "Oh, no. You can't be serious. She's going to be the worst mother ever."

"That's Camden's prediction. But she doesn't plan to keep the baby. She's going to sell it, and I have to get her into a band before she'll tell me the details."

Kary stared at me. "I can't believe it."

"It's the never-ending story."

"Honestly, all these people tossing their babies away! It makes me want to scream. What about the father of Frieda's baby? Does he have any say?"

"That's what I'm going to ask Kit. I'm hoping he can tell me more."

But Kit didn't come in that evening. Monday morning, we didn't see him at breakfast, either, so Camden and I decided to try Comic World again. We put Angie on Rufus Watch. Kary planned to go back to Forest Cove Drive and talk to the woman who'd left the note in her food bag, hoping she'd find out more about the mysterious blonde.

Even though she constantly warns me about being over-protective, I told her to be careful. She promised she would, but she had that gleam in her eye that meant she was hoping for some action. I had to remind myself she'd helped solve several of my former cases, and returning to Forest Cove Drive to ask the neighbors a few questions wasn't as wild as being a magician's assistant or roaming the tunnels beneath Parkland as a superhero.

At Comic World, young men of all shapes and sizes bent over the long boxes of comics and pulled newer magazines from the shelves with all the care of young interns making that first important incision. Kids sat on the floor, deeply involved in what I hoped were kid-friendly adventure stories. Kit sat behind the counter, leafing through something called "Heads on Spikes."

He glanced up. "Oh, hi. New anime on aisle three, Cam. Latest issue of *Lone Wolf and Cub*."

"Thanks." He headed in that direction.

"Randall, you're not here for a comic."

"Nope."

"I see you spoke to Frieda."

"You got any enemy bands we could dump her on?"

"Now, that's a thought." The phone rang. "Hang on." He answered. "Comic World. Yeah, it came in today. Sure." He reached for a pad and pen. "What's the name? Okay, it'll be here. No problem." He listened awhile. "Yeah, that's my band. Runaway Truck Ramp. Yeah, we were killing it last night. I didn't even get home. Stayed up and came on in to work. Cool. Thanks, man." He hung up.

"Runaway Truck Ramp. I like it. I could only come up with Destitute Dolls."

"Takes practice. Let me get this guy's comic." He went to the shelf and returned with something that looked like *Bean Miser and Beads*. He put it in a paper sack and wrote a name across the top.

"I see where you guys come up with lyrics," I said. "Bean miser's about as coherent as pinchers in the circuit."

"Pinchers in the circuit?"

"The Slotted Spoon's big hit."

He put the bag under the counter. "Frieda was an idiot not to join them."

"Any idea what she's going to do about the baby?"

"Here's the weird thing. D.J. wants it."

"D.J.? That's the father, right?"

"Yeah. He says he doesn't, but I know he does."

"Usually teenage boys run away screaming at the idea of being a dad."

"That's what's so weird. I thought D.J. was training to be a redneck. He always pushed me around in school, made fun of my hair, that kind of thing. I get a little more respect now that I'm in a band, but he's still a jerk. But I'm telling you, when I saw him last, he was radiating fatherhood, know what I mean?"

Camden often spoke of seeing emotions radiating from people. "Where could I find D.J.?"

"He's usually here by now. See, I had him pegged as a *Guns and Ammo* kind of reader, but he's a big Spider-Man fan." He pointed to a large inflatable Spider-Man hanging in the window. "Told him he could have that if he fixed the roof." Kit's grin was pure triumph. "It's a kick having him work for me."

"I'll bet so."

"Hang around and you can talk to him."

I went back to the section of the shop devoted to Japanese comics. Camden sat on the floor, reading something I couldn't pronounce.

"Frieda's boyfriend should be here soon," I said. "He wants to keep the baby."

Camden kept his eyes on the comic. "I'm glad somebody does."

I looked through the garish covers featuring big-eyed characters with unnatural amounts of flowing hair. "Maybe I'll find a way to help him out."

Camden closed the comic book and pushed his hair out of his eyes, which were darker than usual. "Too many babies floating around. I don't know if we can find them all."

"Don't go all cryptic and gloomy on me. I'm not giving up."

I left him in the midst of whatever the hell it is he reads, and wandered to the mystery section. Comic World keeps a good supply of best sellers and magazines as well as comic books. Maybe I could get a clue.

I'd read the first few pages of Carl Hiaasen's latest when a large young man came into the shop. Kit was right. This was the pupae stage of Redneckius North Carolinius: blobby shape, little eyes, and a generous growth of long scraggy hair hanging out from under a baseball cap. Even its call was distinctive.

"Yo! Monkey man! Can I get a Mountain Dew outta the cooler?"

"Help yourself," Kit said. "Guy here wants to talk to you."

"Okay."

I met D.J. at the glass case Kit kept in a corner of the store. Actually, I met D.J.'s butt crack as he leaned over to get a can of Mountain Dew. He straightened and popped the top of the can. I'm six feet tall, and this boy could look me right in the eye. Up close, he looked a little brighter and a lot younger. His eyes were blue and guileless.

"Somethin' I can do for you, mister?"

"My name's David Randall," I said. "I'm a friend of Kit's and Frieda's."

He grinned. "You can't be both."

"Mainly a friend of Kit's, but I'm a little concerned about Frieda, too. I promised her mother I'd look after her, and now I hear she may have gotten herself in a little trouble."

His grin faded. "And she's gotten herself out. She's taking care of things."

"Do you know exactly how she's taking care of things?"

"Don't know. Don't care. 'S'cuse me, I got work to do."

He pushed past me. I followed him out to the side of the

building where he'd set up a ladder. "What if I told you I might be able to change things?"

"How? She's done already set up the appointment."

"Appointment?"

He frowned. "We're talking about the kid, right? Mine and hers? Only she says I got no say in this. She's gonna have the kid adopted by these rich people. They're gonna pay her thousands of dollars. What do I get? Nothing. Now, if you'll get out of my face, I'm gonna fix this roof, take my Spider-Man, and get home in time to see *Wrestlemania*."

"Just a few more questions. Did she tell you the name of these people? Who is she working with to make this deal?"

"I don't know. It's all a big secret. Like I care anymore."

"Okay, thanks."

I turned to go, and he said, "Randall."

"Yeah?"

He started up the ladder. "Nothin.' Forget it."

Camden had moved down to the UFO magazines. He put the magazine he'd been reading back on the shelf, but not before I saw the photo and caption on the back cover: "Have You Seen This Child?" "I can't get anything on Mary Rose, at all," he said.

"You're too close to this subject. There's no way you could be getting clear signals."

"Speaking of close—you're practically fused."

"Instead of brooding about it, let's go do something." I stopped by the counter and thanked Kit for the scoop on D.J.

"No problem."

"What can you tell me about your great grandma?"

He shrugged. "Not much. She wasn't the cookie-making, storytelling kind of grandmother. I was six when she died. I remember going into that big spooky house and all those ugly paintings."

"Is seeing your mother going to take care of her problem?"

"Beats me. I don't think they ever got along. I know Delores didn't like my dad. Mom says Delores was always ragging him about not being a real man because he couldn't have kids."

"He found you and Frieda under a bush somewhere?"

"Nah, man, we're adopted."

Adopted? I'd assumed thin bony Kit and Frieda took after their father.

Kit straightened a stack of bookmarks on the counter. "Wish they'd left Frieda under that bush."

"Camden, how does Delores feel about this?"

He'd been listening intently, all moodiness gone. "Something she told me earlier. I don't think she's ever accepted that."

"Yeah?" Kit made a face. "Too bad for her."

"Delores and her husband, your Grandfather Amos, had your mom, Beverly, but your father wasn't able to have children?"

"That's right."

"So your parents adopted you and your sister." He was silent for such a long time, I wondered if he'd fallen into another vision.

"Camden? What does this have to do with anything?"

"It has to do with those hideous paintings in the Carlyle House. Beverly painted them."

Kit stated the obvious. "Mom's not a very good artist."

"But Delores wanted her to be because Amos was."

I made a time-out sign. "Hang on a second. We're talking about Amos Carlyle, the guy who did the murals in the courthouse? That Amos Carlyle?"

"Delores was very unhappy that Beverly inherited none of his talent."

Kit was right with him. "I get it. Then Grandma gets pissed because Mom adopts two kids who can't paint, either. We aren't Carlyles by blood, so there's no way we could be artists. That's the way she sees it, right, Cam? Only she didn't take into account I'd have musical talent, or this psychic thing."

"You need to come talk to her," Camden said.

"Today would be good," I added.

"I'll see if I can get someone to watch the store. What's your number? I'll call you."

Camden gave Kit his cell phone number and we left Comic World.

I wasn't sure this was going to work. "Okay, so Delores wants to see Beverly to what, apologize? Tell her Frieda's pregnant? Does she even care?"

"I think she wants to make things right, whatever that may be."

My phone rang, and I answered. The woman's voice sounded hesitant. "Mr. Randall? It's Tina Ramola at Dream Vacations. I've found something of Bobbi Jo's I think you need to see."

Chapter Eighteen

"Nobody But My Baby is Getting My Love"

Camden and I drove to Friendly Center where an anxious Tina met us at the door of the travel agency.

"I honestly don't know what to do about this. I'd much rather hand it over to you and let you handle it." Tina motioned for us to come inside. She shut the door and went behind her desk. She handed me a large brown envelope.

"I was cleaning out my files and found this in Bobbi Jo's. I'd completely forgotten she asked me to keep it for her. I took a little peek inside and knew right away I didn't want to have anything to do with those pictures."

I slid the pictures out of the envelope and understood Tina's reluctance. The photos were of a man and woman having sex on the floor. The carpet was unmistakably the puce and liver-colored carpet in Bobbi Jo's house.

Tina shuddered. "You see? Why on earth would she want to keep pictures like that?"

I put the photos back in the envelope. "I don't know, Tina, but hopefully they'll explain why Bobbi was murdered. I'll take them to the police."

Back in the car, Camden and I examined the pictures. "That's definitely Bobbi Jo's carpet, but the woman's not Bobbi Jo," I said.

"How can you tell?"

The woman had her back to the camera. "No Texas-shaped birthmark on her bottom. She must be the mysterious blonde the neighbor saw."

"Who's the man?"

The way the woman was positioned, it was difficult to see the man's face. I took a closer look at the woman. "Uh, Camden, I think I know who this woman is. Blonde, photogenic, helping clean up our fair city?"

He took another look. "Good Lord. That's Chelsea Holt."

The mayor's wife. "Definitely blackmail material."

We sat for a long moment absorbing this depth charge of unwanted information.

Camden recovered first. "Why choose Bobbi's house?"

"It's a crappy neighborhood. The neighbors are totally uninvolved. Bobbi's gone all day. They can come and go as they like. They might have had an arrangement with her to use her house."

"Or maybe she didn't know anything about it."

"We know the guy in the photos isn't Rufus, but this doesn't clear Rufus of any murder charges. The fact that this man chose Bobbi's house in which to have a fling doesn't make him a murderer, either, unless Bobbi planned to show these pictures to his wife or girlfriend, and he didn't like that idea. Maybe he came to the house demanding the pictures, and when she refused to give them to him—" I paused. But she didn't refuse. Bobbi had said, "Here it is." "Camden, the 'it' must have been an envelope like this, not the baby."

"But this envelope was at Tina's."

"You mentioned you felt a sense of triumph. Bobbi must have given him copies. The man might have been planning to get rid of her anyway, so he must have killed her and taken the envelope and the baby."

"So they double-crossed each other. She knew she was giving him copies of damaging photos. He knew he was going to kill her."

"Looks that way." I squinted at the man's hands. "Camden,

I've seen that ring before." I pointed to the horseshoe shaped ring. "I think that's Brian Young."

Camden put the photos back in the envelope. "Jordan needs to see these."

"He can see them, but let's not mention our suspicions about Young. Not yet. Not until we know what's happened to Mary Rose."

I knew Camden didn't like this idea, but he was as concerned about the baby as I was. "Okay."

"I could be wrong. He could've given his ring to someone else. It could be another big hairy man."

"A big hairy killer."

"The fact that he's enjoying himself on that lovely rug doesn't make him a killer, either." I took out my phone. "I'd better call Kary and tell her one part of the mystery is solved."

"That fits with my information," Kary said when I filled her in. "The neighbor recalled that the blond woman always dressed in a fancy suit and heels."

"Anything else on the man?"

"No, sorry."

Camden's cell phone rang, and I told Kary to hang on for a moment.

Camden listened to the caller. "Kit says he can meet us at the Carlyle House in about thirty minutes."

"Tell him we have to stop by the police station first, but we'll be there." I spoke into my phone. "We're going to leave the pictures with Jordan and head back to the Carlyle House if you want to meet us there, Kary."

• ● ● ● •

Jordan gave an exasperated sigh as he spread the photos on his desk. "You'd think people would learn."

"Is that Chelsea Holt?"

"It certainly looks like her."

"Does the mayor have enemies who'd set up something like this?"

Jordan kept his eyes on the pictures. "Yep. Who did you say had these?"

"A friend of Bobbi's. She came across them while cleaning out her files."

"The name of this friend?"

If I wasn't going to mention Brian Young, I'd better not withhold anything else. "Bobbi's friend is Tina Ramola at Dream Vacations. She had no idea what was in that envelope."

"So Bobbi had a little blackmail scheme going, and somebody didn't like it."

As far as Camden was concerned, the case was closed. "This clears Rufus, though, doesn't it?"

"I'd like to say so, but not yet."

"But I'm almost certain Bobbi handed the murderer an envelope like this one right before she was shot. Why would Rufus care about these pictures?"

"Maybe Rufus needed a little extra cash." At Camden's look of disbelief, he added, "I'm paid to think like this, Cam. You know that. You two go home and let me work, okay? I'll let you know as soon as I have any useful information." He switched his gaze to me. "You got anything else?"

"No."

I could tell he didn't believe me. "I hope not."

• • ● ● •

When we arrived at the Carlyle House, Kary's car was parked out front. Kit's motorcycle was in the driveway, and Kit perched on the front steps like a young crow.

He jerked a thumb toward the door. "She won't let me in."

Camden went up the steps. "Let me try."

We were able to get inside and stood in front of the mirror. As before, cloud patterns shifted in the speckled surface.

"Have you actually seen Delores?" Kary asked.

Camden carefully touched the mirror. "Not exactly. There's an image, but it's indistinct. She definitely lets me know what she's feeling, though."

While Camden communed on another level, I looked around at the ugly paintings. I hadn't looked too closely because they hurt my eyes, but a closer inspection revealed a basic understanding of composition and perspective. It was the colors or lack thereof that made the artwork so unattractive.

Colors.

Was it possible?

"Camden, ask Delores if Beverly's colorblind."

"I didn't think women could be colorblind."

"It's rare, but I think they can."

He turned back to the mirror, and after a few minutes, stumbled away from it as if Delores had given him a psychic shove.

"I think you're onto something, Randall. She didn't want to talk about that, at all."

"Maybe Kit knows."

Kit had waited for us on the steps. "Grandma feeling cranky today?"

Beyond cranky, now that we'd hit a nerve. "A little bit. Would you happen to know if your mom's colorblind?"

"Never thought about it. I guess she could be."

"It would explain why her paintings are so bad."

"How do you get colorblind, anyway?" he asked.

I didn't know a lot about colorblindness. "Men inherit it from their mothers, but I don't know how women get it. I've seen Amos Carlyle's work. It's pretty obvious Beverly's dad wasn't colorblind."

Kary knew more. "It's pretty rare, but it can happen. We've talked about it at school. You can become colorblind from an accident or injury, alcohol or drug abuse, sun damage to your eyes, or if you have multiple sclerosis."

Kit was puzzled. "Mom doesn't have any of those things."

"Usually, little girls become colorblind if both parents are."

"Judging from that reaction, Delores must have been," I said.

"But Amos wasn't," Camden said. "He's known for his colorful artwork."

We realized what this meant at the same time. There was one possible conclusion. "Beverly's dad and Amos Carlyle must not have been the same man. No wonder Delores didn't like Beverly adopting children. She must have felt a tremendous guilt over not having Amos' real child. Do you suppose she told him?"

Kit's interest was caught. "Oh, wow. Grandma had an affair?"

"I wouldn't ask your mother about this until we know for certain."

"Hey, I don't care. Did you ask why I can't come in, Cam?"

"Let me try again."

Camden, Kary, and I returned to the mirror, and Camden gently touched the surface.

"Delores, I know this is hard for you, but your grandson would like to come in." She must have said something negative because he winced. "You still want to see Beverly, though, right?" This answer must have been yes, because he pressed on. "Would you tell me one thing? Can you see any colors, at all?"

A loud thump behind us made us turn. One of the pictures swung back and forth before the glass cracked and it fell. Kary picked it up. The picture depicted a rainbow painted in muted shades of grays and browns. The mirror darkened. Camden stepped back.

"I would say no."

• • ● • •

When Camden told Kit that Delores refused to explain why she didn't want to see her grandson, he shrugged.

"She's in a mood. I get it. Maybe once she sees Mom she'll want to see me. Thanks for trying, though. I'd better get back to the store."

When we got home, we were amazed by the cars parked along the street.

"Is somebody having a party?" I asked before Camden pointed out that the front yard of 302 Grace looked like a mini-Woodstock. Dozens of tattered and scruffy-looking teenagers lounged under the trees and all over the porch, smoking cigarettes and Lord knows what else, drinking beer, and making a hell of a racket on assorted stringed instruments.

We had to park way up near the corner. Kary parked behind us and got out. "What in the world is all this?"

Camden stooped to pick up a beer can. "Ellie will have a stroke."

The minute the kids saw us, they crowded around. "Hey, mister," one called, "we got what you're looking for. Get a load of this." He brought his hand down on a jumble of strings that made his guitar sound like an iron pipe scraping across concrete.

Another teenaged boy held his guitar overhead and twanged it like a giant rubber band. "How 'bout this?" Still another held his guitar like a rifle and fired off a series of staccato sounds.

I put up both hands for silence. "Wait a minute. What's going on? Why are you all here?"

"Tryouts."

"Tryouts?"

"For the new band you're putting together."

"I'm not putting together a new band—or an old one. Who told all of you to come here?"

"Couple of women at the Holiday Lounge were handing out flyers."

I looked at Camden. "The Archer Sisters." I turned to the crowd. "I'm sorry, but there's been a mistake. I'm not auditioning bands. I need to find a band that will take a no-talent, unattractive girl."

Most of the kids made rude gestures, groaned, and started to leave, but one overweight boy in a striped t-shirt and baggy shorts beamed at me. "Oh, my God, like, that's us, man. We're the GWA: Geeks With Attitude. We'll take her. Is she real ugly?"

"If she smiled, she'd probably be nice-looking," I said.

"Does she sound real sucky?"

"I've never heard her sing, but I would imagine she does."

The boy motioned to his friends. "Hey, guys, come here!"

The other members of GWA lived up to their name. Two of the girls were human blobs, and the remaining boy gave new meaning to the word gnarly. Compared to them, Frieda would look like a princess.

"Where is she? Can we meet her?"

"Where do you guys hang out? I'll bring her by."

"We practice in my garage, 411 Smith Street."

I told the group we'd find Frieda and meet them there. I helped Camden pick up all the trash and cans, and Kary swept the porch clean of cigarette butts. Then we sat down on the porch, and I asked Camden to call Kit and find out if he knew where Frieda was now. "We'll see if we can get one thing sorted, anyway."

He talked briefly with Kit. "Kit says she should be at home. You want me to call her?"

"Yes, she might relate better to someone from her peer group."

Camden ignored my attempt at humor. "Kit also said the best way to get her to join the Geeks is to tell her they're competing with his band for the same gig. Since she'll do anything to spite him, she'll leap into the Geeks' arms."

"Are you sure you want kids, Cam? What if one of your girls turns out like Frieda?"

"I don't think that's likely."

"I'm guessing Beverly said the same thing."

Lindsey hadn't had the chance to become a teenager. I wondered what I would've done if she'd decided to run a hot dog stand instead of going to college, if she'd turned surly and defiant, if she'd run off and gotten pregnant.

Camden was talking to Frieda and making progress. "Yeah, they're real anxious to meet you. I think they might be competing against Kit's band for a slot at the Cave. It's worth a try, isn't it? Okay, 411 Smith Street." He ended the call. "She said she'd meet us there."

"She'd better. Kary, want to ride along and witness the historic meeting of Frieda and the Geeks?"

"Sounds mind-blowing, but all this about Delores being colorblind really intrigues me," she said. "I'm going to see what I can find out about Amos Carlyle. It's possible he could've been colorblind and found a way to work around it."

• • ● • •

Camden and I met Frieda at 411 Smith Street, where the Geeks With Attitude were beating on various instruments and wailing like lovelorn cats. As I'd hoped, Frieda sized up the other females. I don't know why I didn't think of it before. Instead of being the weakest and most unattractive member of the Slotted Spoons, Frieda could be the Geek Goddess.

"This had better be good," Frieda said.

"Oh, did I happen to mention they need a lead singer?"

Two members of the GWA came to meet us. I introduced them to Frieda.

"Guys, this is Frieda Huntington."

"Oh, wow," Striped T-shirt said. "You didn't tell us she was so hot." He wiped his hand on his shirt before extending it. "The gang calls me Too Large." When he saw Frieda's poison green fingernails, he gulped. "Excellent. We're going over one of our numbers right now, 'Tailpipe Suckers.' Would you care to give it a try?"

Frieda nodded like a duchess. "I wouldn't mind."

Too Large and his friend grinned and backed away.

"Well, what do you think?" I asked Frieda.

"I guess it'll do."

"And your baby?"

"I'm giving it up for adoption. There's this guy who'll pay me a lot of money for it."

"What guy?"

She sighed and rolled her eyes as if answering took too much of her precious energy. "Just this guy, okay? He says they do this all the time. It's no big deal."

"How did you hear about him?"

She shrugged. "Word gets around. You know."

"Who told you this man would buy your baby? Did you see an ad in the Yellow Pages?"

My flippancy didn't register. "There wasn't an ad. Somebody at the nail salon told me."

"Who, Frieda?"

"I don't know her name."

"One of the women who work there?"

"The Japanese people? They barely speak English."

"I believe the women who work there are Vietnamese."

"Whatever. It wasn't one of them. This girl was in to get her nails done, a really tough-looking blue. Cyanide Blue, I think, or maybe Drowned Pleasure."

"I'm sure her nails looked great. Do you remember her name? Anything about her?"

"She was pregnant, too, and we got to talking, and she said, oh, I know this guy who'll pay cash for your baby because that's what I'm going to do. I asked her about him, and she told me her boyfriend was going to set it up and she'd let me know—oh, and she had on this really grotty hat. I mean, who wears a toboggan in the summertime? Her nails looked tough, though."

A toboggan. Blue fingernails.

Dicehead's girlfriend.

That unattractive stomach had been Baby on Board.

Frieda sighed. "Is that all?"

"So you don't plan to tell your mother?"

"No. It's my baby."

"It's D.J.'s baby, too." She looked away. "He wants to keep it."

"That's too bad."

"So all you care about is the money."

She glared at me. "Yeah. So what?"

Too Large called from the garage. "We're ready for you, Frieda."

"Be right there." She turned back to me with one of the coldest looks I've ever received from a female, and we're talking Ellin Belton at her frostiest. "Are we through?"

The thought of never seeing her again helped me survive the deep freeze. "Yes, ma'am."

As she walked away, Camden said, "'Thank you' would have been nice."

"No, what's going to be nice is seeing the end of this. We need to take a ride over to the other side of town."

• ● ● ● •

I remembered where Dicehead's girlfriend lived. She wasn't home. I then drove to the love nest on Pacer Avenue. Dicehead hadn't learned a lot from past experiences. When he opened the door, I could see another woman in the dim light of the living room. She was equally attractive as Toboggan Girl. Dicehead tried to play tough.

"What the hell are you doing here?"

"I need to ask you a few questions."

"I don't have to tell you nothing."

"Okay," I said. "I'll call your wife and tell her what's going on. Or I could tell this lady here about your pregnant girlfriend."

The woman sat up straight in her chair. "What? What pregnant girlfriend?"

"Give me a minute with this guy," he told the woman as he pushed me out the door and shut it behind us. He deflated. "What do you want?"

"The racetrack deal your girlfriend mentioned. That wasn't NASCAR, was it? It was horse-racing."

"Yeah, so what?"

"Who's this man you deal with?"

"Brian Young. I met him at some bar."

"The Cave?"

"Yeah, something like that, and he was looking for people to go in on a horse. He said he'd place all the bets."

"Did you make money off this horse?"

"For a while. Then it didn't run so good."

"You lost money."

"A lot. So this guy says he knows another way to make money."

"If you happen to know a woman willing to sell her baby."

He gulped. "Yeah. Look, man, she don't want it, anyway. We're going to split the money."

"Maybe so, but what you're doing is illegal."

He stared at me. "You're kidding. If it's my kid, who cares what I do with it?"

"I've got a friend down at the police station. Want me to call and check with him on that?"

"Why don't you leave me alone?"

It was my turn to make a deal. "You go back to your wife and your children. Convince your girlfriend to let someone at a legitimate adoption agency find a home for her baby. Then I'll leave you alone."

I left him pondering this weighty ethical matter and went back to the car.

"Brian Young is definitely in the baby business," I told Cam. "Let's see if he'll make a deal with Mr. and Mrs. Fisher."

Chapter Nineteen

"There's Nothing Too Good for My Baby"

Brian Young was happy to hear from John Fisher and said he would arrange for us to see all four houses on Tuesday. I agreed to meet him at Superior Homes at nine o'clock. Next, I called Beverly Huntington and told her Frieda was now lead singer for Geeks With Attitude. "Would you like to meet me at the Carlyle House, or shall I pick you up?"

"Oh, I can't stop by today, Mr. Randall. It's much too late in the day."

"How about tomorrow afternoon?"

"I'm not sure. Let me check my schedule."

"Mrs. Huntington, I found your son a place to stay, and I found a band willing to take your daughter. It's time for you to honor your part of the bargain." This incredibly complex and time-consuming bargain.

"Yes, of course. Tomorrow afternoon." She ended the call.

I must have looked disgusted when Kary came in the office, carrying her laptop. "Uh, oh. Did someone blow our cover?"

"No, I'm fed up with all the Huntingtons. Kit's turned out to be pretty decent, but his mom keeps stalling."

"You'd think she wouldn't mind walking into the Carlyle House for a few minutes."

"Maybe she's reluctant to unleash bad ju-ju on all of Parkland."

"Maybe she doesn't want to look at all those sad pictures."

"If she's colorblind, what difference would that make?"

Kary took a seat in the office chair. "Speaking of that, here's what I found out about Amos. He was a big noise in the local art world, but never made the big-time. His most famous works are the murals he painted for the town hall, which got him a little national exposure, but not as much as he'd have liked. In most interviews I found, he manages to get in at least one complaint about other artists he considered inferior."

I'd dealt with artistic types before. "That's not unusual."

"No, but what I found interesting was he never mentioned his family, and if the interviewer brought up the subject, Amos always said that was a private matter and only wanted to talk about his art." She opened the laptop. "The one time Delores is mentioned is in an old televised interview for a show called *Meet the Artist*." A few clicks and she turned the laptop so I could see. "You can find anything in the world on YouTube."

The footage was grainy, but there was the great Amos Carlyle, all in black, and a young man in a suit and bowtie, both seated in armchairs on a set that looked like someone's living room, complete with paneled walls and an ugly lamp. Amos was a large man with dark hair swept back from a high forehead and keen eyes under black eyebrows. He looked fierce, but the interviewer wasn't intimidated. His first questions were about Amos' plans for the town hall murals, which Amos answered in painstaking detail. Then the interviewer switched topics.

"Mr. Carlyle, I understand your wife, Delores, and your daughter also live in Parkland. I'm sure our viewers would like to know more about your family. Does your daughter also paint?"

Amos sat back in his chair as if stung. "I'm here to discuss my art. I do not discuss my private life. Any more impertinent questions, sir, and I'll end this interview."

Chastened, the young man looked through his notes and asked about Carlyle's future projects. Kary closed the laptop. "See what I mean? As far as I can tell, that's the only time Delores was even mentioned, and Beverly's name doesn't come up at all."

"He might have known about Delores' affair and didn't want any bad publicity."

"That's what it sounds like to me, too. Or maybe he was just a jerk."

Kary, like Camden, has justifiable father issues. It was time to change the subject. "That's enough about Beverly for now. The really sad pictures are those of Chelsea Holt. But who's being blackmailed? The mayor? His wife? How did Bobbi get those pictures? Was she hiding in the house somewhere? Maybe Young's the one being blackmailed. She could've said, give me the house I want, and I'll destroy these photos."

"But you're pretty sure Young's running an illegal baby ring."

"That's what the Fishers are going to find out tomorrow afternoon."

"I can't wait."

"You know, we could make our partnership legal. We could be a real Mr. and Mrs."

"Kary Fisher? I'd have to answer *Star Wars* questions the rest of my life."

"Mr. and Mrs. Randall, and you know it. Good grief, it's been days, and I haven't had a proposal turned down. Let me come up with something." I rummaged in my top desk drawer. "I had a ring in here somewhere."

"Don't worry about a ring."

"You'll marry me without one?"

"No, I mean, don't worry about buying one. I'm not ready to get married, and you need money for your agency."

I thought about the thirty-thousand-dollar prize Delores had promised me if I got Beverly to the house. "That's not going to be a problem." Because I intended to get Beverly into the Carlyle House if I had to carry her in kicking and screaming. "Let's suppose I come into some money. What kind of ring would you like?"

"The only ring I'm interested in right now is the illegal baby ring that we are going to expose and end."

I came around my desk to her. "All right. How about a kiss to seal the deal?"

She stood and leaned into me. Her lips were inches from mine when Ellin came in, beaming with pride.

"You'll never guess who I snagged for the next show! Only one of the world's leading authorities on the Mayan calendar."

Kary gracefully stepped back. "Congratulations!"

I wasn't quite as thrilled. "Isn't that over?" Like my kiss. "I mean, the world didn't end. At least, not that I noticed."

"Exactly. He's going to explain the completion of the Mayan calendar cycle. The calendar's been going for over a million days. The way he sees it, the world has secretly been reborn. He's planning to hold a worldwide consciousness-raising symposium."

"Great. About time."

"Here's the best part! He's going to announce the symposium on the PSN."

"That should thrill all the Mayans in the audience."

She ignored me and went to the island, where Camden was sitting on the sofa reading one of his UFO magazines. He got the same Mayan calendar story and a kiss, the lucky dog. "What have you been up to?"

He certainly wasn't going to tell her about our exciting X-rated pictures, our visit to the Archer Sisters, Delores Carlyle's latest fit, or the invasion of the marginally talented bands. "Oh, you know. Stuff."

"Does any of your stuff have to do with this?" She handed him a bright pink piece of paper. "Mrs. Stewart across the street gave it to me. She asked if we could please keep the noise down next time."

The paper was one of the Archer Sisters' flyers announcing tryouts at 302 Grace Street. Busted.

"All a misunderstanding," Camden said. "Kit needed another band member, and a group of kids showed up here to audition."

Camden is generally not a good liar, but this was excellent for a spur of the moment fib. I gave him a subtle thumbs-up, and Kary rolled her eyes.

"I'll go apologize to Mrs. Stewart," he said.

This earned him another kiss. "Thank you. No need to get the neighbors stirred up. How long do we have to deal with Devil Boy, anyway?"

"Give him a chance. He's doing much better."

"Well, I've got loads of phone calls to make. I want a big crowd for the symposium."

She went up the stairs, cell phone at her ear. Camden went across the street to apologize to Mrs. Stewart. I heard him greet Angie as she passed him on the porch on her way in from work. I helped her with her shopping bags.

"Thanks," she said. "Thought I'd make chicken and dumplings for supper."

"That sounds good."

"I'll help you," Kary said.

I knew Kary wanted to plead her case about keeping Mary Rose. The way my office is situated, it's impossible not to hear what goes on. Of course, I could've shut my door, but where's the fun in that?

Angie was onto Kary, too. "Now, don't start fussing about Rufus' baby. We'll make the best decision we can."

"You know I'm available if you need someone to look after her."

"And we appreciate it." Pots and pans clanged and drawers opened and shut as Angie prepared to cook. "You can go ahead and make the dough. Have you and Randall found out anything?"

"We think we know someone who's running an illegal adoption service. David and I are going to pose as a couple wanting a baby and see what happens."

"So this guy killed Bobbi and took Mary Rose so he could sell the baby? That's harsh."

The refrigerator opened and shut. "We don't know if it's the same guy."

"Y'all be careful."

"Angie, it wouldn't be a good idea to mention this plan to Rufus. He'd come charging in like a one-man SWAT team and ruin our chances of finding the baby."

"I can keep a secret."

They talked about other things, Angie's job, the search for a house, Kary's piano students, and the concert at the Carlyle House.

"How'd it go?" Angie asked. "Sorry I had to work, or I would've been there."

"It went very well. The house is haunted, you know, and Cam's been talking with the ghost."

"She don't want to slide out and get in him like that other ghost did, does she?"

"No, she's trapped in a mirror. Cam and David are going to get her out, but it's a long complicated story."

"I got time."

While the chicken cooked and the dumplings were rolled, Kary related the whole twisted tale from Kit moving in to Frieda rejecting the Slotted Spoons to Camden masquerading as a teen. Several times, Angie laughed and said, "Well, don't that beat all!"

"Did you see Cam's baby picture?"

Kary must have retrieved the photo from the piano because Angie said, "Awww, ain't that the sweetest thing?"

"David took him to Green Valley as part of the deal."

"Does the story end there?"

"The story doesn't end until we get Mary Rose back safe and sound."

I heard the clank of plates and silverware as Kary set the table. Then she came to my door. "David, I just thought of something. What about Frieda's baby?"

Uh, oh. "She hasn't had it yet."

"I know. If we crack this baby ring, she'll have to find another place for it."

"Don't even go there."

She came in and sat down. "Why not?"

"First of all, have you seen Frieda? Her baby's going to look like an angry mosquito."

"David."

"An angry, malnourished mosquito. Do you think she's seen a doctor, or she's taking care of herself?"

"What about the baby's father? Is he ill-natured and scrawny, too?"

"He's a big guy who seems like a decent sort. I think he'd take care of the baby."

"Oh."

I reached across my desk to take her hand. "You're going to drive yourself crazy trying to take in every needy child in this city. The right one will come along. But the right one is not Frieda's. Trust me."

"The right one might be Mary Rose."

I didn't think so, but all I said was, "Let's find her first."

• • ● • •

Tuesday morning, Kary was raring to go to Superior Homes. She looked very elegant in the light yellow suit. She'd pinned her hair up in a fancy twist. She spun around to give me the full effect.

"Mrs. Fisher, you look great."

She patted her hair. "We're supposed to be rich, right? Will this do?"

"Believe me, you look fine."

"Is there anything in particular I need to say?"

"Look especially interested in the children's rooms."

"That won't be hard to do."

Brian Young was waiting for us at the door of Superior Homes. "Good morning. Everything's arranged. We can see all four houses today. Mrs. Fisher, may I say you look lovely in that shade of yellow?"

We got into Young's BMW and rode out to Deer Point Estates. There was no car seat in the back this time. Our first stop was the giant brick home. We saw it all, from massive fireplaces in what Young called a "great room," to the guest house out back, which was larger than all of 302 Grace. Next, the castle in Braeside Acres. It lived up to its name. Even on this hot afternoon, it was cavernous and chilly inside. Kary and I had no trouble expressing our disinterest. The sprawling house in Terrace Lakes—no terrace, and one small pond standing in for a lake—had rooms large enough for skating rinks and bowling alleys. Our last stop was Kary's favorite, the yellow one with the indoor pool, a modern cube with odd angles of glass.

Young pointed out the features. "The kitchen's been totally redone, granite countertops, of course, the bathrooms all have Venetian marble, and there's a wonderful study and home office area. What's your line of work, Mr. Fisher?"

"I own a financial consulting service."

"If you do any work at home, this area is perfect."

It was perfect. The walls of deep golden brown wood, the large computer station, recessed lighting, leather chairs, tasteful prints of forests and mountains—with an office like this, I could do a heap of detecting.

"Is there a nursery?" Kary asked.

"There are several rooms that would be perfect for a nursery. This way, please."

Kary made all sorts of pleased and admiring noises. I stood to one side and attempted to look forlorn. When Kary went down the hall to the next room, Young glanced at me.

"Mr. Fisher, I couldn't help noticing your lovely wife's reaction when I mentioned children. I also noticed how she lingered in the nurseries and children's rooms, and she was especially taken by the playground behind the castle."

"I'm afraid we're having difficulty in that area." I lowered my voice. "Julie is quite emotionally fragile on the topic. She's unable to have children, and we're hitting unfortunate snags in the adoption process."

"That's too bad."

"Yes, the ordinary routes are frustratingly slow. It's to the point where we're desperate enough to try anything." I didn't have any trouble making my next statement sound completely honest. "I'd do anything to make her happy."

"A lovely woman like that deserves to be happy. Perhaps I can help you."

I gave him an inquiring frown.

"Oddly enough, in my line of work, I come across people who are in a position to—shall we say—smooth the adoption process? Would you be interested?"

I was definitely interested. "Yes, of course."

"I assure you, we give the mother an excellent price and a guarantee that her child will be brought up in a good home, a Superior Home." He chuckled at his own joke.

"So you run an adoption agency on the side? Why don't you advertise? This seems slightly shady."

"Oh, my, no, I assure you everything is done properly. Our clients are wealthy people, such as yourself, who don't want to wait forever. There are hundreds of women out there who become pregnant and, for various reasons, don't wish to keep their children. They don't want to abort them, either, so I offer another solution."

"I don't know," I said. "This sounds too good to be true."

"Discuss it with your wife. If it sounds like something you'd like to investigate further, we can start making arrangements."

Oh, this was something I'd like to investigate further, make no mistake about that. "Thank you."

"You folks seem like the type who'd make excellent parents, and any of these homes you've seen today would certainly be spacious enough for a large family. There will, of course, be a fee. Initial up-front costs run around fifty thousand dollars, and I would have to have that in cash."

"That wouldn't be a problem."

"Let me make a few calls. Should I start looking for a dark-haired little boy or a blond little girl?"

"Actually, Julie and I have always wanted a little red-haired girl. Julie's mother has red hair."

His eyes lit up. "Really? I'll see what I can do."

"Thanks. As I said before, money's no object."

We shook hands, and I tried not to bound out the door and dance down the street.

Kary was sitting in one of the lounge chairs by the pool. She'd taken off the suit jacket and looked as cool and poised as a fashion model in her silky white blouse and yellow skirt. "It's so peaceful here."

"I know you'd like to stay," I said, "but we have that reception this evening, remember?"

Kary stood and offered her hand to Young. "Thank you so much for showing us all these lovely houses."

Any thoughts or worries Young might have had faded in the radiance of her smile. "It was my pleasure, Mrs. Fisher. I believe your husband wants to talk to you about this house in particular."

She wound her arm in mine and gave me a little hug. "I knew he'd like it. Thanks, honey."

The things I do for this job. "You're welcome, dear."

Young drove us back to the Superior Homes office. I told him I'd call tomorrow. Kary waved good-bye, and we walked around the corner to the Fury.

Kary tossed her jacket into the back and slid into the passenger's seat. "Did you find out anything?"

"Young definitely reacted when I mentioned a red-haired baby. I think Mr. and Mrs. Fisher are expecting a baby girl."

"Oh, my God. Did he say when?"

"He's going to call."

"So what's our plan?"

I concentrated on the road so I wouldn't be distracted by all my doubts. I wanted to say, our plan is something amazing and daring and triumphant that will solve this mystery, assure justice for Bobbi, and return Mary Rose to her rightful father, but I honestly didn't know what the next move would be.

"I'll think of something."

When she didn't answer right away, I took a quick glance in her direction. Her expression made my heart jump. This wasn't the look of shared amusement when I made a smart quip or used an impressive vocabulary word. This wasn't the look of gratitude when she learned I'd taken Camden to Green Valley. This was something else, something deeper. Something I would call love.

She smiled as she faced front again. "Yes. You will. You always do, David."

• ● ●

I drove home with my thoughts good and scrambled. Aside from wondering if I'd misinterpreted that look, I had all sorts of questions about the case. How did Brian Young fit into all this? Yes, he was having an affair with Chelsea Holt and using Bobbi Jo's house as a badly decorated love nest, but how did he get Mary Rose, if indeed he had her? If he was being blackmailed, wouldn't he have been satisfied with the pictures? Killing Bobbi Jo and taking her baby seemed much too extreme. Then again, I didn't know anything about Bobbi Jo. Maybe she didn't want a child. Maybe she was glad to trade Mary Rose for a Superior Home. But that didn't make sense, either.

Camden was waiting on the porch for the Fisher report, but first, I had a phone call of my own to make. I hadn't heard from Beverly Huntington. When I asked what time would be convenient for her to come by the Carlyle House, I could tell by the tone of her voice she was going to stall once again.

"Something's come up. Could we make it tomorrow?"

"I don't think so. Would you like Kit back? I can bring him over right now."

Apparently not. "Give me about twenty minutes."

Kary said she'd stay home in case Young called. Camden rode along with me. On the way to the Carlyle House, I filled him in on the Fishers' morning activities.

"Sounds as if he has Mary Rose," Camden said.

"I hope he does, because I've got a plan. It doesn't involve Kary, so I'm counting on you to save me from her wrath."

"You're leaving her out of the loop?"

"If my plan works, it'll be worth it. I hope."

He was quiet for a moment, strolling around in my thoughts and having a sneak peek at my idea. "I'll be curious to see how you get out of this one."

At the house, we waited twenty minutes, and then thirty.

I'd had enough. "Okay, I'm tired of her games. It's my turn."

We drove to Beverly's house. I strode up the walk, rang the bell, and when Beverly answered the door, went on the offensive. "I need your help right away. Kit's trapped in the Carlyle House, and your mother says she's not letting him out."

She gaped at me. "Not letting him out?"

"I don't have time to explain. Come on."

She scooped up her pocketbook and keys, locked the door, and hopped into the backseat. "Mr. Randall, what on earth are you talking about? My mother can't do anything like that."

"You can see for yourself. When I told her you weren't coming, she threw a supernatural temper tantrum."

"What was Kit doing there?"

"He wanted to see the house. Trust me, if I'd known this was going to happen, I never would've let him come in."

She sat in tense silence until we got to the Carlyle House. When she hesitated on the doorstep, I pulled her inside and stood her in front of the huge mirror. Immediately, cloudy patterns shifted on its surface.

Beverly stared. "What's going on? Where's Kit?"

Camden touched the mirror. "Go ahead, Randall. She's listening."

I felt ridiculous talking to a mirror, but I was fed up with this entire family and wanted to set things straight. "Delores, I have a little something to say to you. You married Amos Carlyle, hoping the artistic gene you lacked would be passed on to your children, but when Amos loved his art more than he loved you, you found another man." A dark shadow rippled across the mirror, but I was not deterred. "You didn't know this other man was colorblind, like you, but you loved him, and you had his child, a little girl. When Beverly had no concept of color, maybe you saw this as divine retribution." Two more ripples, and a rumbling like thunder. I was hitting major nerves. "So you surrounded yourself with Beverly's ugly paintings to remind you. You've spent enough time punishing yourself. We're cleaning house."

I started taking the paintings off the wall. "Help me out here, Beverly. You know you hate these things."

She stood as if rooted to the floor. "But where's Kit?"

"He's at Comic World. You and your mother are going to end this right now, today."

"But my paintings—"

"Didn't you ever wonder what was wrong? Didn't anyone ever tell you you were colorblind?"

"Yes, but I didn't think women could be colorblind. What was all that you were saying about my mother and another man?"

"The only way you can be colorblind is if your mother and your father are. Your mother was. Amos wasn't."

This took her a few minutes to process. "Are you saying Amos Carlyle was not my father?" She looked into the mirror, but no reflection looked back out of the clouds. "He was always very distant. Never really had much to do with me. I thought it was because he was so caught up in his painting. He was away for long periods of time, going to galleries, art shows…that's when Powell was there…"

The shocked look on her face made Camden wince.

"Oh, my God," she said. "Carl Powell. I thought he was only a family friend of hers. We were always so glad to see him. He was always kind to me, brought me presents. She told me to call him Uncle Carl. He died when I was eleven." She smacked both hands on the mirror. "Why didn't you tell me? Why did you let me go on believing I was the daughter of the famous artist Amos Carlyle when you knew I didn't have any of his talent? I didn't have any talent at all!"

She yanked the nearest painting off its hook. "What should we do with them?"

"I think a nice big bonfire in the backyard ought to do the trick. Camden, start on that wall."

Before he could reach it, the walls began to shudder. We didn't have to take the rest of the paintings down. They fell like ugly autumn leaves, the frames bending, the glass crashing. Camden called for me to get out of the way and pulled Beverly to a corner. There was a sound like a huge intake of breath, and the mirror fell forward like a giant flat tree. When it hit the floor, the crackling of the glass sounded like the crash of surf on the sand. In the silence that followed, I could've sworn I heard a woman sobbing.

Camden held up a piece of broken mirror. The edges caught the light and acted as a prism. Rainbows danced on the bare walls. He pointed to the different colors. "Can you see them now, Delores? That's red, and that's orange, yellow, green, blue, and violet." A tremor shook him. "She can see them, Randall."

"Somebody else needs to see them."

I put Beverly's hand in his. She stared in wonder at the uneven rainbow hovering on the wall. "Oh. Oh, my God. Is that—?" She couldn't say anything else.

"Colors," I said. "Real ones. It's what she always wanted you to see, but she couldn't even see it herself."

Beverly's voice trembled. "They're so bright. Is that what Amos Carlyle's artwork looks like? No wonder she hated mine."

"No, she hated herself for cheating you."

Beverly couldn't keep her eyes off the wall. "But my paintings weren't good, anyway. They would've looked the same, only brighter, I guess." She clung to Camden's hand. "How are you doing this?"

"I'm letting you and Delores see through my eyes."

Outside, the sun went behind a cloud, and the rainbow faded.

"She says good-bye, Beverly." He let go of Beverly's hand and gently touched her shoulder. "She says she loves you and regrets not being able to tell you the truth."

She sighed a shaky sigh. "Those colors. That's what you see all the time? It's amazing. I had no idea." Another sigh, this one of relief. "So I guess that's it, then."

I looked at the piles of shattered glass. "There's a little sweeping up to do."

One painting had survived the fall and still hung from its place by the stairs. I glanced at Camden and he gave a slight nod. "Beverly, let's see if we can find any brooms."

With Beverly occupied in another room, I took the ugly brown landscape from the wall and pressed on the wood paneling. A small part of the panel pushed in. I pulled out a small bag. Inside, jewelry twinkled like a cluster of little rainbows, all the colors neither Delores nor Beverly could see.

I put the bag in my pocket. "Thank you, Delores."

There was no answer or indication Delores was still in the house. I took that as a very good sign.

Chapter Twenty

"Don't Cry, Baby"

After cleaning up and leaving a note for Lauber saying the mirror fell and jarred all the paintings off the walls, we took Beverly home.

She shook my hand and then held it a moment longer. "Mr. Randall, I want to thank you for everything. Finding a place for Kit, getting Frieda into a band, everything." She turned to Camden. "Thank you, too, Camden." She couldn't say anything else.

"I was glad to help, Beverly."

She got out of the car and gave us one last wave before going into her house.

I turned on victory music. "Does that take care of everything? I have my payment, Kit's got a place to stay, Frieda's in a band, Beverly and Delores are reconciled, the Slotted Spoons aka the Destitute Dolls are on their way to glory—what's left? Oh, Janice and her Hot Dog Ghost."

"I have an idea about that," Camden said. "Kit knows how to deal with stubborn teenage girls. Let's let him have a go at the Hot Dog Ghost."

I called Kit and explained the problem.

Kit sounded confused. "There's a ghost that looks like a hot dog?"

"It's a young girl, Camden says. Maybe she'll talk to you. I'll bet your aura's dark enough for her."

Kit met us at Janice's, and we walked around to the back of the restaurant. I didn't see the ghost, but Camden said the minute she saw Kit, she came out and told him her sad story of being misunderstood. When Kit asked her what she wanted, it was an easy request to grant.

"She wants her pocketbook," Kit said. "The restaurant's built over where she hid it, and she can't get to it."

"We can't move the building."

"I think if we take up part of the floor in the kitchen, we can reach it."

Janice agreed to let us excavate. We pried up floorboards and dug where Kit instructed until we hit a small box buried about a foot down. We sat down in a circle and carefully opened the box. Inside was a pair of little slippers, a fan, and a drawstring purse, all faded and brittle with age.

"Ask her why she hid these things," I said.

Camden and Kit silently communicated for a few minutes, and Kit said, "Her mother didn't think she was old enough to have them."

"What does she want us to do with them?"

Another few minutes of silence. "There's a place in the park she likes."

"If we take the box there, will she leave the restaurant alone?"

"She says yes."

We filled in the hole and replaced the floorboards. Then we went to Lilac Park and buried the little box under a cedar tree. While Camden and Kit said their silent farewells to Hot Dog Girl, I looked around at the smooth lawns and the marble statues of fairy tale characters. This park was one Mayor Richard Holt had commissioned during his "Every Child Deserves a Safe Place to Play" campaign. Too bad Chelsea Holt was playing in an unsafe place.

Kit came up, dusting his hands. "Okay, she's gone. Anything else you guys need help with?"

"No, thanks. We'll let you know."

"Frieda really enjoys being Queen of the Geeks. That was a pretty smooth move."

"As long as everybody's happy."

"You're sure I can't help you out on another case? I mean, I'm seeing all kinds of kids, mostly yours, Cam."

I grinned at Camden. "I told you he could probably see your future."

Camden looked pleased. "Do you see three?"

"Yep, two girls and a boy. There's another girl, but I don't think she's yours."

"That's the one we're looking for."

Kit frowned as if concentrating. "Nope, it's Randall's." He paused. "Oh. Sorry, man."

That he could see Lindsey around me was oddly comforting. "Don't worry about it."

"For what it's worth, she's smiling."

Something swelled in my chest. I knew if I said anything, I'd choke on the emotion.

Kit frowned again. "There is one more kid, the one who's missing."

"Anything on her?" Camden asked.

"No, sorry. If I don't stop, I'm going to be seeing every kid in Parkland. You guys be careful around Young, okay? You're going to need a distraction."

When I first met this scrawny, safety-pinned punk, I never dreamed he'd be useful, and, unlike his sister, I could express gratitude. "Thanks, Kit. You helped out on this case, after all."

He shrugged. "No problem."

He hopped on his motorcycle and rode off. Camden and I got back in the car, and I put the Fury in gear. "Let's go back to Janice's and make sure everything's okay."

Janice was all smiles. "No more ghost! And you'll never guess this news. Mother is engaged to Jessie Vardaman! They stopped by while you were in the park. They're going to start their own online fortunetelling business for people and their pets. Mother's so delighted and so busy, she hasn't had time to hassle me in days."

"Just another job for Dragon Man and Snake Boy."

Janice laughed. "Don't forget Mimi the Fox. If she hadn't been so sassy, Vardaman would never have come here and met Mother. I'm playing it safe and leaving fox treats by the back door tonight. You guys want hot dogs? On the house, as promised."

We thanked her and sat down at one of the picnic tables.

"There's only one fairy tale that hasn't ended happily ever after," I said.

Camden looked off into the distance. "Not yet."

"Are you being optimistic about Mary Rose now? What was with all the gloom and doom back in Comic World, then, all that about too many babies floating around and not being able to find them?"

"I may have been over-empathetic."

"Is that a fancy-ass way of saying you didn't know what the hell you were talking about?"

He brought his gaze back to me. "No, it means I was picking up signals from someone else."

"From Kit, you mean? The whole adoption thing?"

"No," he said. "From D.J."

I recalled the boy starting to ask me something and then shrugging it off. Maybe he didn't believe I wanted to help. "Yeah, it's too bad the one teenaged boy in Parkland who wants to do the right thing managed to get involved with Frieda."

"He really wants to be a father."

"Even without your vast psychic knowledge, I could tell that. I say he ought to have that chance." My phone beeped, signaling a text. "This better not be another problem." I checked the message. "It's from Vangie."

"Are the Spoons in crisis?"

"She's says come meet her at Perkie's. She has something to show us."

• • ● • •

The Slotted Spoons weren't wailing away at Perkie's, but not long after we sat down, Vangie scooted up and took the other chair. She plopped a disk on the table.

"Guess what this is?"

"What?"

"It's the Destitute Dolls filmed live in concert at the Cave. Ta-da!"

"You recorded your performance?"

"Actually, Dillon Pennix sent it over. He said we might like to have it. Cool, huh? When we're rich and famous, we can say, here's where it all began. Sorta like the Beatles at that place in Germany. We'll probably laugh and say, 'Look at my hair!' Stuff like that."

"So Pennix recorded you?" I hadn't noticed any recording equipment.

"It must have been up in the light booth. I think the bartender switched it on. He took pictures, too. Look." She pulled a large envelope from her shoulder bag, an envelope exactly like the one Bobbi left with Tina Ramola. For one horrible moment, I thought Camden and I might have to look at more amateur porn. "Some really bitchin' stills we can use for posters."

The bartender. Trace Burwell, nerdy cousin. The one who jumped every time somebody looked at him the wrong way.

"What is it, David? You look kinda funny."

"My latest case isn't going the way I thought."

"None of them do, do they, Cam?"

"Not really." He admired the photos, but I could tell his thoughts were echoing mine. Trace Burwell. Least Likely Suspect.

Vangie pushed back a lock of her dark hair, revealing a set of silver earrings shaped like swords and feathers. "Then here's some good news. Let me tell you, Miss Frieda Huntington is one happy skankette, or as happy as she's likely to be. I saw her with the GWA last night at Don's Light Show at the ExcaliBar, and she was making major dissonance with the Geeks. Sounded like Yoko Ono's little sister being skinned with a cheese grater."

"Okay, so maybe I've had one success."

"Did she tell you what's she going to do with the baby?"

"Sell it, like you said."

Vangie shrugged, her earrings dangling and making silver sparks. "It's probably the only thing of value she's ever going to have. You guys want to watch the DVD?"

"Maybe later," I said. "I've had a breakthrough."

She grinned. "Did it hurt?"

"Not especially."

"You made a real grimace there."

"I'm hoping to make somebody else grimace exactly like that."

Chapter Twenty-one

"Baby, I'd Love to Steal You"

Trace Burwell hadn't checked in at the Cave yet, but Dillon Pennix was in his office, clicking away at his computer keyboard. He glanced up for a moment.

"Checking on Fortune. Looks like we're better off selling our shares."

"Your partner agree to this?"

"He'd better. I know for a fact he's down several hundred thousand."

I whistled my disbelief.

Pennix kept his eyes on the screen. "Yeah, I told him to lay off the poker games, but he wouldn't listen to me. I'm glad none of that money was mine."

"Where does he get his money?"

"Sells overpriced homes."

"Nothing on the side?"

"Not that I know of. I'm kinda busy this morning, so what's up?"

"I was talking to the Destitute Dolls earlier. They appreciated the DVD you sent over."

"No problem."

"Might have been better to ask their permission first before you filmed them."

He stopped typing and looked up, surprised. "I thought they knew. Were they upset? They're not planning to sue the club, are they?"

"No, like I said, they appreciated it. You do this all the time?"

He pushed away from his desk. "Damn, I thought Trace told them. He's supposed to check with the performers and make sure they know about the camera."

"You mind showing us how it works?"

He was willing to do anything if it prevented a lawsuit. He led us out to the club and showed us the switch on the wall. He indicated a small glassed-in area directly across from the stage. "The camera's up there with the lights. All Trace has to do is flip this switch to start it. That way, he's not running up and down steps all night."

"Could we have a look at it?"

"Sure."

A narrow flight of stairs led up to the small light booth. A bank of lights and switches filled one wall. One large cabinet mounted on the wall contained four cassette tape decks, a CD player, and two openings for VHS tapes and DVDs. A slim video camera aimed out the window sat on a tripod. All kinds of wires were gathered in a bundle that ran up the wall into a silver pipe.

"Impressive," I said. "Who installed it?"

"Trace did."

"The Dolls had photographs, too."

"Yeah, he took them from up here. Look, I've got a lot of work to do, so if the Dolls aren't suing me, I need to get back to my office."

We went back down the stairs to the club.

"When will Trace be in?" I asked.

"He should be here by now. Why do you need to see him?"

I looked up at the light booth. "I'm really impressed by that system. I'd like to have one installed in my office."

He relaxed slightly. "Oh, he'll be able to tell you how it works."

"That's what I'm counting on. Mind if we wait at the bar?"

"Suit yourselves."

Camden and I sat down at the bar. When Pennix returned to his office, I slipped behind the bar and looked around. I wasn't certain what I was looking for, but way back in a corner of a shelf I found two very useful things. The first was a Superior Homes Brochure. The second was a large envelope.

I handed the brochure to Camden and pulled out the envelope. "Look at this."

"More photos?"

I opened the envelope and took a peek. "Copies of Love on the Carpet. Bobbi was spreading joy all over."

"You might want to put that back," he said. "Trace is at the door."

I slid the envelope across to him. "I'm going to need it."

Trace Burwell came in and stood quivering between the bar stools. "You're not supposed to be back there." If anything, he looked worse than before. His hands were shaking, and his little moustache was clinging by a thread.

I came back around. "I'm curious what a flyer from Superior Homes is doing behind the bar."

Burwell got behind the bar with the look of a cavalry soldier who'd just made it to the fort. "Bobbi must have left it."

"Are you hanging onto it for sentimental reasons?"

He picked up a glass and began cleaning it furiously with his towel. "She was saving up for a house, one of those big fancy houses like you see in magazines. What are you doing here? What do you want?"

"The Destitute Dolls told me to thank you for the DVD and the pictures."

He nodded. The little moustache waved like a piece of seaweed.

"But I found some other pictures that are much more interesting."

He managed to catch the glass he was cleaning before it hit the floor. "What are you talking about?"

"Camden?"

Camden held up the envelope. "Was it your idea to use Bobbi's house?"

Burwell put the glass on the bar, his hand shaking.

I took out my cell phone. "Okay, if you won't talk to me, maybe you'll talk to the police."

He snorted up tears. "I didn't know she was going to do that! I thought she wanted the camera to take pictures of the baby."

"You showed her how to use the camera. Did you set it up like the one in here?"

"For the baby! When I saw what she'd done, I panicked. I didn't want nothing to do with it."

"So you've seen the pictures. You know who the man is."

He wiped his eyes. "Yeah, it's Brian Young with the mayor's wife. Bobbi had told him about her house, and he asked me if it was a good place to have a quickie, and I said sure. I didn't figure Bobbi would find out."

"When did you decide to blackmail him?"

"It wasn't my idea! It was Bobbi Jo's. She wanted a house real bad."

"Bad enough to sell her baby?"

"No! She wasn't going to do that. She told me she thought about it, but now she had a better way to make money."

"The plans she wouldn't tell you about."

"Yeah, she said she didn't care about losing her job because she had plans." His shoulders slumped. "I didn't know she was going to do this, I swear."

"How did she find out Young was using her house?"

"That day she got fired, she must have come home early."

All she had to do was quietly go in, get the camera, and take a few shots.

"Did Young borrow Pennix's blue truck to go to Bobbi's house?"

"Said it fit the neighborhood better than his BMW."

"Didn't Young go back to the house to look for the pictures? Didn't he ask you about them?"

"Yeah, he was real mad, but I told him I didn't know about no pictures."

"But you did. You had them right here. You planned to blackmail Young, too, and Chelsea Holt."

"No! If he knew I had any pictures, he'd be after me next, and—" he began to cry again "—and I didn't know what happened to the baby. You were really looking for her, and I wanted—I wanted—"

"You wanted to help."

He nodded and rubbed his nose so hard I was afraid his little moustache would come off. Then he held his skinny arms tight around him. "What are you going to do? I haven't done nothing wrong. I wasn't going to blackmail nobody."

"Then why keep these pictures?"

He didn't have an answer for that, and when Pennix stepped out of his office to ask if everything was okay, Burwell grabbed the glass and started cleaning it furiously. If that glass had been made out of wood, Burwell would've started a fire.

I wouldn't get anything else out of him with Pennix glaring in the background. "Everything's fine, thanks. We were just leaving."

Burwell was awfully anxious to pin everything on Brian Young. I wanted to see what he might do next. I moved the Fury down one block where we still had a good view of the Cave. It wasn't long before a blue Bigfoot truck tore out from behind the building and turned onto Emerald Avenue.

I put the Fury in gear. "Think Pennix ran out of beer?"

We followed at a safe distance. The blue truck drove to a shopping center and parked in front of an empty store. I parked three stores down. Pennix got out, carrying the large envelope. He knocked on the door, and someone let him in. After ten minutes, he came out, got into his truck, and drove away. Camden and I walked up to the empty store. Through the window we could see folding tables and chairs set up, cardboard boxes, and unconnected telephones.

"Future home of the Gura campaign," Camden said.

"Damn, you're good."

He grinned and pointed to a small sign at the bottom of the window. It read, "Campaign Headquarters for Raymond Gura, Candidate for Mayor."

"Okay, let's sign up."

I knocked on the door. A serious-looking man peered out. "Yes? May I help you?"

"We're interested in helping Raymond Gura's campaign. Need any volunteers?"

"Thank you, but we won't need anyone until September. If you'll come back then, I'll be glad to put you to work. I'm sure Mr. Gura will appreciate your support."

"He's not here?"

"Not at the moment. Thank you for your interest." He shut the door.

Camden touched the door. "He's there now."

"Looking at those pictures and laughing maniacally."

"'Maniacally.' Good one."

As we walked back to the car, I ticked off the points of this case. "I think we've got an evil axis here with Pennix, Young, and Burwell. They all hang around the Cave. They're all in on this race horse. Young wants a safe place to fool around with the mayor's wife. Trace says, use my cousin's place. She's not home during the day. But Bobbi finds out and takes pictures, or has Trace take pictures, and they plan to blackmail Young so Bobbi can have her dream house. But somewhere along the line, Pennix sees these pictures, knows the woman is Chelsea Holt, and wants to try his own blackmail scheme. He must have something against Richard Holt." I snapped my fingers. "The restrictions! Hasn't he been complaining about the extra restrictions nightclub owners have to follow under Holt's clean city rules? When we first met him, he thought we were from the health department."

"I remember the Archer Sisters said their club didn't have problems like other clubs did."

"Then when he sent you to spy on the other club, he didn't really care about what kind of music they played. He was hoping The Other Side was breaking the law."

"He lost money on the race horse deal, too."

"Couple of things I've got to figure out. One, Bobbi got herself in too deep. Who killed her for those pictures? Two, if the woman in the pictures is Chelsea Holt, how did she hook up with Brian Young? And three, most importantly, does Young have Mary Rose and will he give her to Mr. Fisher? I don't want to make any sort of move against Pennix or Young until Mary Rose is safe." I checked my watch. In about three hours, I would return to the Superior Homes office. Thinking of Superior Homes gave me an idea about question number two. "Camden, do you happen to know where the mayor lives?"

"Village Gardens."

"Let's ride out there."

Village Gardens was another wealthy neighborhood in Parkland. The Mayor and Mrs. Holt lived at the end of a winding drive. I recognized the house.

"That's a number six twenty-three, a little model called 'Suburban Castle.' I've been looking at houses for days now. I know a Superior Home when I see one."

"If Brian Young sold the Holts this house—"

"Then that's how Young met Chelsea."

That left me with two questions to answer.

• ◦ ● ◦ •

When we got home, Rufus and Angie filled up most of the porch steps.

Rufus turned his head to spit a stream of tobacco juice into the bushes. "We want to thank you for all you've done, Randall." He reached into the pocket of his overalls. "Got a little money for you. It's not much, but we'll get the rest."

I thought of the handful of rainbow jewelry I had in my pocket. "Don't worry about it. I just got paid for solving another case."

"Take it."

I folded the bills into my other pocket. "Thanks."

"Angie and I've been sitting here trying to decide what to do should you get this baby and it turns out to be mine."

"What do you want to do?"

"We been round and round about it. We're just not sure."

"Let me find her first."

Rufus pulled out his tobacco pouch for another wad of tobacco. "Jordan came by earlier today. Said there might be new evidence that could clear me."

"Yeah, some interesting photos have come to light, and I didn't have to hide in the bushes to find them."

His brow lowered as Angie's eyebrows went up. "Hide in the bushes?" she said.

"Figure of speech," I said with a grin at Rufus. "I've been looking everywhere."

It was Camden's turn to make supper, so lasagna was in our future. I stayed on the porch with Rufus and Angie and filled them in on the latest news. I told them about the Destitute Dolls being filmed at the Cave and that Trace Burwell had taught Bobbi how to use the same kind of camera.

As Rufus' brow lowered even further, I said, "Don't go running to the Cave to squash Burwell. He thought Bobbi wanted to make videos of the baby. But since she had a nice little setup already in place, it was easy for her to get incriminating pictures of the mayor's wife."

"Easier and sneakier than using her cell phone," Angie said.

Rufus spat another wad of brown goo. "Damn. I can't see Bobbi as a blackmailer."

"She wanted a house for herself and her child. I guess she figured as long as Chelsea Holt paid, and the pictures never came to light, no one would get hurt. But Pennix is in on this, too, and has his own copies. Camden and I followed him to Raymond Gura's campaign headquarters. You can imagine what Gura would do with those pictures."

"Is that what got her killed?"

"Somewhere along the line, things went wrong. I don't know if she tried to double-cross Young, or Pennix, or even if she had a deal with Gura."

"Have you told Finley all this?"

"He's got the pictures Bobbi left with her friend at the travel agency, but I didn't tell him what I know about Young. I want to find out if he has Mary Rose first."

"What do we do?"

Angie put a huge hand on his arm. "You are doing nothing, remember? Sounds like Randall's on the right track to solving this."

• • ● • •

At supper I told everyone about Delores and Beverly's reconciliation moment over the rainbow, and Camden related the Tale of the Hot Dog Ghost. We filled Kary in on our afternoon adventures and brought her up to date on the case.

She passed the lasagna to Rufus. "So you have three good suspects—Pennix, Burwell, and Young—and every one's got a motive for blackmail. I sat here all afternoon and Brian Young didn't call. Maybe he was out peddling more X-rated pictures. I hope he's not on to us."

If the Fishers' cover was blown, I wasn't sure how I'd get Mary Rose. "We'll go back and try again."

"Rainbow Wishes never called, either. My reputation as an ace investigator must have gotten around."

"Or they're the scumbag organization you prayed they would be."

My cell phone rang during dessert, so I excused myself and went to my office to answer it.

Brian Young did not sound as if he'd discovered the Fishers were fakes. He sounded satisfied. "Mr. Fisher, I have good news. Can we meet tomorrow afternoon? Would two o'clock suit you? I know you and your wife are going to be thrilled."

"I appreciate this, Mr. Young. You have no idea."

I put my phone back in my pocket and glanced toward the dining room. Kary passed the cake to Angie, who cut a huge slice for herself and one for Rufus.

"Be your birthday before long, won't it?" Rufus said to Kary.

"Next week," she said. "June 22."

"Better have a bigger cake than this one."

I was determined she'd be around for her birthday. She'd be mad as fire, as Rufus would say, but if Young had Mary Rose, I needed to make my move, and I couldn't put Kary in a dangerous situation. So my plan was and always had been to go by myself.

Tomorrow at two o'clock.

Chapter Twenty-two

"Baby, Take a Bow"

For Christmas, I'd given Kary a bracelet with little stars, which I was pleased to notice she wore fairly often. For her birthday, I thought matching earrings might be perfect, and since Ellin had a large collection of celestial jewelry, she was the one to ask.

We were the only two up early Wednesday morning. Ellin liked to be the first one at the PSN, and I hadn't been able to sleep, thinking today might be the day I'd find Mary Rose. Then what? If Rufus and Angie decided not to keep her— My mind kept shutting off at that point.

I sat down at the kitchen counter with my coffee and yawned. I was still in my pajamas and hadn't shaved. Ellin, as usual, looked perfectly put together. "Ellin, where's good place to find star-shaped earrings?"

"Have you checked Royalle's?"

"No, I've gotten a late start on the birthday gift-buying."

She brought her coffee cup over to the counter and sat down. "If Royalle's doesn't have any, try Sparkles in the mall. I've found quite a few beautiful things there."

"Thank you."

"Do you know where this baby is?"

"I think so."

"Cam isn't going with you?"

"Kary and I have posed as a couple wanting to adopt."

She gave me a look as if to say, I know whose idea that was. She stirred her coffee. "Cam tells me he doesn't think Rufus and Angie will keep the baby."

"Yeah, that's going to be tough on Kary."

"And on you."

Ellin and I have an odd, prickly relationship. She thinks I'm a bad influence, and I think she's too uptight. But we've gotten used to each other, and occasionally, she says exactly the right thing.

"I'll be okay."

Her second look said, Oh, really? But she changed the subject. "Do you have any idea who might have killed Bobbi?"

"There are several possible suspects." Including the fellow I'm going to see this afternoon.

"Don't you think you ought to let Jordan in on this?"

"I'm afraid if the police go barging in, we'll lose Mary Rose. I want to try it my way first."

Kary had left *Tales of a Chinese Grandmother* on the counter. Ellin gave the book a glance. "Cam tells me Kit was able to get rid of the ghost that was haunting Janice's restaurant."

"He's turned out to be really helpful."

"I wish I'd gotten a camera crew over there."

"Kit and Camden were the only ones who could see her."

"Still, it would've been an interesting story." She took another sip. "Cam also told me he and I are both Snakes."

I wondered what she thought of that. "If you believe in the Chinese zodiac."

"It would make a good program. Do you think Janice would come on the show?"

"No, but her mother would be delighted. She and Jessie Vardaman are an item now, did you know that? They could do a double act, the Chinese Zodiac for Your Pet. They could tell which animal was which animal." I liked this idea. "So your dog could've been born in the Year of the Horse."

"Leave the program planning to me. Snakes trust no one to run things for them."

"See? The perfect sign for you."

"So, how's your agency doing?"

She *was* in a good mood. "I'm thirty thousand dollars richer, thanks to Delores Carlyle."

Her eyebrows went up. "I'm impressed. Now you can pay Cam the rent you owe."

"I plan to settle up with him as soon as possible."

She looked as if she didn't believe me. "Other than finding Mary Rose, do you have any other cases?"

"No."

"This doesn't bother you, this hit-or-miss occupation? You got lucky this time, but how often do clients come through with real money? Is this how you want to spend your life?"

I didn't want her to know this was exactly my concern. "Keeps things lively."

"You need to think about something else you could do. I'm sure you have other talents. Actually, I'm not sure. Do you have other talents?"

Ah, the old Ellin had returned. "You got an opening at the PSN?"

"Janitor, maybe."

"I like you better when you're snarky."

She decided this wasn't worth an answer. She gave me a pitying look, finished her coffee, and hurried out.

I went back upstairs to shower and shave. When I finished my shower and was drying off, I noticed some words had been written on the steamy bathroom mirror and grinned. Had Kary slipped in to leave me a love note? I was always leaving little "Marry Me" signs in odd places. Maybe she'd finally said yes.

"David Randall."

Okay, no need to be so formal, but it was cute.

"Will Contact You Soon."

Wait a minute. These words were writing themselves. Suddenly cold, I wrapped the towel around me. What the hell?

"Delores Sent Me."

I threw on some pants and yelled up the stairs for Camden to come have a look. He was already halfway down the stairs. The words had faded, but all he had to do was touch the mirror and there they were.

Was my career was about to take an unexpected turn? "What does it mean? Am I the Dearly Departed Detective Agency now?"

Camden did not look concerned. In fact, he was grinning. "Guess you'll find out."

"Guess you'll run interference. You're enjoying this, aren't you?"

"Now I'm not the only one seeing things."

"Fine by me, especially if these ghosts have more hidden wealth to spare." Too bad Ellin wasn't here to see that word had gotten around in the spirit world that I was the man to hire. Or did I want Ellin or anyone to know? "Let's keep this between us until I see where it leads."

"Like the return of my telekinetic power."

"Oh, you haven't shared that info with Ellin?"

"I didn't think it would be wise—unless I want to star in a PSN series." He sighed. "I thought it was gone. I don't know what's going to happen now."

"New and unexplored realms of wonder."

"New and painful psychic episodes."

Or something new and wildly exciting, which I found, to my surprise, I was curious to investigate.

● ● ● ● ●

That afternoon was one of longest afternoons I'd ever experienced. Camden and I tried to watch *This Island Earth*, which is usually perfect for laughs and smartass comments, but our attention wasn't on the movie. At one-thirty, I got up from the blue armchair.

"Anybody need anything from the store?"

"I need another box of Pop-Tarts," Camden said on cue.

Kary had been crocheting little multi-colored squares. She set a finished stack aside. "I can't believe Young still hasn't called. He must be on to us." There was no way her eyes could squint like Rufus', but she gave it a good try. "Where exactly are you going?"

I'd had time to think of a good story. "Okay, you got me. I've been so busy with this case and all the running around to placate the Huntingtons, I haven't had time to get your birthday gift."

"'Placate.'" She turned to Camden. "Thirty points?"

"More like fifty."

"Which is why you can't come along right now," I said. "Young might call while I'm gone. Then you can alert me, and we'll go."

"All right. But no sneaking by Superior Homes without me."

"This sting operation doesn't work without you. I'll be right back."

Camden followed me to the door. I looked at my watch. "She's going to be mad, but there's no way in hell I'm taking her with me. And you can't come, either. It'll look suspicious."

"What about backup? Kit said we'd need a diversion."

I'd taken Kit's warning seriously and planned to make a quick stop by Comic World. "Don't worry. I know a good one."

Brian Young greeted me at the door of his office. I noticed the receptionist wasn't there. "Good afternoon! Come in, come in. Mrs. Fisher not with you?"

"She's not feeling well this morning. She's very excited, though. I'm supposed to take notes and report back as soon as possible."

He smiled. "Oh, we can do better than that. Of course, we have a package of legal documents and lawyers who'll set up the adoption with the courts."

"I'm prepared to sign any papers today."

"With fees, that'll run an additional thirty-five thousand."

"I understand. That's acceptable."

"But let's do that tomorrow. Have a seat. I'll bring her out."

I was surprised to find my heart beating faster. Bring her out?

Young went into the next room and returned carrying a small bundle. "Here you go."

He put the baby in my arms. The infant was a perfect little rosebud of a girl with a wisp of red hair. I could hardly believe I'd actually found her.

"She's beautiful."

The baby cooed and smiled. Her tiny fingers grasped mine. I was overwhelmed.

"Mr. Fisher?"

It took me a long while to process Young was speaking to me.

Get up! Move! If you let yourself get caught in the past, you'll never save this little future!

"What do you think?"

I stood, holding the baby close. "She's perfect. Thanks."

And I ran like hell.

As I'd hoped, Young was so startled he didn't react until I was out of his office and out of Superior Homes and halfway down the sidewalk. Then he came charging after me and ran right into D.J. Goins, who caught him by the arm.

Young struggled, but D.J. was much stronger. "Let go of me! Who are you?"

He tightened his grip. "I'm the father of Frieda Huntington's baby, the one she's not going to sell to you."

I stood a safe distance away. Young glared at me. "Who are you people? What do you want?"

"We're friends of Bobbi Jo Hull," I said. "This is her baby, isn't it? At least you weren't enough of a monster to kill the baby, too."

He turned pale and stopped struggling. "Gentlemen, let's go inside and discuss this rationally. I'm sure we can work out a satisfactory arrangement for all of us."

"We can talk out here. The baby needs some sunshine."

He looked up into D.J.'s set young face. "Miss Huntington didn't tell me of your wishes. I can certainly stop my dealings with her. As for you, Mr. Fisher—if that is your name—your wild accusations are untrue."

"I have pictures of you and a certain blonde."

This time he managed to break D.J.'s hold and dashed back into Superior Homes, slamming the door. D.J. followed and began pounding on the door. The noise made little Mary Rose start to cry. I bounced her on my shoulder as I called Jordan.

"There's a disturbance at Superior Homes."

"Do I hear a baby crying?"

D.J. had taken out his screwdriver and was working on the hinges of the front door.

"You're going to hear even more crying when you get here."

• ● ● ● •

Jordan arrived before D.J. had gotten into Superior Homes. As he and the other officers led Brian Young out in handcuffs, Young glared at D.J.

"Keep that hoodlum away from me! He doesn't know what he's talking about. He should be arrested for attempted assault."

D.J. made another move toward him and found his way blocked by Jordan. "Stand back, son. We'll take it from here."

D.J. stood back, but I could tell he didn't like it.

Young transferred his angry glare to me. "Who the hell are you? You don't know what you're talking about, either. I didn't kill anyone."

"As I said, I'm a friend of Bobbi Jo's. You didn't have to murder her to get a baby."

"I didn't kill her! Besides, she planned to sell it to me, anyway. We had worked out a deal."

I was sick of all these deals. "I think she found a better way to make money. Wasn't she planning to blackmail you with pictures of you and Chelsea Holt? Isn't that why you borrowed Dillon Pennix's truck and went over to her house?"

"I'm not saying anything else until I have my lawyer."

"Fine," Jordan said. "We're going to make a stop at Raymond Gura's headquarters and have a word with him. Randall, the baby needs to go to the hospital."

"I'm certain she belongs to Rufus."

"Let them check her out first. Before we can hand her over to Rufus, there'll have to be tests to prove he's the father."

As Jordan reached for Mary Rose, I found myself pulling back. I hadn't held a baby since Lindsey, and I was amazed by how close to tears I was. Jordan paused and gave me a look of complete sympathy before saying gruffly, "It'll work out."

I managed to let go. I called Rufus and told him to meet Jordan at the hospital. With Mary Rose taken care of for the moment, and my emotions locked down, I headed over to the Cave. I needed to have a long talk with Dillon Pennix.

● ● ● ● ●

When I entered the bar, Pennix was up in the light booth, leaning over the controls programming one of the machines.

"I need to talk to you," I said.

No answer. Okay, so he wanted to play dumb. I wasn't going to let him ignore me. I went up the narrow stairs and halted in the doorway. Pennix wasn't going to answer my questions. He wasn't going to answer anyone. He sat as if frozen to the metal control room chair. From the way his hands and teeth were clenched, I guessed he'd had a pretty bad shock.

Trace Burwell uncurled himself from the corner, wild-eyed and shaking. "It was an accident! He was messing with the wires. I told him he didn't know how to do it."

"I don't think it was an accident."

"He didn't know what he was doing."

"With the wires or with those pictures? He wasn't supposed to take them to Raymond Gura, was he? That was supposed to be your deal."

"They wouldn't let me in on the race horse, either! Thought I was too stupid. Didn't pay me for the use of Bobbi's house, and that was my idea! Then Pennix said Bobbi shouldn't have taken those pictures. Said she stole his idea."

I couldn't decide who was more greedy, Pennix or Bobbi Jo. "Blackmail's not a very bright idea."

"Next thing I know, she's dead. He killed her."

"If you believed that, why didn't you go to the police?"

"He told me if I said anything, he'd do something to the baby."

I stayed very still in the doorway. "Pennix went to Bobbi's house to get the pictures, right? You're saying he killed her for stealing his idea? Why not split the blackmail money with her instead?"

"I don't know. Pennix lost a lot of money on that race horse. Said Young gambled all the profits away, and it would serve him right to get caught. He knew Young had a thing for the mayor's wife ever since he helped the Holts find a house. Never did like that mayor anyway, and all his rules and restrictions."

This led me to believe Young had been set up from the beginning. "Did Pennix ask you to video Young and Chelsea Holt?"

"I never did! I told you I thought Bobbi wanted the camera to take pictures of the baby."

Bobbi may not have been interested in blackmail. She hoped to exchange those pictures for a new house. Pennix, on the other hand, had bigger plans, including a deal with Holt's opponent, Raymond Gura.

"So Pennix took Mary Rose and gave her to Young. Why?"

"Young owed him a lot of money. He was supposed to give Pennix half of what he got for the baby. Did you find her? Is she alive?"

"Yes." I wanted to get him out of the light booth and away from any more wires. "Would you like to see her?"

"You got her with you?"

"She's in the car." I backed down the stairs, keeping my eyes on him.

As I'd hoped, Burwell followed, pathetically eager. "I kept telling Bobbi she ought not to try anything. Guess I ought to be glad I didn't have part of that race horse. Everybody lost a pile of money on that nag." He paused. "You know you shouldn't leave a baby outside in a car, especially in this hot weather."

"I didn't."

Burwell gave me one frightened glance and then ran for the door. I was certain I could catch him, but at the last minute, he zigzagged to the bar, grabbed a handful of glasses, and began pelting them at me. The first one bounced off my arm, but the next ones hit the tables and floor and shattered in a spray of glass. I picked up a chair to use as a shield and moved toward him as he continued to fire away, throwing everything he could, the entire inventory of glasses, followed by beer mugs and bottles.

I wondered what he'd do when he ran out of ammunition. Did he have a gun stashed behind the bar?

He worked his way down to the cash register, which I knew he couldn't lift. I thought he'd throw money next, but he ducked down and came up with a weapon. Not a gun, but a vicious-looking crowbar. Skinny Trace Burwell hefting a crowbar might not have looked dangerous, but the man was running on what must have been years of repressed anger. His moustache stood straight out as he screamed.

"Come on! Try it!"

I put down the chair. "Take it easy. You've already killed someone today, and you've taken out the bar. Tell the police your story. You might be able to plead self-defense."

He brought the crowbar down on the bar with a smack that left a dent in the wood.

"He deserved to die! He killed Bobbi and stole her baby! I'm glad he's dead! He should have been dead a long time ago!"

Okay, self-defense was out. Maybe he'd like to try for insanity. I slowly reached for my phone.

"Don't do that!" Burwell whammed the bar again and then, to my surprise, leaped over the bar and attacked, swinging the crowbar like a baseball bat. I dodged his first swing, caught his arm, and tried to force him to drop the crowbar. We struggled for control, Burwell cursing and screaming. Maybe I couldn't overpower him in full berserker mode. I should've told Jordan where I was going.

Suddenly, Camden and Kit grabbed Burwell from behind. Their combined strength knocked Burwell to the ground. Kit snatched the crowbar and threw it as far away as he could. Then he and Camden sat down on top of Burwell, who deflated like a popped balloon.

I staggered up. "Thanks."

"I got the message about the same time as Cam," Kit said. "I stopped by the house and picked him up."

"Glad to know the psychic relay is working."

Kit looked down at Burwell, who was gasping, his moustache wavering like a piece of seaweed. "Who is this guy?"

Someone who'd finally had enough of being overlooked. "His name is Trace Burwell, and he killed the club owner, Dillon Pennix. That's him up there in the light booth, well-done. Pennix killed Rufus' ex-wife, Bobbi, because she double-crossed him with those photos of Brian Young and the mayor's wife that Camden and I discovered."

"Then Pennix took Mary Rose to Brian Young," Camden guessed.

"That's right. He wanted half the money Young would get for selling the baby."

"Sounds like a real creep," Kit said.

"Yep, and Burwell's not the double blank Rufus thought he was."

We had to wait three days before DNA testing proved Rufus was Mary Rose's father. By then, Kary had forgiven me for leaving her behind, and Trace Burwell had spilled the entire twisted story to the police and had been charged with the murder of Dillon Pennix. While Brian Young wasn't involved in Bobbi's murder, he was convicted of running an illegal baby ring. Jordan paid a visit to Raymond Gura, and the incriminating photos of Young and Chelsea Holt mysteriously disappeared. I guess that while Gura wouldn't mind using pictures of his opponent's wife caught in a compromising position, he could not be associated in any way with a murder and kidnapping case.

When Rufus brought Mary Rose home, we were all waiting on the front porch. It happened to be Kary's birthday, and she was ready.

"Oh, she's beautiful!"

"I knew you'd want to hold her first."

She cradled the baby in her arms and sat down in a rocking chair. Then she began to sob.

Camden's smile faded. "Uh-oh."

"It's okay," I said. "Kary, please, it's all right."

"I'm so happy she's alive."

"She's safe now. Please don't cry."

We couldn't get her to stop crying or to let go of Mary Rose. She clutched the baby. "Promise me you won't give her away. Promise me we can keep her."

Rufus looked at Angie in dismay. "What are we going to do?"

Angie patted Kary's shoulder. "Kary, honey, I know you're upset. We're trying to decide what's best for the little girl."

"We're the best thing she could ever have."

"Rufus and I, we're not real sure we're ready to be parents."

But no one is. No one's ready. You make it up as you go along and hope it works out. Sometimes it works out. Sometimes it doesn't.

"Here," Rufus said, "let me have her."

He was probably the only one who could have gotten Kary to relinquish her hold. He took Mary Rose in his large hands and held her up. Mary Rose gurgled and spit right in his eye. Rufus roared with laughter.

"Gonna chew and spit like your old man, huh?"

Kary managed a smile. "Now you have to keep her."

• • ● ● •

The rest of the afternoon, we took turns holding Mary Rose. Rufus and Angie went to the store for baby food, diapers, and formula. Camden convinced Kary to take a rest inside on the island sofa. Ellin sat on the porch swing, the baby in the crook of her arm.

"How does it feel?" I asked.

"Not bad."

"Give you any ideas?"

"I don't know." She shifted Mary Rose to her other arm. "That other boy, D.J., the one who helped you catch Young. What about his baby?"

"It's not here yet. That's something he and Frieda will have to work out." Now that Brian Young was no longer in the baby-buying business, I hoped Frieda wouldn't choose more drastic measures to rid herself of the baby. "Some people aren't cut out to be mothers," I said before I thought.

Ellin looked annoyed. "Give me a break, Randall. Motherhood is not really high on my list right now."

"At least you're considering it, though."

She looked down at the tiny girl snuggled against her. "It's a huge responsibility."

For eight wonderful years, I was the best father Lindsey could have had.

Before I sank too far beneath the waves, Camden came out. "Kary's asleep."

"Is she all right?"

"She will be. You know she was remembering her own baby."

The one she never got to hold.

Camden looked at Ellin holding Mary Rose. "Now there's a nice picture."

"Don't get too used to it." She smiled. "Could you bring me my tea, please? I left it in the fridge."

"Okay. You want a drink, Randall?"

"Yeah, I'll come get one."

I started around to the kitchen when something new caught my eye: Camden's baby picture, framed and on the mantel. Ellin had bought one of those special sterling silver frames with a design of ABC blocks and little cars, exactly the kind of frame proud parents would've chosen for their little boy. It was engraved with his birthday and his name. She'd set it between the picture of Kary as Miss Panorama, and the photo of herself and Camden, all dressed up for PSN's first anniversary party. His one and only baby picture. Mary Rose would have thousands.

"Randall, come here." Camden stood at the bay window in the dining area and looked out across the dark backyard. He pointed to a little animal near the hedge. I thought at first it was a stray dog. "It's Mimi."

We went outside. Mimi the Fox approached cautiously.

"What's that in her mouth?"

It was a fox cub. Mimi set it down, and after giving it a few licks, looked up at me as if expecting a compliment.

Camden was silent a moment and then said, "She brought her baby by especially for you to see."

I'm presenting you right now,
Baby, take a bow.

"Thanks, Mimi. It's really cute."

The fox cub rolled in the grass, sneezed a huge sneeze, shook itself, and ran to its mother. I think it might have performed more tricks if Ellin hadn't called out the back door.

"Cam? What are you two doing out here?"

He turned to answer. "Communing with nature."

I called over my shoulder. "Checking on another red-haired child."

When we turned back, Mimi and her baby were gone.

"And the fox fairies have vanished as mysteriously as they appeared," I said.

Ellin came out into the yard, Mary Rose on her shoulder. Her eyes, usually smoldering, were alight with impish humor. "Okay, I've got one for you. I can't believe you boys missed it."

I couldn't believe she was about to make a joke. "What?"

"Our new boarder's real name is Christopher, right? His nickname is Kit."

"Right," Camden said.

"And Randall insists his mother looks like a beaver."

"She does," I said.

Ellin started laughing. "That's what beavers call their babies. Kits!"

We couldn't stop laughing, and hearing us, Mary Rose turned her head and made a happy little baby sound, a sound that made me want to keep laughing and start crying all at once. Was this little girl the one? Was this the baby that was going to heal everyone?

Camden suggested he and Ellin take Mary Rose back to the porch and sit on the swing together. "It'll be good practice." Ellin gave him a look but agreed.

Kary was still asleep on the sofa. Rufus was bringing Buddy and more of his pals by to see the baby. I didn't want Kary to be disturbed by all the fuss, so I gathered her in my arms and carried her upstairs to her bedroom. I carefully eased her down on her bed. I thought she was still asleep, but as I turned to leave, she caught my hand.

"Don't go, David."

As much as I wanted to stay, I didn't want to take advantage of her fragile emotional state. "You know I love you, but this is probably not the best time."

"No, it's all right."

"Maybe Mary Rose isn't the answer to all our problems, but we'll find that answer, I promise."

"I know we will, and I want you to stay."

"I want you to be sure. No regrets. No buyer's remorse."

This made her smile. She gave my hand a tug and pulled me down beside her. She loosened my tie and unbuttoned my shirt. "I know what I'm doing."

"I see that." I tossed shirt and tie aside and stretched out beside her, feeling the warmth of her smooth skin, the silky feel of her hair.

"You're what I want, David," she said. "No more deals. No bargains. No price to pay."

I put my arms around her and leaned in for the first of what would be many kisses. "You win."

To see more Poisoned Pen Press titles:

Visit our website: poisonedpenpress.com/
Request a digital catalog: info@poisonedpenpress.com

CPSIA information can be obtained
at www.ICGtesting.com
Printed in the USA
BVOW08s2235150317
478656BV00001B/8/P